"Steven Ma~ ~ a gift for expressing through his writi~ ~ complicated and transcendent beauty of the human experience with poignant clarity."
– Yolanda King,
eldest daughter of Dr. Martin Luther King

"Steven Manchester's *Goodnight, Brian* is a poignant, inspiring story about resilience and faith and one family's enduring love that should be a model for us all."
– James S. Hirsch,
bestselling author, *Willie Mays: The Life, the Legend*

"An amazing writer...with *Goodnight, Brian*, Steven Manchester has yet another winner on his hands!"
– Noonie Fortin,
1SG, USAR (Ret); Author and Speaker

"*Goodnight, Brian* is a heart warming story about the power of love."
– Tami Brady, TCM Reviews

"Steven has once again proven his deep insight into human emotions and relations and his ability to craft a well written and entertaining story that also has the power to inspire courage and hope. *Goodnight, Brian* is a fine read."
– Bob Price, WPZZ Radio Personality

# Goodnight, Brian

# Goodnight, Brian

# by
# Steven Manchester

THE
STORY PLANT

The Story Plant
The Aronica-Miller Publishing Project, LLC
P.O. Box 4331
Stamford, CT 06907

Copyright © 2012 by Steven Manchester

Jacket design by Barbara Aronica Buck

Print ISBN-13: 978-1-61188-061-8

E-book ISBN-13: 978-1-61188-062-5

Visit our website at www.thestoryplant.com

First Story Plant Printing: January 2013

Printed in The United States of America

## Also by Steven Manchester

Twelve Months

For my children –
and unconditional love

## Acknowledgments

First and forever, Jesus Christ, my Lord and Savior. With Him, all things are possible.

To Paula, my beautiful wife, for loving me and being the amazing woman that she is.

To my children – Evan, Jacob, Isabella and Carissa – for inspiring me. It's only one life – make it an incredible one!

To Mom, Dad, Billy, Randy, Darlene, Jeremy, Jenny, Jason, Philip, the DeSousa's –
my beloved family and foundation on which I stand.

To Lou Aronica and Peter Miller, for giving me another priceless opportunity to share my writing with the world. I am forever grateful to Lou for mentoring me, and continuing to champion my work.

"God knows...and that's enough."
— Mama

# Chapter 1

## Winter 1976

Two streets from a choppy Narragansett Bay, Frank pulled the station wagon in front of his mother-in-law's cottage and shut off the engine. Joan grabbed her swollen belly and turned to face the backseat. Ross wore a bulky snowsuit and was strapped in to an even bulkier car seat. "We're at Mama's house," she announced to the small boy. From beneath a wool hat, he stared at her but never uttered a sound. Then – jumping into some choreographed fire drill – Frank grabbed the boy, Joan grabbed her worn purse and, braving the angry biting winds, they hurried for the front door.

Mama lived on the low end of a very affluent community; a row of summer cottages that had been winterized and converted into year-round dwellings. Her place started out as a tiny summer cottage, but had evolved into something much greater over the years. To combat the lack of space, there were three additions made to the house. Each one was smaller than the one before it, creating a telescopic effect. Long and narrow, the exterior was stained a weather-beaten white with teal blue shutters. It looked odd, but it was heaven – containing so much more than the massive houses that sat down near the shore.

The name HORIZON was carved into a wooden board and nailed to the front of the house. A brick pathway, now covered in salt and patches of black ice, led past a statue of St. Jude that welcomed all guests. As the front door flew open and a blast of heat spilled from the house, the distinct smells of sweet Italian sausages and fresh baked bread hit the young family.

Angela DiMartino – all 4'10" of her – stood in the doorway, waiting. She had a crop of curly gray hair that added at least two inches to her stature. With pencil-thin lips, her subtle smirk revealed her mischievous sense of humor. She was heavyset and well endowed, and wore her usual flowered smock. She smelled like a mix of garlic and dryer sheets. Her dark brown eyes, illuminated by a strong inner light, shined when she saw her grandson. After pinching Ross' cheek, she turned her own cheek to the little boy and asked, "You gotta big smack for Mama?"

"Okay, but just a kiss," he said, "No biting this time!" Tentatively, he kissed her cheek.

"I don't bite," she whispered in his ear, "I only nibble." As she helped him off with his jacket, she gave his neck a loving chomp.

Tickled to laughter, he fled toward the living room.

Chuckling, she turned her attention to her daughter. "So when am I gonna be able to nibble on my new grandbaby?" she asked, rubbing Joan's massive mid-section without permission. "You look like you're ready to pop."

"Soon...I hope," Joan said, still trying to catch her breath from the short jaunt to the cottage.

After running her blotchy, gnarled hands over Joan's belly one last time, Mama leaned into it – until she was an inch from it – and whispered, "Enough stalling already. It's time to come home, little one."

Joan exhaled deeply. "You've got that right," she said.

~ ~ ~ ~ ~ ~ ~ ~

In Mama's cucina – the family hub – the obnoxious red wallpaper offset the worn linoleum. The kitchen table had a yellow Formica top, surrounded by five faux leather-bound chairs. While Joan contemplated sliding into one of them, Mama gestured that she take a seat. "Get off your feet, while I finish the gravy," she said – above Dean Martin crooning in the background.

As Mama headed for the large pot of red sauce, Frank playfully teased her. "And that's gonna be son number two, Ma," he boasted, pointing toward Joan's large belly.

"Well, isn't that something, Frank," the old lady teased, "already calling your unborn child a boy."

"These genes are too strong to produce a girl," he said.

"You may be right, Frank," she said with a shrug. "The good Lord knows what He's doing, and I suppose He'd never let you ruin a little girl."

Joan laughed aloud. Frank shot her a look, but didn't dare consider a comeback in front of her sharp-tongued mother. Instead, he stepped into his mother-in-law's bedroom and dumped their coats onto her bed, careful not to disturb the trays of spinach pies that were covered with dish towels and cooling on top of a plastic tablecloth. As he turned to leave, he noticed a silver tray filled with pill bottles that sat on the nightstand. "So that's what's keeping her alive," he snickered, and headed for the living room to be alone with the T.V.

~ ~ ~ ~ ~ ~ ~ ~

While Mama worked away at the stove, Joan pointed at the hideous porcelain rooster – with wooden spoons sticking out of its head – sitting among the many bottles of olive oil and spices on the counter. "You need to throw that ugly thing out, Ma," Joan said, "or donate it to the Salvation Army."

Mama shook her head. "Can't do it," she said, with her back to her daughter. "He wakes me up every morning."

"Yeah, right. You've gotten up every morning at five o'clock for as long as I can remember."

"And you've never gotten up earlier than 6:00, so how could you have ever heard my rooster crow?"

They both laughed.

Mama turned from the stove to face her daughter. "So you think Ross is ready for a new brother or sister?" she asked, beginning their weekly tradition of getting caught up on every detail of each other's lives.

"Well, we've definitely talked a lot about it." Joan shrugged. "He's become very clingy, but I have this sense..." She paused.

"Go on," Mama said.

"It's gonna sound strange, Ma, but it's like he's more protective of the baby than jealous."

Mama smiled. "Now that doesn't sound strange at all." She nodded. "That just sounds like the love of a big brother to me."

As if on cue, Ross walked into the kitchen and approached his mother. After giving her belly one quick rub, he headed back to the T.V.

"Well, isn't that something," Mama said.

Joan smiled proudly. "He watches over me like a hawk," she whispered. "He's always by my side, trying to pat my stomach or talk to the baby."

Mama nodded again. "He's going to be a good brother. The baby's very lucky."

There was a loud knock at the door. Mama wiped her hands on her apron and answered it. It was her son, Bob, and his wife Bev, along with their two daughters, Steph and Heidi. No sooner had the door opened when the girls shot through, excited to visit with their Aunt Joan's big belly.

Steph had the dark eyes of a gypsy – Mama's eyes – which lit up like Christmas when she smiled. With olive skin and full lips, she was beautiful. Her raven-black hair was curly and pulled back in a pony tail. Though her mom dressed her in frilly dresses, she hated it and everyone knew it.

At seven years old, Heidi was one year younger than Steph – almost to the day – but they could have easily passed for twins with their matching hair and eyes. Heidi was a bit heavier, with the olive skinned face of a Mediterranean angel. Unlike her big sister, she was a girlie-girl who loved to wear nice things – lacy dresses and ribbons in her hair.

Wrestling off their coats and hats, the girls paid their grandmother a respectful kiss before speaking gibberish to their unborn cousin. Bob waited in line to greet his mother with a peck on the cheek. Bev followed suit.

Once the usual greetings were exchanged, Mama headed to the living room to change albums. Within seconds, Frank Sinatra was singing *Summer Wind* and Mama was swinging Ross around in his first dance lesson. The living room walls were covered in dark wood paneling, but it was tough to tell. There were framed photos of family and friends covering every inch of the place. While their dead ancestors watched on, Ross squirmed and fidgeted, trying desperately to escape his grandmother's arthritic grip. "Please, Mama," he pleaded. "I'm too tired to dance."

Without missing a step, she laughed so hard she nearly launched Frank from the worn gray armchair. She had a distinct laugh that started from her diaphragm and worked its way up until it escaped in a roar. It was larger than life and startled those who weren't used to it. Frank looked up at her and shook his head. It was shocking to hear something so loud coming out of someone so tiny – not to mention, she was blocking the T.V.

The girls watched Ross and Mama's dance and considered joining the pair. They decided against it when Heidi spotted two stained cardboard boxes – marked CHRISTMAS DECORATIONS – sitting off in the corner. She elbowed her sister and pointed toward the great find.

"Mama!" Steph gasped. "Christmas stuff?"

The old matriarch paused for a moment and smiled. "Mama starts decorating for Santa Claus next week," she confirmed with a nod.

Ross took the opportunity to break free and hurry off to his mother to make sure she was okay. The girls quickly followed their young cousin.

~ ~ ~ ~ ~ ~ ~

While the women talked over each other at the kitchen table, Steph took a sip of Kool-Aid and spilled the red drink all over the front of her yellow dress. Bev rushed toward her. "I saw that, Steph! You did it on purpose," she said through clenched teeth.

"No I didn't, Ma," Steph swore.

Concealing her smile, Mama hurried to the rescue. "It was an accident, Bev," she testified and shot Steph a secret wink. "I'll get some dry play clothes for her."

In the safety of her grandmother's bedroom, Steph threw on the faded pair of dungarees and long-sleeved shirt, while Mama handed her a warm spinach pie. "Mama, I didn't..." Steph began.

The old woman placed a finger to her lips. "Shh-hh... it's fine. Just eat your pie before it gets cold."

Finally comfortable, Steph smiled – and meant it.

Upon returning to the kitchen, Bev gawked at her clumsy daughter with a suspicious eye until Mama slapped her on the backside. "Let it go," the old woman whispered. "There are greater tragedies – trust me."

~ ~ ~ ~ ~ ~ ~ ~

Halfway through a feast of cheese raviolis, sweet Italian sausages, meatballs and Mama's famous spinach pies, Joan excused herself to go to the bathroom. Ross started to get up to join her. "Finish eating, honey," Joan told him. "Mommy doesn't need her helper right now, okay?"

He nodded and stuffed another bite of ravioli into his mouth.

Mama entertained the children by daydreaming aloud. "When you kids get a little bigger, you know that Mama's going to take you to Italy, right?"

The adults exchanged skeptical grins. The kids, however, were hypnotized by her descriptive tales.

"Fall is the season of *sagre*, with food festivals throughout the province. During mid-September, they have a giant wine festival in the town square of Greve in Chianti. And in October, they gather all the grapes for winemaking. This is known as the *vendemmia*."

"You like wine?" Steph asked between chews of bread.

"I sure do and Tuscany is world famous for its wines. Chianti is probably the best known, but they make every kind."

"What kinds of food will we eat when we're there?" Heidi chimed in, speaking just as fluently with her hands.

Mama clasped her hands together and took a deep breath. "Oh, just imagine tomatoes ripened under the Mediterranean sun, freshly picked basil, cold pressed extra virgin olive oil, black truffles and pecorino cheese…"

"Huh?" the girls wondered.

Mama smiled. "They have the most delicious ice cream in the world. It's called *gelato*."

"Gelato," Ross repeated. "Gelato. Gelato. Gel…"

"That's enough," his dad warned. "Just finish your dinner."

As Joan returned to the table and reclaimed her seat, Mama stood and announced, "I just finished two more photo albums that I want to show you guys." She wasn't two steps from the table when she turned back to the kids. "And we also need to plan our Christmas visit to Boston," she added, and hurried off to retrieve her picture books.

For Frank, this was the perfect cue to excuse himself. Throwing his napkin into his empty plate, he looked at his brother-in-law, Bob. "Join me on the porch for a cigar and a game of pitch?"

Grinning, Bob stood and started for the porch.

Frank looked at Ross. "Want to join the men?"

Ross shook his head, and slid his chair a few inches closer to his mother.

"Suit yourself," Frank muttered, and left the room.

Mama returned to the table and wasn't even seated when Heidi and Steph dove right into the new photo albums, excited to hear whatever vivid stories their grandmother cared to share.

~ ~ ~ ~ ~ ~ ~ ~

The afternoon whipped by and, after devouring a warm batch of Cornflake cookies and some cappuccinos, Mama interrupted the card game on the porch. With Joan and Bev in tow, she pointed to a spot out in the front yard. "That's where the new baby's tree will be planted in the spring...right between the girls' trees and Ross'. This way, I can see all four of them when I'm sitting in Papa's glider."

~ ~ ~ ~ ~ ~ ~ ~

Nausea and cold air that caused goose bumps on her arms yanked Joan from her sleep. She opened her eyes to obnoxious fluorescent lighting. *Where am I?* she wondered. It took a few moments. She could tell by the occasional moan that other women shared the maternity ward room, separated by white curtains that ran from the ceiling to the shiny linoleum floor. She coughed once and winced from the sharp pain in her abdomen and crotch. Her entire face felt dried out; her mouth, nose and throat were caked in dried mucous. She gagged again and looked up to find the young candy striper shoving a straw into her mouth. She sucked once and gagged some more. Her tongue was heavy with a metallic aftertaste and the nausea became worse. She tried to sit up, but it felt like a razor blade shot across her lower torso. She collapsed back into the pillows. "Where's my..."

An older nurse approached and took the cup of water from the candy striper. She pointed the straw toward Joan's lips. "Here, just take a small sip."

Joan tried to sit again, this time ignoring the pain in trade for some relief from her desert-chapped throat.

"How do you feel?" the smiling nurse asked.

"Huh?"

"How are you feeling, Mrs. Mauretti?"

"My baby?" Both words came out in a rasp between sips.

"He's fine, Mrs. Mauretti. You have a healthy baby boy."

Joan smiled. "My husband? Has anyone..?"

"Yes. I believe he's in the waiting room handing out cigars to anyone who will take one. I'll send him in."

"And my baby?"

"He's with the pediatrician now. I'll bring him in just as soon as they're done."

"Thank you." She took another sip and gagged.

~ ~ ~ ~ ~ ~ ~ ~

At two hours old, Brian Francis Mauretti was wheeled into Joan's room. He wore a light blue knit cap and was wrapped tightly in a white receiving blanket with alternating pink and blue stripes. The nun lifted him out of the glass bassinette and gently placed him into his mother's arms. Joan felt overwhelmed with joy. "Good morning, Brian," she whispered and removed his soft cap. He had his dad's black hair and plenty of it, but his head was cone-shaped. Before the nun left the two alone to bond, Joan looked up for an explanation.

"Oh, he's fine...stubborn, but fine," the nun teased. "Your son liked it so much in the birth canal that he stayed there for as long as he could. The doctor had to use forceps. His head will return to a normal shape within a day or two. No need to worry."

"Thank you," Joan said and kissed Brian on the point of his head.

As the kind woman departed, Joan unwrapped the tight swaddling and counted ten fingers and ten toes. She kissed each one. "Mommy's been waiting a long time to meet you, Brian," she whispered. The baby squinted to look at his mom. "And you have your brother's chocolate brown eyes," she said, excited over the new discovery.

The white curtain parted and her husband walked in, wearing a giant smile. "How's my new boy?" Frank asked, swollen with pride.

"Perfect, Daddy." She kissed Brian's tiny face again. "Just perfect." She patted the bed for Frank to sit. "Come meet your son." Together, they smothered the newborn in hugs and sobs of joy.

Allowing his wife to rest, Frank cradled the boy in his arms and took a seat in the chair beside Joan's bed. Searching his new son's eyes, he told him, "Just wait 'til your brother gets a look at you. We're gonna go fishing together and play baseball and..."

It felt like seconds had passed when one of the meaner looking nuns entered the room to escort

Frank out. "It's time for you to go, Dad," she announced. "Mom needs to feed your son and they
need time to get to know each other."

Frank's puppy dog eyes pled for more time, but
he had no shot. He was dealing with the maternity
warden. Shrugging, he turned to Joan. "I'll be back
this afternoon," he promised, and smiled. "Great job
today, Mommy. I love you."

Joan kissed him. "I love you, too. Can you please
call my mom and let her know that she's going to
have to wait a little while longer for another little
girl?"

He laughed. "Oh, don't you worry about that. I
plan to go by the cottage just as soon as I leave here
and let her know in person," he said with a grin, and
headed for the door. As he reached it, he turned and
smiled at the nun. She never smiled back.

Under the warden's eye, Joan tried several times
to get the baby to latch onto her nipple. He had dif-
ficulty, losing his grip each time. She shifted to get
comfortable. It was no use. Her body throbbed in
pain. Finally, the little one got the nipple positioned
to where he wanted it and began to suckle. While he
fed, Joan sighed in relief and rocked him back and
forth. The nun continued her watch. Brian fed for
three full minutes, but Joan was unsure whether he'd
gotten enough. She questioned the old nun.

"Trust me, he'll let you know if he's still hungry.
Is he your first?" the woman asked.

"No. We have another boy at home."

"You didn't nurse your first?"

"I did, but it's been a while. I just want to make sure that I'm doing it right."

"Give it a few feedings. It'll come back to you. It's been shown by many studies that breastfed infants are healthier. They can get the occasional cold, but they generally stay healthier." For the first time, the woman smiled. And with an approving nod, she left Joan and Brian to figure out the rest together.

When Brian finished suckling, Joan placed him in her lap, unwrapped the receiving blanket again and took another inventory. Thrilled with the results, she quickly wrapped him back up and lifted him up until they were face-to-face. "I can't wait to show you everything, Brian," she whispered into the newborn's ear. "You're going to love it." She kissed his plump, rosy cheek and then placed him on her chest to sing him his first lullaby.

# Chapter 2

## *Spring 1977*

Mama sang completely out of tune, "A, you're ador-able, B, you're so beautiful, C, you're a cutie full of charms. D, you're a darling and E, you're exciting. F, you're a feather in my arms."

Dressed in a white satin baptism gown, Brian cooed. Joan and Bev fussed over the baby, tying the shiny ribbon on his little white boots.

"G, you look good to me, H, you're so heavenly, I, you're the one I idolize. J, we're like Jack and Jill, K, you're so kissable, L is the love-light in your eyes. M, N, O, P...you could go on all day. Q, R, S, T...al-phabetically speaking, you're okay. U made my life complete, V means you're very sweet – W, X, Y, Z. It's fun to wander through... the alphabet with you... to tell you what you mean to me."

Frank stepped into the room and looked at his son lying on the bed. Grinning, he shook his head. "I'm letting you ladies know right now that this is the last time my son wears a dress."

Bob, Brian's godfather, placed his hand on Frank's shoulder and shrugged. "You never know," he teased.

Everyone laughed – except Frank.

~ ~ ~ ~ ~ ~ ~ ~

At four months old, Brian Francis Mauretti was welcomed into the Catholic Church through the sac-
rament of baptism. As the late April rain promised
a season of new beginnings, the entire family converged on Mama's cottage to take part in the usual
overindulgent celebration.

Many of Mama's famous dishes lined a long rectangular table, camouflaged in her mother's lacy table
cloth: There was an enormous antipasto salad; roast-
ed red peppers marinated in extra-virgin olive oil,
balsamic vinegar, fresh herbs, capers and kalamata
olives; a crock pot of homemade meatballs and another crock pot filled with sweet Italian sausage and
onions, with a basket of fresh rolls between them.
There were also dozens of warm spinach pies; a tray
of her heavenly white pizza squares; and a giant bowl
of ziti in a red gravy – with tomatoes, fresh basil, and
her secret spices – that had simmered all day. For
the kids, a sweating pitcher of sun-brewed sweet tea
sat beside a stack of plastic tumblers. For the adults,
there were two pitchers of Sangria, slices of fresh
apples and oranges floating at each brim.

While Bob and Uncle Sal filled their cups, they
talked politics. "Well, hopefully Jimmy Carter will
make a difference. I couldn't stand Ford, the clumsy
oaf," Bob said.

Sipping his Sangria, Uncle Sal shrugged. "They're
talking about opening the Alaskan pipeline this year.
I hope that helps with gas prices. Sixty-five cents a
gallon is ridiculous! If it keeps going, I might have to
trade in the Cadillac."

Bob chuckled. "So I may actually witness the day that hell freezes over then?"

Uncle Sal grinned. "You might."

Throughout the day, cousins of cousins and friends from long ago dropped in to welcome the little one into the family. As if she were performing miracles, Mama kept the food hot and replenished. A dozen different conversations competed with scratchy, old Italian albums. The combination was deafening and chaotic – glorious.

~ ~ ~ ~ ~ ~ ~ ~

Mama hurried into the kitchen to refill the meat-balls when she noticed Joan at the stove, heating a baby bottle in a saucepan of water. "What's this?" Mama asked, scooping meatballs out of a giant pan into the crockpot.

"I stopped breastfeeding a few days ago. It's been four months, so I figure Brian's gotten the co-lostrum he needs to boost his immune system," Joan explained. "I don't know if it's a growth spurt, but he's been feeding eight to twelve times a day...about every two to three hours." She stared at baby Brian in her arms. "I hope he's getting enough," she worried aloud. "I'm afraid he's..."

"Don't you worry about that," Mama said, tending to her food. "He'll let you know if he's still hungry." She abandoned her chore, plucked the baby out of Joan's hands, picked him up to eye level and inspected him. "Isn't that right, big boy?" She looked back at Joan. "How much has he gained?"

"Last weigh in...just over six pounds."

"That's my boy," Mama said, and gave the baby's belly a nibble. But Joan shook her head and Mama caught it. "What is it?"

"I don't know...maybe nothing. It's just that since I put Brian on the formula, he's been irritable and even cries sometimes after feedings. And that's not like him."

"His tummy's probably just getting used to the change in diet. Just watch it and..."

"He threw up this morning after I fed him, Ma."

"Babies throw up, Joan. Your brother cost me half my wardrobe because he couldn't keep anything down," she said, handing the baby over.

Joan laughed. "I guess," she mumbled, adjusting the tiny boy in her arms. "Frank says to stop worrying, too."

"Give it a few more days and if it doesn't change, call the pediatrician and bring him in," Mama advised, placing one hand on her daughter's shoulder, while juggling the crock pot in the other.

"Thanks, Mom." Joan tested the temperature of the formula on her forearm and began feeding Brian.

~ ~ ~ ~ ~ ~ ~ ~

Joan did give it a few more days. In fact, she gave it nearly a week, but each day proved worse than the one before. Brian exercised his lungs and screamed louder than any baby should have been able to. After each feeding, he vomited and then wailed until he physically exhausted himself. It didn't take long before everyone's nerves were frayed.

"Why did you ever stop breastfeeding?" Frank asked after dinner one night. He popped the top on another can of beer and awaited the answer.

"Whaaa!" Brian screamed from his infant seat.

"I told you why!" Joan exploded. "It was time... that's why!" She lifted Brian out of his seat and began swaying with him. "Do *you* want to try to breast-feed him, Frank?"

"Whaaa!" Brian added.

Frank shook his head, got up from the table and headed for the living room. "I'll look after Ross," he mumbled and left the room.

"Whaaa!" Brian added.

"Okay, sweetheart," Joan told the baby, standing at the sink and filling a bottle with lukewarm tap water. "Mommy's going to figure out what's wrong."

"Whaaa..."

Joan thought about Frank's question – the very same question she'd been asking herself since she'd stopped nursing – and felt the stinging bite of guilt.

~ ~ ~ ~ ~ ~ ~ ~

The following night, Brian was asleep in his infant seat, giving Joan a few precious moments to straighten up the house. The telephone rang. *Oh, God,* she thought. Her heart jumped into her throat and she hurried for the phone. The phone rang again.

"Whaaa..." Brian wailed.

*Damn it,* she thought, and picked up the phone. "Hello?"

"Whaaa!"

There was a brief pause. "Someone doesn't sound happy over there," Mama said.

Joan rolled her eyes, but decided not to tell her mother that she was the cause. Instead, she buried the telephone into the crook of her neck, picked up Brian and began to rock him in her arms. "It's been hell, Ma. For the last week, he's thrown up after each feeding and then he starts crying. And I mean, really sobbing."

"Whaaaa!" Brian added for effect.

"Maybe he gets scared from vomiting?" Mama suggested.

Joan shook her head, while tears welled in her eyes.

"Whaaa!"

"I don't think that's it, Ma. I think..." Joan said, dancing the baby around the kitchen. "I think it's because he's starving." She paused. Putting the thought into words made every fiber of her maternal being wince in pain.

"Whaaa!"

Frank stomped into the room and startled Joan. He looked at Brian screaming and then at Joan on the phone, and shook his head.

"Ma, I gotta go and try to figure out how to quiet this baby," she said, glaring at Frank. "God forbid he bothers his father anymore."

There was quiet on the phone, Mama picturing her son-in-law standing there, staring down her daughter. "Okay, sweetheart. I'm here, if you need me."

"Thanks," Joan mumbled and slammed the phone into its cradle. As she walked past Frank, he said, "I'm sorry, but..."

"But nothing, Frank!" she snapped. "You're not the only one suffering, you know," she added, and brushed past him like an icy wind.

~ ~ ~ ~ ~ ~ ~ ~

On Friday afternoon, Frank took two hours off from work to drive Joan and Brian to the doctor's. Although he wasn't happy about having to take the time off, he knew they were lucky to get the last minute appointment.

After they dropped Ross off at Mama's cottage, he thought about his young son. Ross had been caught trying to feed chocolate pudding to his baby brother. When he'd scolded him for it, the little boy's reply shocked him. "Brian's hungry!" he yelled, furious. "Mom says it all the time."

Frank pulled into the parking lot and shook his head at the lunacy. *I'd take a month off, if I knew it would stop the crying*, he thought and turned off the ignition.

After Joan grabbed the sleeping baby from the car seat, he lounged back and closed his eyes, hoping to reclaim some of the sleep he'd lost during the week. *Take your time*, he thought and could feel his mind slip into its own pool of warm pudding.

~ ~ ~ ~ ~ ~ ~ ~

Joan sat in the pediatrician's crowded waiting room. Careful not to wake Brian in her arms, she tried to calm her nerves by flipping through one of the parenting magazines. On page ten, there was an ad for a new soy milk formula called *Neo Mulsoy*. She read: *Perfect for sensitive tummies that cannot tolerate a milk based formula, Earth's Best Organic Infant Soy Formula with DHA & ARA is made with high-quality protein, carbohydrates, vitamins, minerals and essential fatty acids, including DHA & ARA – special nutrients found in breast milk that are critical to baby's mental and visual development. Easy to digest, this formula meets all FDA requirements for infant nutrition with the added benefit of being organic.*

"Brian Mauretti," the nurse announced, holding a blue folder.

Joan put the magazine down and adjusted Brian in order to stand without waking him.

The nurse smiled. "The doctor will see you now."

~ ~ ~ ~ ~ ~ ~ ~

Doctor Carvalho, the pediatrician, hurried into the room as if he didn't have a moment to lose. He was a scarecrow of a man with a pronounced beak and round spectacles. His off-white coat was faded with years of baby deliveries and unnecessarily worried moms. He studied Brian's thin folder and looked at Joan. "So why are we here today?"

For whatever reason, at that moment, Joan felt silly for wasting the busy man's time. "Well, I stopped breast feeding a week or so ago and I think my son's having some trouble digesting the formula."

Doctor Carvalho placed both hands on the side of Brian's neck and pressed.

"Whaaaa!" the baby cried out, angry over the rude awakening.

"What kind of trouble?" the scarecrow asked, as he continued to prod the squirming boy.

"Whaaaaa!"

"He throws up...after I feed him, and he never did that when he was breast feeding. He cries a lot now and he's...well...he's just not himself."

The man looked up at her like she'd just passed wind. "Not himself, huh?" He placed his cold stethoscope to Brian's mid-section and listened.

"Whaaaaa!"

"You have him on a milk-based formula?" he asked over the screaming.

"Yes," Joan answered, completely intimidated.

He pressed on Brian's belly and the baby wailed even louder. "Any diarrhea?"

"No," she answered, swallowing hard.

He pressed on Brian's belly again, making Joan squirm with anxiety. He finally stood, handed the baby back to her and shook his head. "A lot of babies have digestive issues, but I guess we can try him on a soy-based formula. I'll have the nurse send you home with some samples." He scribbled something into Brian's folder and muttered, "He'll be fine." And in a flash, he was gone.

The smiling nurse returned with two cans of Neo Mulsoy formula. One can was blue and the other was orange. Both had the word *improved* on the label, with a picture of a cute little yellow duck.

"Whaaaaa!" Brian complained.

Joan rocked him back and forth in her arms, trying desperately to soothe him. "The doctor's going to make you feel better, sweetheart," she promised. "No more belly aches."

~ ~ ~ ~ ~ ~ ~ ~

Joan pounded on the station wagon's passenger window. Frank jumped out of his sleep. Dazed, he wiped the drool from his face. "Help me get him in the car," she yelled, struggling to balance two cans of formula and their screaming infant.

Frank jumped out, ran around the car and fastened Brian into his seat. "How'd he do?" he asked, as he took his position back behind the steering wheel.

"Whaaa!" Brian wailed.

"Well, he's not happy, but the doctor thinks that he's lactose intolerant."

Frank's brow wrinkled in confusion.

"He can't have milk or anything made from milk," she explained.

"Whaaa....whaaa..." Brian cried, his volume winding down from sheer fatigue.

"So what does that mean?"

She lifted one of the cans of formula. "It means that he's on a new soy-based formula."

Frank offered a hopeful nod, started the car and pulled out of the lot. "Home?" he asked.

Joan thought about it and glanced toward the back seat. Brian's heavy eyelids were fighting sleep. *The car ride will definitely finish him off*, she pondered. *He'll be sleeping in a matter of minutes.* "Stop by the market, so I can get more formula. Two cans aren't going to go far."

·    Frank nodded again and pointed the car's nose toward the closest A&P.

~ ~ ~ ~ ~ ~ ~ ~

At the checkout counter, without even realizing it, Joan began shuffling her feet. There were three people in front of her. She looked out the store's giant front window – between the many advertisements – but couldn't tell by her husband's body language whether Brian had awoken yet. Suddenly, she felt a tap on her shoulder and jumped.

"Hi Joan," Katy, an old high school friend, said. "I'm sorry. I didn't mean to frighten you."

"Oh...hi, Katy," Joan replied, leaning in for a quick, awkward hug. "That's okay."

Katy smiled. "I heard that you just had another baby. Congratulations! Boy or girl?"

Joan placed six cans of the soy formula onto the conveyer belt and reached into her purse for her wallet. "Boy," she said. "We named him Brian."

"Wonderful. And everyone's good?"

Joan paid the cashier. "Couldn't be better. Thanks." She looked out the window toward the station wagon and, thinking that Brian might now be awake and screaming from starvation, she actually felt guilt take another bite. She looked back at Katy. "And how have you been?" she forced herself to ask her long-forgotten friend.

"The same..." Katy sighed. "I'd love to finally meet a good guy. There aren't any out there, you know."

Joan's nervous eyes alternated between the slow, elderly bagger and the station wagon. The old man bagging the groceries smiled at her. Although she felt like crawling out of her skin, she returned the smile. *I need to get out of here and back to Brian.* She looked back at Katy again. "Good men...they're out there," Joan said and snatched the heavy paper bag filled with cans of formula. "Don't give up looking."

"I wish that were true, but..."

"Katy, I don't mean to be rude, but I need to leave and feed my baby. He's hungry." Without waiting for a reply, Joan turned on her heels and marched out of the store.

Katy's mouth hung open – until she spotted the cashier smiling at her; a woman who looked like she might be a really good listener.

~ ~ ~ ~ ~ ~ ~ ~

Less than an hour after Brian consumed his first bottle of Neo Mulsoy, Joan changed his diaper to discover that he had diarrhea. It was like dark muddy water that had just run out of him. "Oh, God," she said, but decided not to complain to Frank just yet. Nervous, she grabbed a pen and paper, and jotted down the date and time. *If we have to go see the doctor again*, she thought, *this time I'll have the information to back up my claims.*

As she filled another bottle with tap water, more guilt gnawed at the core of her maternal being.

~ ~ ~ ~ ~ ~ ~ ~

After nearly two weeks of being on the soy-based infant formula, Brian still experienced frequent vomiting – only now, he also suffered from severe diarrhea. He wouldn't stop crying and rarely slept. Joan spent her waking hours trying everything to console him and stop him from waking up Frank and Ross. Most of the time, it was no use. "Do something, Joan!" Frank screamed from their bedroom. "I have to work in the morning!"

But there was nothing she could do. She just sat in the dark with her son and wept along with him. Her breast milk had dried up and the guilt she carried for it was overwhelming.

~ ~ ~ ~ ~ ~ ~ ~

At wit's end, she finally called Doctor Carvalho's office and nervously explained, "My baby won't stop crying and he hardly sleeps. When he's not vomiting the soy formula, he's passing it as diarrhea. I'm sick with worry and I need to bring him in to see the doctor right away."

An hour later, the nurse who had taken down the information called back and told her, "The doctor would like you to stick with the Neo Mulsoy."

Joan slammed the phone into its cradle and gasped for air. Her heart began to beat hard in her chest. She didn't know what was wrong. For a few terrifying moments, she couldn't breathe. She couldn't think. With a sweaty face and shaking hands, the vicious wave crashed over her and left just as quickly as it had arrived. Although she felt dazed and confused, she still realized that it was fear; panic for her helpless baby boy.

# Chapter 3

*Summer 1977*

Joan checked the wall calendar and cringed. Since Brian's first bottle of soy-based formula, he was now suffering from weight loss, lethargy and severe chest congestion. She picked up his medical diary and flipped through its pages. It was filling fast – dates, times, detail after brutal detail.

To her surprise, on one of the pages of Brian's medical diary, Ross had drawn two stick figures. It was a picture of him and his baby brother. Her eyes filled with tears of love and sorrow. *Poor Ross*, she thought. The little boy was now forced to sleep on the couch in order to get any rest at all. Most nights, he'd stay by his brother's side for as long as he could – until Joan forced him out to the living room where the couch had been converted into a temporary bed. "Please, Ross," she told him. "Little boys shouldn't have bags under their eyes. Mommy will take care of Brian. I promise."

Fortunately, Frank was also aware of the situation. Fearing that Ross was getting lost in the chaos, he suggested, "How 'bout I take him out on Friday for a boy's night out? We'll get some pizza and then go catch a movie."

"I think that's a brilliant idea." Joan said, and kissed her husband tenderly. "Which movie?"

"Well, it's between Star Wars or Disney's new film, The Rescuers."

"Isn't Ross a little young for Star Wars?"

"Yeah, but I'm not," he joked.

Joan slapped his arm, playfully.

"Okay, then an adventure about two little mice, it is."

~ ~ ~ ~ ~ ~ ~ ~

Just as expected, Casserta's was jam packed. Frank ordered a small pepperoni pizza and two spinach pies, and then felt like he hit the lottery when he found a small empty table in the back of the cafeteria-style dining room. While they waited for their food, he asked Ross, "So what's new in your world, little man?"

"Number 75," the intercom belted. Frank checked his receipt. *Too early*, he thought. *Can't be us*. He was right.

As if he carried the weight of the world upon his narrow shoulders, the little boy shrugged. "I wish Brian was happier," he admitted. "He's always sad."

*Unreal*, Frank thought.

"Number 77," echoed through the dining room.

Placing his hand on his son's knee, Frank explained, "Brian has some boo-boos in his belly, buddy, but the doctor will figure out what's wrong. You don't need to worry about it. He'll get better."

"But what if he doesn't?" Ross asked, peering into his father's eyes.

"He will," Frank said, "I promise."

"Number 78," the intercom called out.

*Though God only knows when*, Frank thought. He stayed locked on his son's gaze until belief registered in the young boy's eyes.

"Number 79."

Frank checked his receipt again. *We're up next*. He turned his attention back to Ross. "I know Mom and I usually don't let you drink soda, but you can have whatever you like tonight, okay?"

A spark of joy ignited in Ross' eyes. "Coke?" he asked.

"Number 80."

Smiling, Frank stood. "Sure. Two Cokes...one for me and one for you." He held out his hand and Ross grabbed it.

"Thanks, Dad," Ross said, as they made their way toward the counter. "And I won't tell Mom and get you in trouble, okay?"

Frank laughed. "That's okay, buddy. But we don't keep secrets from Mom, right?"

"Right," Ross said, with a subtle shrug.

~ ~ ~ ~ ~ ~ ~ ~

It was a mild summer evening – the air, warm and sweet. While the world peacefully slumbered away, Joan kept a strict vigilance over her ailing baby. Throughout the night, Brian's diarrhea had become so severe that she had to change his diapers five times and his bedding twice.

Just before dawn, she laid him on his belly in the crib and patted his backside until he finally drifted off.

It felt like she'd just closed her eyes when she awoke with the late morning sun on her face. *Ouch!* Her lower back throbbed in pain. It took a moment to realize that her body was contorted in the chair. She sat up straight and stretched her legs to work out the knot in her back. As she yawned, she spotted Brian lying motionless in his crib, a zombie's expression on his face. "Oh God!" she screamed and leaped to her feet, nearly tripping from the lack of blood in her legs. Her baby was gray, with big, black circles under his eyes. He'd lost so many bodily fluids through the night that he was scratching at death's door.

Besides the pins and needles in her legs, all the symptoms of another panic attack – pounding heart, shallow breathing, overwhelming feelings of doom and darkness – ambushed her. But she pushed them away. *There's no time*, she thought. *Brian's in trouble and he needs help now!*

She lifted him out of the crib and hobbled toward the kitchen phone to call for an ambulance. With trembling hands, she called Doctor Carvalho's office to inform them of the situation. "Either you admit him, or we're camping out at the Emergency Room...and we're not leaving!"

She looked down to find Ross standing there, panicked.

"Brian has to go to the hospital," she told him. "Go get dressed."

He ran back to his room.

She then left a message for Frank at work before she dialed her mother's house. "Ma, Brian's being admitted into the hospital. I need..." Her strength had finally left her and she broke down in a wounded sob.

"Okay, I'll meet you there," Mama promised and hung up the phone.

The sound of an approaching ambulance was the first welcomed wail in weeks.

*I need to get dressed,* Joan thought, looking down at her pajamas. *I'll just throw on some sweats over these.* She then looked down the hall. "Hurry up, Ross!"

~ ~ ~ ~ ~ ~ ~ ~

While Ross was escorted into the nurse's station away from the action, Brian was so dehydrated that two nurses had to strap him to a wooden, infant-sized board. They worked at a frantic pace, placing intravenous needles into his arms and legs to feed him the fluids and nutrients that his tiny body screamed for.

"It might be more comfortable in the waiting room," the younger of the two nurses told Joan.

Joan looked up at her, but never uttered a word. Instead, she squeezed Brian's hand tighter and firmly planted her feet.

Both nurses looked at each other, the older of the two nodding that it was okay for Joan to stay. After checking his monitor, they quietly left the room.

Mama arrived before Frank. When Joan spotted her, she collapsed into her arms. "I just know something is seriously wrong with Brian, but nobody will listen to me. Everyone just keeps telling me that I worry too much...that I'm overanxious. Frank, Doctor Carvalho..."

Mama pulled her daughter into her chest. "I'm listening, Joan. I'm here and I'm listening." She nodded. "Everything will be okay."

~ ~ ~ ~ ~ ~ ~ ~

With Joan sleeping in a chair on one side of the hospital bassinette and Mama sleeping in a chair on the other, Brian stayed overnight for observation. Although he felt terrible for not staying, Frank returned home to watch Ross.

In the morning, Doctor Carvalho entered the room with Brian's chart in hand. "I'm going to prescribe a syrup to bind him up." He wrote out the script and handed it to Joan. "I just signed your son's release, so you're free to go home." He looked her straight in the eye. "Your son will outgrow his digestive problems, Mrs. Mauretti. Hang in there."

Joan was stunned. She opened her mouth to argue the point, but was interrupted by the busy doctor. "He'll be fine...and he needs to go home." The pediatrician turned and hurried out of the room.

As if she were six years old again, Joan looked toward her mother with scared, desperate eyes. Mama merely shook her head, squirming with the same anxiety that her daughter had been suffering. "We'll figure this out," she finally said. "We will."

~ ~ ~ ~ ~ ~ ~ ~

Long days turned into unbearable weeks. The syrup ran out and the diarrhea returned. Brian depended on Neo Mulsoy formula as his sole source of nutrition for nearly six months, and he never did outgrow the digestive problems. In fact, they became worse. The nights of screaming were endless, with Joan feeling helpless to ease her baby's discomfort.

Mama finally told her, "Doctor Carvalho is a good pediatrician, but maybe you should get a second opinion from someone younger? I know a younger doctor might lack experience, but he'll be up on the new procedures and products on the market."

Without hesitation, Joan contacted a new pediatric practice two towns over, requesting a second opinion on her son's digestive nightmare. After explaining her son's condition, the receptionist said, "Looks like I can squeeze you in on Monday afternoon... ummm...two o'clock. Is that okay?"

"Yes," Joan choked out. "We'll be there." She hung up the phone and felt the first ray of light touch their dark world.

~ ~ ~ ~ ~ ~ ~ ~

With short-cropped hair and crystal blue eyes, Doctor Alexander looked like he'd just graduated from high school. Joan second-guessed her decision until the young man spent more time examining Brian in one session than Doctor Carvalho had in all of their appointments combined. At the conclusion of the exam, he actually took a seat, looked at Joan and said, "So tell me everything."

Her eyes filled and she nearly hugged him for his genuine concern. "I could explain it, but I'd rather give you this." She reached into her pocketbook, retrieved Brian's battered medical diary and handed it to him. "I documented everything," she said.

He opened the book and read the first two pages before skimming through the rest. With a heavy sigh, he stood and asked, "May I keep it for a day or two to read through it thoroughly?"

"Of course."

"I'm going to help your son, Mrs. Mauretti," he promised. "Whatever it takes, we're going to find out what's wrong with Brian."

Joan's knees nearly buckled. "Thank you," she whimpered. *Thank God.*

~ ~ ~ ~ ~ ~ ~ ~

A slew of tests were conducted on Brian and the initial screens turned up nothing, but Doctor Alexander was a man of his word. He was relentless in his pursuit of answers; for the truth.

The baby gave blood, urine, stool samples and more blood. He squirmed during an abdomen ultra sound and screamed during a scary CT scan. Joan felt pieces of her soul shrivel up and die each time her baby was prodded. The only saving grace was Mama. The old lady never left their sides.

Initially, a diagnosis of Bartter's Syndrome was made.

"Dear God...what's that?" Joan asked.

"It's an inherited defect in the renal tubules that causes low potassium and chloride levels," Doctor Alexander explained. "We'll need to start Brian on supplements right away. Let's set up an appointment for later in the week and discuss in detail. For now, I'll call the prescriptions into the pharmacy."

"Okay then," Joan said, confused.

But the young doctor was still skeptical about the initial diagnosis. For the next few weeks, while Joan prayed that the new supplements would help, he continued his research, reading through current medical journals and making phone call after phone call to colleagues throughout the country. Finally, he discovered several similar cases in Tennessee. A Memphis pediatrician had noticed that three sick babies with strange symptoms had all been depending on Neo Mulsoy as their primary source of nourishment.

According to the Memphis pediatrician, all three infants were unable to gain weight and failed to thrive. He also noticed that all three were being fed the same brand of soy-based formula. To further investigate the possible correlation, he contacted the Center for Disease Control in Atlanta and reported it. The CDC advised that similar infant cases, scattered throughout the country, had been diagnosed with metabolic alkalosis.

After notifying the CDC and the Food and Drug Administration to report his suspicions about Brian, Doctor Alexander telephoned Joan once again and told her, "Mrs. Mauretti, I hate to tell you this but I think we need to conduct a few more tests."

And the nightmare continued.

~ ~ ~ ~ ~ ~ ~ ~

Brian was eleven months old when Doctor Alexander summoned the Mauretti family into his office to deliver the final verdict. Mama insisted that she be there. No one objected.

It was a late winter afternoon, a howling wind knocking on blocks of ice that were once windows. Doctor Alexander sat behind his tidy desk, looking distressed. Joan nearly cried when she saw his demeanor and immediately leaned on Frank for support. Avoiding initial eye contact, the young doctor was clearly having trouble offering his prognosis. He cleared his throat and finally reported, "We've discovered that Brian has metabolic alkalosis."

"He has what?" Frank asked.

"Metabolic alkalosis is a blood disorder that affects an infant's ability to digest properly and gain weight. It's caused by a lack of chloride, or sodium, in the diet."

"So what does that mean for Brian?" Joan asked.

"Several of Brian's tests have shown some abnormality in the frontal area of his brain."

Joan, Frank and Mama's silence begged for the man to embellish. The doctor took another long pause, making Joan feel like her heart was going to explode. She tried to slow down the hyperventilating. It was no use.

"Your son's development has been severely damaged," he finally told Joan and Frank directly. "And at this point, I believe it's irreversible."

"Irreversible? I don't understand?" Joan screeched, frightened for her baby boy's future. She felt so light-headed that the room began to spin.

Doctor Alexander shook his head. "It means that Brian will never walk."

"Never walk?" Frank repeated, his face instantly bleached to white.

"I'm sorry, but we don't believe he will." He scanned the reports in front of him and took another deep breath. "It's also doubtful that Brian will ever talk or communicate effectively."

Joan looked toward her mother again, her terrified eyes begging for help. Mama got to her feet and took a defensive posture.

Without acknowledging the old woman, the doctor went on, "Brian may never be able to do what normal children – or adults – are able to do." He paused again. "We believe it may have been caused by the Neo Mulsoy formula. The low chloride concentration in his urine is substantial proof that the sodium deficiency within the soy formula has been the primary cause of Brian's medical problems."

While the doctor tried to explain further, Joan wailed, "Oh God, what did I do to my boy?"

"You didn't do anything," Doctor Alexander and Mama vowed in unison.

The doctor backed off, allowing the old lady to take over. She grabbed her daughter's panicked face. "This wasn't you," Mama promised. "You did nothing wrong!" She shook her head. "And this is only one opinion. There are other doctors...more tests."

While Joan wept sorrowfully, Frank rested his hand on his wife's leg and stared helplessly at the doctor. "But Doctor Carvalho prescribed the formula to Brian," he muttered in a wounded voice, as if it would make some difference.

"There's no way he could have known at that time that it would have caused your son harm," the man replied.

"You say he'll never walk?" Joan cried.

"Sorry, but I really don't believe he will," the doctor answered, sadly.

"Or talk?" Joan gasped, trying to breathe.

The man slowly shook his head. "I have to believe that the damage to your son's frontal lobe will prohibit any real speech."

As Joan struggled to continue her panicked line of questioning, Mama shook her gray, curly head. "That's crap!" she said, loud enough for everyone to hear.

The young doctor turned his attention to her. "I realize that this is..."

"You're wrong!" Mama insisted, taking a step toward him.

"Excuse me?" he asked. "I know this isn't easy to hear, but..." The man shot her a kind smile, but Mama wasn't swayed. "I'm so sorry, but Brian is now mentally disabled," he concluded.

"No. I don't think you understand," Mama replied, staring straight into his sapphire eyes. "Our boy is going to walk. He's going to talk. He's going to ride a bike, swim, and learn to do everything that

any other kid can do. It might take a little more doing, but I guarantee it!"

Although it was the slightest movement, the
doctor shook his head at her foolish hope. "Believe
me, I wish that were true, but..."

"Wishing won't have anything to do with it. No,
this'll take faith and determination, and the love and
support of our entire family."

Unable to do more, Doctor Alexander turned
back to Joan and Frank. "I'm here for whatever you
need."

"For what?" Frank barked, his shock turning to
rage. "It was a doctor who ruined my son's life!" By
this point, Joan was nearly rolled into the fetal position, her body paralyzed from the devastating news.

Doctor Alexander nodded compassionately and,
handing Frank a piece of paper, concluded, "This is a
different soy-based formula that you folks can start
Brian on, as well as an additional chloride supple-
ment. We'll talk about solid foods and other alterna-
tives during his next visit." Patting Joan's shoulder,
he said, "I'm so sorry," and stepped out of the room.

Mama watched the back of him disappear down
the long hall and nodded herself into the slightest
smirk. In that one moment, she realized her life's
mission had just begun.

While Joan sobbed and convulsed, Frank held
his head in his hands, trying to process it all. Mama
grabbed her dejected daughter's face again and forced
Joan to look into her eyes. She spoke sternly. "Joan,
you listen to me right now. That doctor's wrong! Brian's going to write his own story. He's going to sing

his own song and no one's going to sing it for him. It's his life and it's between him and God...not some fool doctor who's had so much schooling that he's forgotten the power of faith."

Joan shook her head. "But, Ma..." she sobbed. "You heard him. Brian's brain has been damaged." The final word made her wail out in pain.

"Your Nana said that she had such a difficult time bringing me into the world that she nearly died. And the horse doctor who assisted in the birth told her that I just wouldn't be right."

Frank looked up from his spell and began to quietly weep.

Mama nodded again. "Yep," she said, with burning determination. "Brian's going to be as right as rain. I guarantee it. Only God knows how...but that's enough."

~ ~ ~ ~ ~ ~ ~ ~

In the months that followed, Brian's case was introduced to a world-renowned pediatric specialist located at the Children's Hospital in Boston. For the family, it was a time of living out of suitcases and eating in hospital waiting rooms. Each of their waking thoughts was filled with the hope that – no matter how slim the chance – Doctor Alexander was wrong. Dozens of additional tests were conducted on Brian, and twice as many prayers were prayed. Tragically, the final result remained the same – "Irreversible brain damage."

Forced to face reality, Joan and Frank returned home to mourn the loss of their son's normal, healthy future. Mama, however, returned to her cottage by the bay with a different mindset. Before the front door slammed shut, she was already on the telephone, dialing Liz DeSousa, her old floor lady at the textile mill.

"Hi, Liz, it's Angela. Do you have any seamstress work you can send my way?" She paused. "Nope. I'm coming out of retirement. I need the money." She shook her head. "Actually, today's that rainy day...and it's pouring out." There was another pause, followed by a nod. "Thanks," she said. "I appreciate it more than you know."

Mama stepped into her bedroom and took three pills before slowly easing down to her knees. With clasped hands, she prayed, "Father, please bless this family. Forgive us of our sins and have mercy upon our souls. Shroud our children in your angels and protect them from all harm..." The last words were forced through a wave of raw emotion. She paused. "Lord, please bless Brian. I honestly don't under-stand why this has happened to a pure and innocent child; why such enormous obstacles have been set before him...but I place my faith and trust in you. And I will lean on that faith, believing that there are reasons that reach beyond our understanding. Please, Father...grant our family the love, faith and strength to help Brian through this difficult world. Let us teach him to walk and talk and live..." The tears flowed feely now. "...to love...and be able to receive our love in return. I ask this in the name of your son, Jesus. Amen."

The God-loving woman struggled off her knees and rolled into bed. For a long time, she stared at the crucifix that hung above her bedroom door. "Please let me live long enough to help Brian fly," she whispered, and then closed her weeping eyes.

# Chapter 4

### Late Spring 1978

The newspaper reporters were starting to knock, followed by even louder knocks from an army of attorneys. Even a producer from the Geraldo Rivera show contacted Joan and Frank to gather information on the Neo Mulsoy formula that had now poisoned one hundred thirty babies nationwide.

Joan called Mama and asked, "Is there any chance you can let the boys stay with you tonight?"

"Of course."

There was a pause before Joan went on. "And maybe Ross can stay with you for a few extra days? The phone's been ringing day and night, and I think it would be nice for him to get some much needed attention."

"Sure...but how 'bout we plan for a week? I'll talk to Bob and Bev about letting the girls stay over, too. The four of us will kick off the summer with a real adventure."

"Summer?"

"It's early, I know, but after the winter we've had..."

~ ~ ~ ~ ~ ~ ~ ~

That night, as the bay winds were picking up and the sun was going down, Mama sat out on the three-season porch with her four grandchildren. As they played Parcheesi and shared silly stories, she sat with Brian in her lap. She looked up from the baby and smiled. "What do you guys think about staying at Mama's for a full week?"

"YES!" they screamed.

"That's what I thought. So what do you think about starting it off with our own little adventure tomorrow?"

"What adventure, Mama?" Heidi asked, for all of them.

Mama shrugged, teasing them.

"Come on, Mama," Ross whined.

"Please?" Steph pleaded, knowing that this one magical word could get her almost anything from the woman.

Mama nodded. "Okay," she said. "We're getting up early tomorrow and going on a whale watch."

All three kids sprang from their chairs and began to dance. Ross sang, "We're goin' on a whale watch. We're goin' on a whale watch..."

"Yes, we are," she chuckled and returned to her sewing. As she worked, she began their preparation for embarking upon the high seas. "You guys will each have to bring an extra jacket or sweater," she told them.

"But it's starting to get warm out, Mama," Steph said.

"True, but it's still early in the season and it gets cold out on the water, so we have to dress in layers."

The kids nodded.

"You'll also need hats because the sun reflects off the water and can burn your skin. And be sure to wear your sneakers, so you won't slip on the deck of the boat."

They nodded again.

"I'll bring the binoculars and a camera." She thought for a moment. "But we'll leave the watch at home."

"What about food?" Heidi asked.

"There's a galley on the boat that sells sandwiches, drinks and snacks. I'll bring the money, okay?"

They all giggled.

Suddenly, Mama spotted a doe and her fawn standing on the front lawn, looking out onto the bay. She placed her finger to her lips. "Shhhhh," she whispered. "Look." She slowly pointed at them. "That's two of the Lord's gentle spirits."

"Ahhhh," the kids whispered.

As both deer grazed, Mama shook her head and whispered, "How folks can hunt them is beyond me."

The doe looked up and ran off, the little one hurrying behind her.

"Okay, guys. If we're going to tackle the open seas tomorrow, then it's time for bed."

"Awww," they complained.

"What do you guys think about having supper at McRay's Clam Shack tomorrow after the whale watch?"

All three began their celebratory dance.

"But none of it's going to happen until you get a good night's sleep. Now, go get cleaned up and I'll be in to kiss you good night."

~ ~ ~ ~ ~ ~ ~ ~

With the kids tucked in and Brian nestled safely in her lap, Mama picked up the local newspaper and read the first of many articles about her grandson:

> Baby Formula is Discovered Toxic and a Rhode Island Family Suffers
>
> by Steven Herberts, Staff Reporter – Narragansett Gazette
>
> For more than six months, the Mauretti family of Narragansett fed their new-born son, Brian, a soy-based formula called Neo Mulsoy. What they didn't realize is that the company that man-ufactured the formula removed too much chloride from its two formulas, Neo Mulsoy and Cho-Free. As a re-sult, Brian, along with thousands of other babies nationwide, has been placed at risk to suffer poor muscle control, slowed growth, learning dis-abilities and perhaps even lifelong speech and language disorders.
>
> After his birth, Brian thrived and gained weight while Mrs. Mauretti breast-fed him. Once she stopped nursing and

Brian rejected a milk-based formula, however, the Maurettis quickly conferred with their pediatrician.

Mrs. Mauretti said, "I knew something was wrong right after the doctor prescribed the soy formula. Brian was sluggish and had black circles under his eyes. He would cry for hours at a time and there was nothing I could do to comfort him. And the diarrhea just wouldn't stop, making him so weak. I always knew there was something seriously wrong, but the doctor just kept telling me that I worried too much."

Fed to an estimated twenty thousand infants nationwide, Neo Mulsoy lacked sufficient amounts of chloride, or sodium: an essential ingredient in an infant's brain development.

"What babies eat during their first six months of life is crucial and any damage caused usually can't be repaired later," Dr. Bernstein, a renowned pediatric researcher, reported. "Infant formula has to have everything a baby needs because it is normally the sole source of nourishment during peak brain development. The brain gets bigger right after birth and by the age of two, it's close to adult size. Essentially, our future depends on what food we take in as an infant. With the wrong nourishment, the consequences could prove devastating and last a lifetime."

Neo Mulsoy's manufacturer, Syntex Corp., acknowledged that they had reformulated the soy mixture to reduce its sodium content. Unfortunately, they failed to properly test the new formula.

Syntex, a market giant which sells nearly $400 million in infant products annually, refers to the issue as "an error in judgment."

Unable to find answers with the doctor who prescribed the toxic formula, the Maurettis sought the opinion of another local pediatrician. Tests were run and rerun. Initially, a diagnosis of Bartter's syndrome was made. However, Dr. Alexander had heard about several cases in Tennessee where a Memphis pediatrician noticed that three sick babies all shared the same strange symptoms, and all three were dependent upon Neo Mulsoy as their primary food source. He immediately notified the Food and Drug Administration (FDA) and reported his suspicions.

"This poor family had suffered terribly and just couldn't find any answers for their baby's chronic symptoms," Dr. Alexander said. "I wanted very much to help them."

After more tests, Dr. Alexander diagnosed Brian with metabolic alkalosis. The sodium deficiency within the soy formula had been the cause of the Mauretti's nightmare, as evidenced in the low chloride concentration within the baby's urine.

The FDA, however, permitted Neo Mulsoy to remain on many supermarket shelves for months after it was reported.

"Neo Mulsoy is not a poison at all," Charles Woods, an FDA spokesman said. "Only a fraction of the babies who consumed it might suffer long-term issues."

Dr. Erickson, deputy chief of the birth defects branch of the federal Center for Disease Control (CDC) in Atlanta, stated, "We now know that the lack of chloride may have caused metabolic alkalosis, which is a blood disorder that affected the infants' abilities to digest properly and gain weight. We also believe that the babies who were on the soy based formula, but also eating solid foods, are fine. More than likely, they received enough of the chloride to avoid any problems."

He added, "It is possible that some infants could suffer permanent brain damage, as well as learning disabilities."

The CDC has currently identified one hundred thirty affected babies, with Brian Mauretti at the top of that list.

According to Dr. Erickson, this is the first time a significant number of babies have suffered a chloride deficiency, and he said it might take years before any real results are yielded.

Although the Rhode Island Dept. of Health advised that only a small percentage of infants were placed at risk, there has been widespread concern over Neo Mulsoy and its adverse affects. "That doesn't help my son," said Frank Mauretti, Brian's father. "I can't believe that the company didn't properly test for the right levels of sodium or that the FDA even allowed it on the market for as long as they did." He and his wife are determined to help other families ensure that it never happens again.

At least a dozen lawsuits have been filed against Syntex, seeking millions of dollars in damages. Several Rhode Island families are involved in legal action as well. The Maurettis are one of those families. "Considering the challenges my son now faces, at the very least he shouldn't have to worry about money, too," Mr. Mauretti said.

Congressional hearings are being called for, proposing laws that would mandate formula-producing companies to submit test results to the FDA before being allowed to release their products into the market. The legislation will also require that a certain amount of specific nutrients be included in all formulas. Currently, such test results are not required to be sent to the FDA and the nutrients – for now – are only "recommended." The reforms won't help Brian Mauretti, though.

At more than a year old, Brian Mauretti still can't crawl, pull himself up, stand or walk. He doesn't speak and his future is quite uncertain. He now suffers with metabolic alkalosis and celiac disease, an intestinal problem aggravated by certain foods. With a new change in diet, Dr. Alexander is hopeful he'll begin thriving. It is not yet certain, however, the permanent effects that this tiny Rhode Island infant will suffer.

His parents, no doubt, will continue to suffer for years to come.

~ ~ ~ ~ ~ ~ ~ ~

Mama placed the newspaper down, looked at Brian who was snoring quietly in her lap and kissed the top of his head. "*Uncertain* future, my backside," she grunted. "Enough talk. Our work begins." She took out her rosary beads, blessed herself and took the very first step down the long, hard road before them.

# Chapter 5

### *Early Summer 1978*

Enough time had passed for the shock of Brian's condition to wear off. Joan had stumbled beyond the grieving process and had given up negotiating with God. She was now at a place called rage. Mama sat with her daughter at the kitchen table, trying to help her make sense of it all. "Maybe Brian's a test from God?" Mama suggested.

"Why would God test a little baby who's never done a thing wrong? Why would He test an innocent child?" Joan snapped back.

Mama shook her head. "I didn't say God was testing Brian," she said evenly. There was a thoughtful pause. "Maybe He's testing everyone around Brian?"

"I don't want to hear that!" Joan roared. "My son will never be able to enjoy the life of other people who don't..."

Mama slapped her hand on the Formica table, stopping Joan in mid-sentence and turning her face into that of a seven-year-old girl's. "Not another negative word, do you hear me?" she yelled back, quickly grabbing her daughter's hands and holding them tightly. "Positive, Joan – everything must be positive! Negative calls for negative and positive brings forth

positive. Brian's already facing some unfair challenges. We have to be positive, Joan. We just have to be!"

Joan wiped her eyes. "But what if the doctor's
right, Ma?" she muttered in a tortured voice. "What
if..."

Without letting Joan's hands go, Mama took a
deep breath and started in on her own tirade. "The
doctors don't know what the hell they're talking
about! I had a grandmother who lived her whole life
as a brittle diabetic, but she ate anything she wanted.
She died three days before her eighty-fifth birthday.
Your grandfather supposedly had cirrhosis of the liv-
er, but lived with his bottle for forty more years until
old age took him. They don't know beans! Besides,
we need to have faith in a higher source." She pulled
her crucifix away from her neck and kissed it. "You
have to believe, Joan. Before any of the healing can
take place, you have to believe that it will." She nodded and lowered her tone. "Only God knows how...
and that's enough."

Joan placed her face in her hands and began to
cry. She was now completely removed from her rage
and safely returned to the stage of grief. "I'm...just...
so...scared," she stuttered, sobbing.

Mama stroked her hair. "Don't you worry, love.
They say that children are raised by a village." She
nodded her gray, curly head. "I think it's about time
we had a village meeting."

~ ~ ~ ~ ~ ~ ~ ~

The following Wednesday night, the DiMartino/
Mauretti family meeting took place right in Mama's

kitchen. After three giant meatloaves and two trays of her famous white pizza had been devoured, Mama scanned the table and locked eyes with each person seated with her, commanding their full attention. She finally addressed them as a group. "As Brian grows up, he's going to need our help...all of us." Although it sounded like she was asking, everyone knew better.

Except for Frank, the nods fell like dominoes.

"For years, every Wednesday and Saturday night, this family has gotten together in this little cottage to break bread and share our lives. Although I expect that to continue, I'd like to set some new rules going forward."

Everyone stared at her, careful not to make any moves that could be interpreted as an objection. She was setting out instructions to be followed without question. Frank's face was slowly turning crimson.

She turned to her small grandchildren. "From now on, no one has to help clear the table or dry the dishes after dinner."

Heidi started to celebrate when her dad's hand stopped her.

"Instead, I want each of you to spend the time with Brian," Mama explained. "You can either talk to him and teach him how to use his mouth to form words, or help him to learn how to crawl." She looked down at the baby seated in Joan's lap and rubbed his head. "Eventually, we'll even get him to walk."

Joan gasped at her mother's impossible prediction. Frank shook his agitated head.

Mama ignored it and waited for a reaction from the kids.

"How will we know what to do?" Steph asked, innocently.

"Yeah, how can we help?" Heidi joined her sister.

Mama pointed to Ross. The little boy was seated beside Brian and his mother at the table, holding his brother's hand. "That's the type of love and attention that we need to pay Brian," Mama explained. "Just watch Ross. He'll show you what to do. He always thinks about his brother before himself. It's instinctive for him."

Although the silence remained, Bob and Bev joined the girls' nods.

Mama turned to Joan and Frank and announced, "I also plan to hire a speech therapist."

"Speech therapist?" Frank repeated. "I think it's too early..."

"No, it's not. I've already spoken to a few of them and have been assured that it's not too early, and that it's time for him to start forming words."

"But how much..." Joan began to ask.

"I'm going to cover it," Mama interrupted. "Weeks ago, Liz was good enough to give me some piece-work."

"But Ma, you shouldn't..." Joan began to object.

"I want to do this. And I don't want to hear another word about it."

Frank was now shaking his head even harder, clearly upset with where the discussion was going.

For the moment, Mama ignored it and scanned the table. "I also know that Brian's only going to get a fraction of what he needs from outside of this family. Most of what he's going to learn will come from us, so we need to be well aware of that and put in the extra effort every chance we can."

Frank half-rose and began to rebel against his mother-in-law. "I appreciate what you're saying, Ma, but my son's future is for your daughter and me to decide."

With a gentle hand upon his shoulder, the stubborn old lady diplomatically explained, "But you're not always going to be around, Frank. You need to work and provide for your family...for your son. So he's going to need others to teach him, as well." She patted his shoulder. "It's going to take everyone, Frank. And I know you want the best for Brian."

"That's it! I've heard enough," Frank said. With a huff, he rose from his seat and headed for the door. "I'm going for a cigarette," he grumbled and slammed the door behind him.

Ross watched his father storm out of the house, but quickly returned his attention to his little brother. Everyone else, however, looked to Joan. She simply shrugged. "Let him go and sulk. I really don't care. Brian comes first." But her face told a different story. She loved Frank too much to dismiss his feelings so easily and everyone knew it.

Mama shook her head. The first crack had revealed itself in the foundation of her daughter's strained marriage.

~ ~ ~ ~ ~ ~ ~ ~

Uncle Sal – Mama's brother – pulled his cherry red Cadillac in front of the house, parked and spotted Frank sitting on the front steps. Although Frank was sucking on a non-filter, Sal could see the smoke coming out of his ears. He strolled over and took a seat beside him. "What's going on?" he asked.

Frank never hesitated. "Your sister's in there trying to run the show, as usual…telling me and my wife what's going to happen with Brian."

Sal nodded. "Yeah, she told me that you guys were meeting today to discuss the little guy."

"Too bad I didn't know ahead of time. I could have avoided it!"

"Frank, if you put your pride aside for a few minutes and think about your boy rather than yourself, you'll see the amazing opportunity that's right in front of you." Ignoring Frank's angry gaze, he shrugged. "Angie may be the most stubborn, pig-headed person I know, but she's also got a heart as big as your head…and that's exactly what you need with the tough hand that Brian's been dealt." There was a thoughtful pause. "If anyone can help your son, it's your crazy mother-in-law. She loves that boy more than her own soul. She'll pull the best he has out of him and help him fit into this screwed-up world."

Frank flicked his cigarette butt onto the lawn, stood and started for the car. "Maybe…but she's not going to run my life in the meantime."

~ ~ ~ ~ ~ ~ ~ ~

From the living room window, Joan and Mama watched as Frank and Sal finished their animated conversation. Mama turned to her daughter. "Let the boys stay tonight."

"Brian, too?" Joan asked, surprised.

"Brian, too," Mama confirmed. "You don't think you're the only one who can change a diaper, do you?" Mama rubbed her daughter's back. "Besides, it looks like you could use a good night's sleep."

Joan stared at her husband, who now sat waiting in the parked car at the curb. "Thanks, Ma."

Mama turned to Bob and Bev. "Do you mind if the girls stay, too...just for the night?"

"Okay," Bob said. "I'll be by to pick them up first thing in the morning."

While the kids celebrated, the adults headed for the door. Mama watched from the window, as Joan and Frank exchanged some heated words. She looked down to see Ross also watching his parents argue. The little boy looked up at his grandmother. She half-shrugged, telling him, "When the elephants are mating, it's best for us little people to stay out of the high grass, or we might get hurt."

Ross' big eyes showed even more confusion.

Mama smiled at him and nibbled on his neck until he squealed. Frank and Joan pulled away from the curb and drove down the road. *Like marriage isn't hard enough*, she thought and turned to find the girls playing with Brian on the floor.

Heidi and Steph were taking turns trying to show the toddler how to push himself up onto his knees from his belly. Mama's eyes filled when she saw it.

As they played, Brian flopped onto his back and – although he tried real hard – he couldn't roll himself back onto his belly. Steph grabbed him and started to flip him over when Mama stopped her. "Let him do it, sweetheart."

"But he can't..."

"No such word as *can't!*" she blurted. "Brian is abled, not disabled...and we're never going to treat him like he's handicapped. Let him learn to do it for himself, please."

Each young face stared up at her, betraying a mix of confusion and disappointment.

Mama slowly took a seat on the floor with them and took a deep breath. "Do you guys like butter-flies?" she asked.

They all nodded. "They're my favorite!" Heidi said.

"Mine, too," Mama confirmed with a smile. "But butterflies start out as fuzzy, crawly caterpillars."

"Yuck," Heidi said.

Steph smiled. "That's cool," Ross agreed.

Mama chuckled. "And when the time's just right, each caterpillar forms its own cocoon. About two weeks later, when it's time for them to fly off into the world as a butterfly, they have to struggle with all their might to break out of that cocoon. And believe me, they can't fly until they've struggled for a very long time." She searched their faces. They seemed to be following her. "If they didn't have to struggle," she explained, "then they wouldn't be able to build up the muscles that they need to help them fly." She looked at Brian and rubbed his belly. "We don't want our little boy to be a caterpillar forever, right?"

"No, Mama," they sang in chorus.

"That's right," she said. "Brian's our butterfly, so he's going to have to learn how to break out of his own cocoon."

There were still some questions in their eyes, so Mama took a more direct approach. "We just need to be careful not to do everything for Brian. We have to allow him to do for himself, and this isn't going to be an easy thing to do. Trust me, it breaks Mama's heart sometimes to watch you guys struggle. But unless I let you struggle, you'll never learn and be able to do for yourself and survive in this world. And that's what we need to give Brian...that's what he deserves. Breaking out of his cocoon is going to take a lot of hard work, without other people doing it for him. You guys..."

Although they continued to nod, they'd returned to playing on the floor. She'd reached the end of their attention spans and laughed. "Okay then," she said. Stretching out on the floor with them, she gladly joined in their games.

# Chapter 6

*Early Summer 1978*

Breakfast was a team effort, with each kid taking his or her assignment very seriously. Heidi set the table and then fed Brian, while Steph worked the toaster, lathering each burned slice of bread with globs of butter. Ross worked slowly at the counter, mixing plastic tumblers of flavored milk. Mama scrambled a frying pan of fluffy eggs and watched as one mess after the other was being made. It would have been easier for her to do it all herself – *but what would that teach?* she thought.

Although he did his best to avoid it, Ross knocked over a full cup of milk. "Sorry, Mama," he said, looking up from the brown puddle.

She glanced over her shoulder with indifference. "You don't need to apologize to me," she said. "You're the one cleaning it up."

With a nod, he mopped up the new mess before taking another shot at his breakfast treat – cold milk and the perfect amount of sweet coffee syrup.

Before they sat down to eat, Mama insisted that the bigger messes get cleaned. And like some brilliant orchestra conductor, she ensured that it all got done before the eggs grew cold.

As they claimed their seats around the table, Mama took over for Heidi and finished spooning out the bowl of mush to Brian. She waited for the questions to begin. It didn't take long.

"Mama, what did the doctors say about Brian? I mean, what did they really say about him being sick?" Heidi asked.

Mama never hesitated with the truth. "They said that he won't be able to do what other kids can do...that he *can't*."

Ross shook his head – visibly upset.

Mama grabbed the little boy's hand and peered hard into his eyes. "Ross, we just talked about this. What does the word *can't* mean to you?"

"Nothing," he answered, defiantly. "You always tell us there's no such word as *can't*."

She smiled. "That's right. For us, there is no such word as can't. Do you believe that?"

"Yes," he replied, confidently.

She looked at the girls.

"We do," they promised in unison.

"Then there's nothing to worry about! If you really don't believe something, then it just isn't true, is it?" She looked at Brian and beamed with love. "I can't tell you how excited I am to see what this little guy is going to teach us...what he's going to show those foolish doctors."

The kids were still agreeing with her when Mama jumped up from the table and began searching for something in the back of the cupboard beneath the sink. She grabbed one of her giant glass pickling jars and a single shot glass. She placed the small glass into the bottom of the massive jar and filled it with water, making sure that the shot glass stayed upright. She then hurried off to her bedroom, returning with a full jar of pennies. Catching her breath, she looked at each of them and explained, "They say it's impossible to drop a penny into this jar and hit the shot glass." She handed them each a penny. "Go ahead and try it."

Each child dropped their penny into the jar, but none of the copper coins came close to landing into the shot glass. Their shrugs quickly turned to mumbled complaints.

"So are you going to quit after only one try, or are you going to give it another shot?" She gave them each a handful of pennies and smiled. "Remember, nothing's impossible. And if I were you, I'd spend every penny I had to prove it."

Steph hit the shot glass on her eleventh turn and squealed in delight. Ross hit the shot glass seven turns later and celebrated like he'd just scored the winning touchdown at the Super Bowl. Heidi dropped penny after penny into the jar, but couldn't hit the shot glass. No matter how carefully she aimed, the small coin always drifted to one side of the target or the other. She finally ran out of pennies and began to sulk.

Mama turned to Ross and Steph. "Well, are you going to help her out or not?" she asked.

They immediately slid the rest of their pennies over to her.

On the very next turn, Heidi hit the shot glass.

While the three kids danced in celebration, Mama said, "Sometimes, you have to give it all you have. And you might even have to rely on the help of family. But there is nothing that's impossible!"

They all nodded, each understanding her clever lesson and the message it was meant to impart.

~ ~ ~ ~ ~ ~ ~ ~

That afternoon, on the front porch, Mama played Parcheesi with the kids, while Brian watched from her lap. Between moves, Heidi innocently asked, "Now that we have to spend our time helping Brian to talk and walk, will we still be able to go on our adventures?" She'd finally popped the question they were all wondering, but didn't dare ask.

Mama smiled. "Oh yes, we'll go and Brian will come with us. And keep in mind, Brian will be the greatest adventure of all for us."

Heidi high-fived her sister and cousin Ross.

After the next move, Steph looked up from the game and asked Mama, "Why did God do this to Brian?"

Mama sat back in her chair and stared into space for a few moments. "I don't know," she finally answered, honestly.

They were shocked. Mama knew everything.

Reading their faces, she embellished, "Only God knows why Brian was chosen to face such challenges. We just need to have faith that it's a good reason; faith that God knows what He's doing...and that's enough."

"What's faith?" Ross asked.

There was much less hesitation this time and she jumped at the opportunity to share her deepest beliefs. "Faith is believing in something you can't see with your eyes."

They were baffled, but took a break from the board game to wrestle with the idea.

"But how can you believe in something that you've never seen?" Steph asked.

"Do you guys love me?" Mama asked the group, grinning.

"With all our hearts," Heidi answered.

"But how do you know? It's not something you can see, right?"

"But we can feel it," Steph finally answered, proudly.

"Right. And I can always feel God's love, so I know He will watch over me and the ones I love. And that's called *faith*...knowing without having to see." She paused to sip her tea. "Without faith, there would be no hope. But with it, we can do anything... and so can Brian. And I believe that more than anything I've ever seen with these tired eyes."

The kids sat back, looking at each other, trying to understand.

Mama concluded, "We are each a single ray of light in this world and Brian's spirit burns as brightly as any I've ever seen. Trust me, faith is stronger than any prediction a doctor can make. We just have to believe."

"We will, Mama," Ross muttered. The girls quickly agreed.

Mama's eyes misted over. She bent down, kissed Brian's head and whispered, "You now have everything you need, little caterpillar."

~ ~ ~ ~ ~ ~ ~ ~

At first light the next morning, the phone rang. It was Joan. "How were the boys?" she asked.

"Angels...the both of them." There was a pause. "How was Frank?"

"Better now." She paused. "We had a long talk and a lot of things that needed to come out – came out."

"That's good," Mama said. "There's nothing more toxic than feelings that are left unsaid."

"We argued for a while and then actually shared a good cry...something we should have done a long time ago. In the end, we agreed that whatever the future holds, we have to face it together...as a family. The boys need..."

"From what I've learned," Mama interrupted, "common ground is the only place you'll find your footing in a marriage and..." She was also stopped in mid-sentence.

"Good morning, Mama," Ross said, standing in the doorway and wiping the sleep from his eyes.

"Good morning, love," Mama told him, and then directed her attention back to Joan on the phone. "Looks like some of your common ground just woke up."

Joan chuckled. "Listen Ma, I just sent Frank to pick up meat pies from Sam's Bakery and then he'll be over to pick up the boys. Please be nice to him."

"I'm always nice," she teased.

"Then nicer," Joan countered.

"Relax," she said, "I'm not here to make trouble. I'm here to help."

# Chapter 7

*Summer 1978*

Mama's house was the kind of place where each summer became the best summer of your life. And each year, Heidi, Steph and Ross spent the better part of the summer months at the cottage. It started off as weekends, but after enough begging on behalf of the kids these eventually turned into full weeks. By late August, their parents had finally surrendered and it was one giant slumber party.

Mama's front yard was plain – except for the four trees she'd planted to celebrate each grand-child's birth and a two-seat glider built by her late husband, now gone for ten years.

At the front of the house was the beloved three-season porch where the grandkids slept on air mattresses during spring and summer. At twilight, to the sound of rushing waves, they could hear whis-pered conversations in the darkness; neighbors sit-ting out, enjoying their safe little world. In the morn-ing, they were usually greeted by robin red breasts foraging for food, or the occasional seagull begging for handouts just outside the screens. Beyond the screen house, at the very tip of the property, was a small wooden deck filled with mismatched chairs painted in different pastel colors.

A statue of St. Jude, the patron saint of desperate cases and lost causes, welcomed all guests at the beginning of a brick pathway that led to Mama's sanctuary in the back yard. A day never passed when Mama didn't kiss her index finger and place it on his weather-beaten head.

Plants and wild flowers sprung up everywhere. Just past the rose-covered arbor sat a small concrete bird bath with a weather-beaten Adirondack chair facing it. The chalk-red brick meandered in several different directions, but each path led to a round table in the middle of the courtyard, protected by a giant maple arbor. This table hosted hours upon hours of card games, rounds of Parcheesi and priceless conversation.

Fire-red sea grasses grew out of black mulch. Mama loved ceramic frogs and there were a dozen or so carefully placed around the secret garden. There were also a half-dozen bird feeders hanging about. Dragon flies and everything from blue jays to yellow finches claimed the place as home – or at least their summer home. The occasional seagull screeched overhead, drowning out the portable radio that Mama stuck in the window to listen to the Red Sox – or "my boys," as she called them. An outdoor shower abutted the house and, if you came in from the beach, you weren't allowed in the house until you got under it and rinsed off every grain of sand.

Bees pollinated the hydrangeas surrounding a big green lamppost that came on at dusk, creating even more atmosphere. Some nights, Heidi, Steph and Ross spent time there in silence, listening to the crickets and peepers. Most nights though, they chased fireflies with empty mayonnaise jars, while Mama sat in her chair cheering them on.

It was such a magical place that even the occasional horsefly attack was worth the risk of spending time there.

~ ~ ~ ~ ~ ~ ~ ~

While Mama hemmed a laundry basket filled with men's slacks, Heidi, Steph and Ross played in the backyard. Mama placed a blanket on the grass and put Brian on his belly. She then dropped his favorite toy – a plush puppy that squeaked when you squeezed its belly – on the far side of the blanket across from him. For hours on end, it looked like he was swimming, but going nowhere. "Eventually, he'll learn to crawl," Mama promised. To the untrained eye, this would have appeared awfully cruel, but Mama cared too much not to give him the tough love that he needed to make progress.

After Brian spent countless hours struggling and failing to crawl, Heidi finally spoke up in her tiny cousin's defense. "Mama...please. It's too hard for him."

"Nonsense," she said. "It looks like he isn't going anywhere, but he's actually learning about perseverance; about never giving up."

Steph looked down at the blanket to find Brian paddling hard to nowhere. "Well, he hasn't given up yet," she admitted.

"And he won't!" Mama promised. She took a break from her mending and searched each of their tanned faces. "Here's the real secret to succeeding in life: You get knocked down, you get back up. You get knocked down again, you get back up. It's not getting knocked down that's the problem. Life does that to everyone. It's when you don't get back up that you're in trouble." She looked down at the struggling toddler and smiled proudly. "Fortunately, Brian refuses to stay down."

As if on cue, Brian looked up, grinned and then set his sights on the stuffed puppy again. Legs kicking, arms stroking – he continued to give it everything he had.

"That's Mama's boy," she told him. "You just keep pushing, Brian. You'll get there."

~ ~ ~ ~ ~ ~ ~ ~

The summer went by in a flash and it was perfect. After each breakfast, Heidi, Steph and Ross left the cottage and played all day, taking their lunch in the backyard and washing it down with the water from the garden hose. They didn't even consider going in until the streetlight came on. They climbed trees and fell from branches. They suffered their cuts and bruises, cried for as long as Mama allowed it, and then headed back out into the wild to eat worms that squirmed out of mud pies. They made friends with kids up the street and were allowed to walk to their houses, as long as they "stayed together." And, as a treat, they sometimes shared a cola, drinking from the same green glass bottle and learning how to share as they did.

By late July, both Heidi and Steph finally learned how to ride their bikes without training wheels – or helmets. Mama threw a backyard cookout to show off the girls' new skills.

They also spent a lot of time down by the bay. The girls watched Brian in the shade, while Mama taught Ross how to swim. It didn't take long for the daredevil to paddle off in the shallow water – all by himself.

While the girls joined Ross in the surf, Mama grabbed Brian, painted him white with sun block and then marched him into the water until she was up to her waist. For the longest time, she just stood there holding him in the water, while he flopped and flailed around.

Standing in the surf, Steph nervously asked, "What are you doing, Mama?"

"Taking away Brian's fear. Once the water starts to feel natural to him, then the swimming will come natural to him. Right now, we're just removing the fear." She looked down at him. "Right, buddy?" she asked.

Brian contorted and thrashed, struggling violently against the water.

~ ~ ~ ~ ~ ~ ~ ~

It was the last week of August when the kids – Heidi, Steph and Ross – presented Mama with a priceless gift. "Come out to the yard," Heidi, the group's elected representative, told her. "We have something we want to show you."

Expecting to sit through another one of their backyard plays, Mama stepped out into the yard to find Steph and Ross kneeling before Brian on the blanket. The baby was propped up on his bum, with a rolled towel wedged behind him, allowing him to stay seated. *But there are no costumes or props*, Mama thought. As she and Heidi took a seat on the blanket beside them, the old lady looked at the kids and shrugged. "What's up, guys?"

Ross began giggling and couldn't stop. Heidi grabbed him by the shoulders, "Shhhh, Ross. Let Steph show her."

Intrigued, Mama looked toward Steph. "Show me what?"

Steph never answered. Instead, wearing a giant smile, she turned toward Brian and clapped twice. Nothing happened. She clapped twice more. "Come on, Brian," she whispered, obviously pleading for him to comply.

The little guy looked directly at Mama, brought up both of his hands and quickly clapped them together.

Mama's mouth dropped open, but before she could get a word out, Steph clapped at the baby again. Brian responded with another clap. This time, he added a laugh.

"Oh, sweet Jesus," Mama gasped, and her eyes immediately filled with tears. This was no small feat.

*Brian's learning to mimic*, she thought. "He's learning!" she said aloud.

The kids looked up at their grandmother for her approval.

"It's the greatest gift I've ever received!" she cried out and meant it. While Brian applauded, she hugged each one of them.

After a half hour of clapping with Brian and round after round of tearful kisses, Mama stood and stretched out her creaky back. "We need to call Aunt Joan and Uncle Frank." She shot them a wink. "And after that, I'm treating you guys to McRay's for supper. Whatever you want to eat, it's yours!"

"Anything?" Heidi asked.

"Anything," she said, smiling. "You've earned it."

Once Brian returned home, the other three kids ate enough sugar to launch any one of them into a diabetic coma. It was a glorious – and somewhat discreet – celebration.

~ ~ ~ ~ ~ ~ ~ ~

As the leaves turned from green to bright red and orange, a yellow school bus sadly carried the squeals of summer down the road. Life went back to normal and the family returned to Mama's cottage every Wednesday and Saturday night. Inspired by Brian's recent progress, the kids kept their promise and spent hours working with him on developing his speech.

"Say Ma, Brian," Heidi told him.

"Say Ma," Steph repeated.

"Say Ma. Ma. Ma. Ma..." Ross added.

It was mind numbing to listen to, but the relentless repetition was exactly what he needed. Occasionally, Frank would chime in, "No, say dah dah," but he didn't have a shot in hell with the overwhelming push for the boy to say "Ma."

Before long, Frank began to miss some of the weekly get-togethers. As time went on, his absences became more frequent and Joan's excuses became less believable. No one ever commented on it – not even Mama.

The weeks turned into months and countless hours were spent trying to teach Brian to utter a word; hours upon hours spent failing again and again.

"Say Ma, Brian," Heidi told him.

"Say Ma," Steph repeated.

"Say Ma. Ma. Ma. Ma..." Ross added.

Brian refused to speak. Still, not one of the kids gave up. Each one of them refused to stay knocked down.

~ ~ ~ ~ ~ ~ ~ ~

It was a Sunday afternoon in early November, a few short months before Brian's third birthday. Frank was out in the backyard, taking a break from raking the few remaining leaves on the ground to teach Ross how to swing a golf club. Joan was in the kitchen, cleaning up from the pumpkin carving when Brian looked up from his oversized high chair and said, "Ma."

Joan spun on her heels to face the baby. "Did you say *Ma*, Brian?" she gasped, hoping against all hope that she hadn't been hearing things.

He banged a spoon on his tray, but didn't repeat it.

With a heavy sigh, she reluctantly dismissed it as nothing and turned her back on the little guy to finish the cleaning.

He didn't like it. He threw his spoon and yelled, "Ma!"

She dropped the sponge onto the floor and hurried to him. "You did call for Mommy!" she said. "You're learning to talk," she squealed in joy. "Can you say it again?" she asked. "Can you say..."

"Ma," he said, and grinned at her like he'd merely been teasing everyone for all these months.

"Oh, God," she cried. "You're talking." She smothered him in kisses.

He laughed. "Ma...Ma..."

After composing herself, she called Frank and Ross in from the yard. By then, Brian was on a roll. "Ma...Ma...Ma...Ma..."

Frank stepped into the kitchen, heard Brian speak and hurried over to him. He lifted his son out of the high chair and spun him in circles. "Daddy's so proud of you," he whimpered. "So proud..."

"Ma...Ma..." Brian answered.

Ross was so excited that he couldn't speak. He simply nodded, while his eyes filled with tears. Joan kneeled down and hugged him. "Thank you for helping your brother," she told him. "He could have never done this without you."

Ross nodded again, proud tears streaming down his cheeks.

"Ma...Ma..." Brian said.

While Frank danced Brian around the kitchen, Joan grabbed the telephone and dialed her mother's house. "Ma, you need to get over here right away." She paused. "No, there's nothing wrong. It's just that...well...Brian has something he wants to say to you."

~ ~ ~ ~ ~ ~ ~ ~

Mama was at the house in record time. She hurried through the door and threw her tattered jacket onto the couch. "Where is he?" she panted.

With a grin, Frank pointed toward Brian's bedroom.

As she entered the room, she spotted Joan and Ross changing Brian on the bed. Mama bent over and gave Ross a kiss. "What's the..."

"Ma...Ma...Ma...Ma..." Brian said, answering for his mother.

Instantly, Mama began crying and just stood there – shaking her head for the longest time. She grabbed for the crucifix around her necklace and kissed it. "Stupid doctors," she finally said, sobbing, "what do they know?" She picked up Brian to give him a squeeze and a nibble. Ross hugged her. Joan hugged her. And then she began crying and laughing – all at the same time. "All that money for a speech therapist and he's learned the same way as any oth-er kid...just by hearing it over and over again." She ruffled Ross' hair. "You did this, you know. You taught your baby brother how to speak."

Ross nodded, proudly.

"And I need to tell your cousins the same," she added.

"Ma...Ma...Ma..." Brian agreed.

Frank stepped into the threshold and smiled. Mama handed Brian to Joan, marched over to her son-in-law, stood up on her toes and gave him a long, hard hug. Joan froze, unsure of how her husband would receive the unexpected display of affection. He surprised everyone and hugged her back just as hard. It was a moment that transcended all barriers and hard feelings.

In the background, Brian sang, "Ma...Ma...Ma..."

Mama pulled away and wiped her eyes. "We just need him to string them together a little quicker and he'll have my name down, too."

"Then can we work on Dada?" Frank asked, playfully.

She nodded. "I guarantee it."

"Oh, I believe you," he said. "And I'll never doubt you again."

"And from what I can tell, he'll be crawling by the first snowfall," she said with a wink.

# Chapter 8

*Winter 1978*

Before the DiMartino/Mauretti clan knew it, winter had arrived and it was Christmas time again. Although she always displayed the same spirit, this was Mama's favorite time of the year. She spent a solid week decorating the cottage. There was a holiday village that took up a corner of the dining room, with real plants and tiny white lights mixed in. She gift-wrapped doors, and hung a red and green garland over each doorway. And she had to have a real tree. "They might be messier," she admitted, "but the smell of pine is worth the extra effort of cleaning up the needles." She demanded an angel on top of the tree, and used lots of tinsel with strands and strands of colored lights that made the house shimmer in a festive glow.

The smell of Christmas Butterballs filled the air, while quarts of eggnog filled the fridge – though no one ever drank it. Ribbon candy, chocolate covered cherries, thin mints and candied almonds sat in bowls and were replenished throughout the holiday season. Mama loved her black licorice, too. If you took one, though, you had to hide it and eat it in secret. She was generous with everything but her black licorice.

Christmas music played all day, rotating between Nat King Cole, Dean Martin and Bing Crosby. And even after her husband had passed, she still hung lights outside – in the snow and the bay's freezing winds. All of this, however, seemed no more than a prelude to her annual pilgrimage to the old neighborhood.

~ ~ ~ ~ ~ ~ ~ ~

It was the first snowfall when Mama suggested that they visit Little Italy for Christmas. Frank and Bob opted out, so Mama, Joan and Bev brought all the kids into the city.

With the kids forming a human chain – hanging off of Brian's oversized stroller – Mama led her ducklings out of the gray subway and stepped onto the bright, bustling street. Like living dolls, the girls were dressed in wool coats and fur-lined hats. Ross and Brian wore red and black checkered flannel coats with hats to match. Mama inhaled the cold city air and smiled. Since she could remember, her favorite Christmas tradition was to visit the old neighborhood to see the twinkling lights and familiar faces. For her, the real gift of the season was taking a stroll through Little Italy. The lights were nothing spectacular, but she still brought the kids every year. The seasonal decorations were just a convenient excuse for her to take a stroll down memory lane.

The North End – Little Italy, as most knew it – was a magical land. For a place so congested, it possessed a wonderful feeling of freedom. Those who were baptized within its confines rarely ever left and usually died in the same flats that they were born in. In total, it was no more than five city blocks, yet it was an island all unto itself; a safe harbor in a sea of giant skyscrapers.

Strings of white lights were hung across the glistening streets. Giant wreaths were strapped to each lamp post. As they started down Hanover Street, Mama gawked at a row of warmly-lit brownstones where her childhood memories lined up like one movie scene after the next. By the glow in her eyes, Joan, Bev and the kids could see the old film reel playing in her mind.

Clay pottery and wrought iron café chairs sat on balconies and fire escapes, betraying hints of warmer days. Colored Christmas lights framed most windows and were payment enough to endure the frigid air. Mama's smile was contagious.

An old man whistled at her.

"Ooooh," Bev teased. "Looks like you have a gentleman admirer, Ma."

Mama shook her head. "Yeah, sure. Just like a dog chasing a fire truck. If he ever caught me, he wouldn't know what to do with me."

They laughed.

As they strolled along, Mama turned to both Joan and Bev. "Any reason Frank and Bob decided not to join us today?"

"Bob said it was more of a girls' night out," Bev answered, before hurrying the kids ahead – until they were a safe distance from Joan's explanation.

Not wanting to continue the lies, Joan struggled for the words. "It's just that..."

"It's okay, Joan. I know Frank hates me," Mama announced, bluntly.

Joan shook her head. "He doesn't hate you, Ma. He just...he just doesn't know how to handle all of this with Brian. He never has. I can't imagine the torment of feeling uncomfortable around your own son. He's had a difficult time with it all and he's too proud to admit it." She shook her head again. "Deep down, he knows you're right...but it kills him that he can't give Brian the same tough love."

Mama nodded. Although Joan expected a verbal barrage to follow, the old woman never uttered another word about it.

~ ~ ~ ~ ~ ~ ~ ~

Just past Dominic's Bar, Mama led her willing flock into the butcher shop. As they entered, a brass bell rang. The paunchy, middle-aged man hunched behind the glass case stood erect to greet his new customers. He wore a white coat, stained red above the pockets, where he'd obviously wiped his bloody hands a hundred times. He was bald with two black clumps of hair just above his ears. When he recognized Mama, he gave her a big smile, displaying a wide gap between his two front teeth. "Angela, what'll it be this year...ham or turkey?"

"Ham, two of them, and the biggest you have. And leave in the bone on both of them. I know how you butchers like to steal the flavor from the meat and then sell it again to someone who wants to make the same soup that I can make."

He laughed. "You hurt my feelings, suggesting that I'd..."

"You'd have to have feelings for that," she teased.

He laughed again, wiped his hands on his filthy coat and headed for the back room to get the full hams.

Mama bent down to the kids, who were fogging up the butcher's meat case. "Don't ever let anyone take something from you that you're not willing to give."

They each nodded, oblivious to her intended lesson.

"Amen to that," Joan mumbled.

~ ~ ~ ~ ~ ~ ~ ~

Three blocks down Hanover, they arrived at Saint Anthony's Church. At the black wrought iron gate, Mama pressed the buzzer. In the bitter cold, they waited a few minutes before she became annoyed. She pushed the buzzer again, this time longer than needed.

A young priest appeared in the rectory's threshold. He descended the stairs, turned up the collar on his jacket and scurried across the short courtyard to the gate. "Good afternoon, Mrs. DiMartino. What can I do for you today?" he asked, as he struggled to open the gate.

She looked into both butcher's bags and handed him the bigger of the two hams. "Father, this is for the family who needs it most this Christmas...in my mother's memory."

"You're very kind, Mrs. DiMartino. Thank you."

"I just thank the good Lord that I'm still able to do it."

"Amen," the priest said and hurried back toward the warmth of his rectory.

As Mama started to walk away, Steph looked up at her grandmother. "Why did you do that?" she asked.

"It's been a tradition for years now," she explained. "After my mother passed away and went to heaven, I needed a way to honor her memory on the holiday that she loved most – Christmas. So I decided to help a less fortunate family in her name, and buy them the biggest turkey or ham that the butcher had in his shop." She shrugged. "I've been doing it every Christmas since."

Each of the children nodded again. This time, the lesson was understood.

"In some ways, it's a selfish act on my part."

Their heads flew up in confusion.

"By giving to others, it fills a need inside of me," she explained.

They walked for a bit until Steph finally suggested, "But it's a good type of selfish, right? Like how we feel when we teach Brian something."

Mama nodded. "Exactly! It's the only good type of selfish there is," she said, and then stopped to look down at them. "We don't take money to the grave – only our deeds. And what we do for others before ourselves are the greatest deeds of all. Remember that." She looked down at Brian and winked. "Someone very wise taught me that."

They each nodded, but their thoughts were already set on Mike's Pastry Shop just up ahead.

Mama smiled and took a quick left into Mike's. Biscotti, anise cookies, bags of almond candies, and dozens of decadent cream-filled, chocolate frosted pastries lined the glass shelves. The kids squealed in delight at the promise of a sweet surprise.

~ ~ ~ ~ ~ ~ ~ ~

As they continued their hike, everyone devoured their treats and took in all the details of a world that was locked in a different time. Beyond the gelato shop – with a rainbow of colors in the front window – they passed an empty lot that sold Christmas trees and handed out free cups of steaming cocoa. An old man waved from his makeshift office. "Hey Angie, you out slumming tonight?"

Mama stopped. "Out shopping for my four babies," she called out. "How 'bout some hot chocolate for these angels?"

Right away, he started pouring out a Styrofoam cup from the dented, silver urn. "Come and get it," he told the kids.

~ ~ ~ ~ ~ ~ ~ ~

One block from the end of Hanover Street, Pleasant Drugstore displayed the latest Christmas decorations in its giant window. Ross' eyes begged his mom to go in. With a nod, Joan set him loose.

Following Ross, Mama led the kids upstairs. Fake Christmas trees, decorated in all the latest lights and ornaments, were lined up like some fairyland forest. Three mirrored walls created the illusion that the plastic forest went on for acres. Ross loved the place so much that he plopped down in the middle of the trees and drifted off into a deep hypnotic trance.

"Get up, Ross," Heidi began to warn him. "We..."

Mama stopped her with a hand on her shoulder. "It's okay. We have time," she whispered. "Ross thinks he's at the North Pole right now and who are we to tell him that he's not?" She patted Brian on the head. "Trust me, the harder you believe in something, the more real it will become."

While Joan and Bev nodded, Steph took a seat beside her little cousin and stared at all the twinkling, colored lights. Everyone knew that Mama wasn't talking about Christmas trees.

~ ~ ~ ~ ~ ~ ~ ~

Mama's next stop was at the statue of the Virgin Mother, whom she adored. Some threw change into the fountain at her feet and made wishes – but not Mama. While the kids looked on, she kneeled on the frozen concrete and offered her prayers. And no one had to guess who most of those prayers were for. While Joan ensured that Brian stayed bundled up in the stroller, Bev and the kids joined the old matriarch on the ground.

When Mama blessed herself and struggled to stand, Steph inquired, "Asking God to make Brian better?"

Mama looked down at her and smiled. "Nope. Thanking God for all of you...and for allowing Brian to walk."

"But he hasn't yet," Heidi interrupted.

Mama stopped in her tracks and turned to face her granddaughter.

Heidi cringed, expecting to be scolded.

Mama smiled. "That's right – *yet*. See, you believe it's going to happen, too." She pinched Heidi's cheeks. "Now that's *faith*, sweetheart."

The young girl's neck shot a wave of heat up her face. Compliments from Mama were more valuable than any present found under a twinkling tree.

~ ~ ~ ~ ~ ~ ~ ~

During their hearty lunch at Rosa's, Mama shared a story to teach her grandchildren a glimpse of where they came from. "When my mother – your great grandmother – was a little girl, she was sad after hearing that baby Jesus had nowhere to sleep. So, she asked her mom for some tin foil and formed it into a small bed. She then put a soft cotton baby blanket inside it and placed the homemade manger under their Christmas tree..."

"So baby Jesus would have a place to sleep?" Ross asked.

Mama nodded. "That's right."

Joan and Bev looked at each other and smiled. Mama's simple teachings instilled more spiritual learning than a dozen of Father Benton's monotone sermons.

"Is that why you put the aluminum foil manger under the tree every year?" Steph asked.

Mama nodded. "Family traditions are important. And it's even more important that Jesus knows He's welcome in our home."

Rosa flew out from behind the red door and approached the table. "How was the lunch?" she asked.

Mama curled each of her fingers into her thumb and kissed them. "*Perfecto*," she said, and then opened her hand. Watching this, each of the kids did the same. Brian, however, kissed his fist and then threw it forward in a different display of gratitude.

Rosa laughed. "You a good boy," she told him.

On the way out, Mama pointed up at the oil painting of the Italian countryside and daydreamed aloud. "Someday, Mama's going to hit the lottery and take you all there." Her eyes grew distant. "Siena and San Gimignano are two of Italy's beautiful medieval towns. They say Siena is like a postcard, with its red terra cotta rooftops and cobblestone streets. They host a world-famous horse race each summer, where neighborhoods compete against each other to win a portrait of the Virgin Mary. And just south of Siena, there are thermal springs or baths that were used to cure sickness during Roman times. San Gimignano is known as *the Medieval Manhattan* for its skyline of towers. Twelve of the original towers are still standing. Noble families actually competed with each other to build the tallest one. The city is laid-back and was made famous in the movie, *Tea With Mussolini*..." Mama looked up from her daydream to find the children considering the possibilities of visiting

Italy, while Joan and Bev exchanged their usual smirks. She laughed and guided them back out to their walking adventure.

~ ~ ~ ~ ~ ~ ~ ~

When the happy group reached the end of Hanover Street, they came upon a brick-faced three-story tenement. An old abandoned restaurant named Lucia's was on the first floor, its green and white striped awning stained and torn. Mama stopped in her tracks and stared at the building the same way that Ross had gawked at the Pleasant Drugstore Christmas trees. She breathed deep and let out a long sigh. "My Aunt Lucille and Uncle Bob used to own this place," she began to explain. "My mom ran the kitchen, and me and Uncle Sal were raised on the second floor. There wasn't a better place to grow up. Families were very tight-knit and protective of each other, and everyone was somehow related to everyone else. The person you knew the least still called himself your third or fourth cousin." She scanned the street behind them. "On Hanover Street, it seemed as if we were untouched by the tragedies of the world, as if there were invisible walls that protected us...and nothing could hurt us as long as we stayed within its borders. Back then, it wasn't uncommon for a small child to walk the street at night – either to return a borrowed dish or deliver a package to a neighbor – and still be safe. During the day, everyone peddled some type of goods right in the street – from shoe shines and ice to vegetables, fish and cookware. People rarely had to leave the neighborhood to get

whatever they needed. Even for the most special oc-
casions, the corner jeweler could find just the right
gift and throw it on the passbook so that customers
could make small payments each week." She nodded
and smiled. "We had parades in the summer and
Christmas lights in the winter. This street was just
as much a part of home as anything that happened
within the tenement houses. There are so many
wonderful memories here. It really was a beautiful
place to grow up..." Her voice trailed off and became
as distant as her eyes.

Joan, Bev and the kids quietly stood by, allowing
her the time she needed.

She wiped her eyes, looked down at her grandchildren and paused for their full attention. "Enjoy
every minute you have together because it goes by
faster than you could ever imagine," she promised.
"And always be there for each other...always!"

The kids promised that they would.

Mama took one more look at the apartment
house and then turned around to face the long walk
back down Hanover. She sighed heavily, summoning
the energy to make it back to the train, and held out
both hands for the kids to latch on. "Okay then, let's
go home and get ready for Santa Claus."

~ ~ ~ ~ ~ ~ ~ ~

It was later than they planned when they returned to
the cottage with the kids. Before Mama even took
off her coat, she filled a large pan with water and
put it on the stove to boil. She then removed another pan from the refrigerator and pulled back the

cellophane wrap. It was her red gravy, or at least the start of it. She submerged her finger and then stuck it into her mouth. "Mmmm," she said, smacking her lips together. "This batch could make Rosa jealous."

Without having to be told, the kids dumped their coats onto Mama's bed and stampeded into the bathroom to get washed up. While Bev headed for the kitchen to help her mother-in-law start dinner, Joan stripped Brian out of his snowsuit and placed him on the living room floor.

After throwing their coats onto Mama's bed, she returned to find Brian sitting only a few feet from the coffee table. "Can you be a good boy for a few minutes, while Mommy helps Mama finish supper?" she asked him, before grabbing at her rumbling abdomen.

He never responded, nor did he even look up to acknowledge her. He was too busy staring at the coffee table's skinny legs.

"I'll take your silence as a yes, then," she said, and left him to play.

Mama was chopping onions and Bev was preparing the garlic bread. Joan stood in the kitchen doorway for a minute. *Something's wrong,* she thought. A sudden sensation had come over her − instinctive and maternal − that made her spin on her heels to see what it was.

Both of Brian's small hands were gripped on the lip of the coffee table and he was actually pulling himself up. With a final grunt, he stood erect and wobbled. Joan's eyes flew open and her jaw went slack. For a moment, Brian just stood there. And then he looked over at his mother. "Ma...Ma," he said and shot her his million-dollar smile.

"Ma!" Joan screamed. "Come here...quick!"

Mama and Bev came running from the kitchen and caught Brian's mischievous smile just before he wobbled once and went down on his bum.

While the kids looked on in the living room doorway, Mama turned to Joan. Together, they both started crying. "I'm telling you, Joan," Mama whimpered, pulling her daughter to her chest. "Your son's going to walk tall and proud."

"Oh, Mama," Joan moaned, overwhelmed. It felt like this one moment was the culmination of countless hours of worry, patience and prayer. "Thank God."

"Thank God, is right," Mama said. With bent hands that stunk of onions, she grabbed Joan's face and kissed her forehead. "Brian's entire life is a miracle. It has been from the moment he was born." She thought about it and snickered to herself. "And to think that the doctors sentenced him to fail..."

Ross ran to his brother and hugged him long and hard. Everyone else quickly joined in. While they celebrated his miraculous feat, Heidi blurted, "But he only stood for a second before he fell down,"

"And he's going to keep falling for months," Mama said, "maybe even years. But he's going to walk! As sure as the good Lord's watching right now, he's going to walk and we've just witnessed his first step, sweetheart."

Joan and Bev nodded in agreement. "He couldn't crawl for almost two years, but he's getting around pretty good now, isn't he?" Joan added, trying to compose herself. She hurried for the telephone to call Frank.

Brian was now on the floor, scurrying on all fours toward the kitchen.

Mama went after him. "He must smell my red gravy," she joked, and swept him up into her arms on the way. "Okay, buddy, now that you can stand, we need to see about getting you out of those stinky diapers." She nibbled his plump belly.

He squealed in laughter.

~ ~ ~ ~ ~ ~ ~ ~

Joan returned to the living room and said, "Frank's on his way from..." She stopped, covered her mouth with her hand and ran off to the bathroom.

Mama followed her in and watched, as her daughter retched over the toilet bowl. "What's the matter with you?" she asked.

Joan looked up from her knees and shrugged. "I don't know. All of a sudden, I feel so nauseous and..." She vomited again.

Mama grabbed her hair, pulling it away from her face and the toilet. She studied Joan's face and smiled.

Joan never noticed. "I must have caught some bug," she said.

Mama nodded. "Do you think that maybe Frank could've given you that bug?"

Joan thought for a moment and her face turned a pastier shade of white. "Maybe," she admitted, and threw her head into the bowl again to empty whatever remained of Rosa's manicotti.

## Chapter 9

### Summer 1979

Joan – the self-proclaimed Neo Mulsoy watchdog – and two other Rhode Island mothers formed a group called *Mothers of Neo Mulsoy Babies*. They met twice a month to share their knowledge, as well as their fears. They met just enough for Frank to label it his wife's "new obsession."

"Why is this such a problem for you?" Joan finally asked, frustrated over his snide comments. "I thought you'd be happy that I'm making good use of my time."

"But that's all there is now – Neo Mulsoy. It's completely consumed you and I've just about had enough of it!"

~ ~ ~ ~ ~ ~ ~ ~

It wasn't long before Frank was dropping the boys off at the cottage again. This time, he sprinted back to his car.

"How far apart are the contractions?" Mama called out after him.

"About twelve minutes, but I want to get her to the hospital right away!"

"You just be sure to drive safe, Frank," she yelled. "You have plenty of time."

~ ~ ~ ~ ~ ~ ~ ~

After a solid hour of teasing the boys, Mama couldn't make either one of them consider that they might be having a baby sister – not even for a second.

"Can I watch TV?" Ross finally asked, bored with the baby talk.

"Yes, but no Three Stooges. You don't need any more bad ideas," she said. "If you need us, your brother and I will be working on his pronunciations." With a grunt, she lifted Brian and started for the porch.

~ ~ ~ ~ ~ ~ ~ ~

Brian stared at the old lady, carefully watching as her pencil-thin lips formed each word. Through mind-numbing repetition, he echoed every sound she made.

"Ross," Mama told him.

"Rin."

"No...Ross."

He nodded. "Rin."

"Try it again. Ross."

He took his time and carefully said, "Riiiin."

She shook her head and chuckled. "Okay, how about Steph?"

"Ot."

"Oh, come on. You can do better than that, Brian." She paused. "Steph."

"Ot!"

"Really? How can you possibly get *Ot* from Steph?"

He giggled. "Ot," he said. "Ahhhhhht."

"And Heidi?"

"Biddy."

She clasped her hands over her heart in a show of gratitude. "Now we're talking! That's very close. Good job, Brian."

He put on his proudest smile and nodded.

"Heidi," she said again.

"Yets. Biddy," he countered.

Mama watched as Ross got up from the chair in the living room, walked to the TV and turned up the volume. She laughed. "Looks like your brother's getting sick of listening to us silly parrots."

Brian looked into the living room. "Rin," he said with a smile.

"That's right...Ross," Mama said. "Try it again. Ross."

"Riiiin," he said, slowly.

With a deep breath, Mama dug in her heels and prepared to go another round.

~ ~ ~ ~ ~ ~ ~ ~

Two hours later, they emerged from the painful lesson – exhausted but alive. Mama asked him one final question. "What do you say we make a deal?"

He just looked at her, awaiting the terms.

"What do you say that you and I have a discussion every night from now on...say around eight o'clock? This way, you can tell me how good you're doing and fill me in on all the details of your day. Deal?"

He nodded.

"What does that mean?" she asked, mimicking his nod.

"Yets," he said.

"You promise?" she asked, raising her pinky finger to seal the pact.

With a giant smile, he wrapped his baby finger around hers and shook it. "Yets, Mama."

She kissed his hand. "Then it's a deal!"

~ ~ ~ ~ ~ ~ ~ ~

Ross was finally saved by the bell when the phone rang. Excited, Mama somehow made her way across the house and picked it up before the end of the second ring.

"It's a girl!" Joan announced, her voice content but exhausted. "And we've named her Angela Louise." She paused. "We're going to call her Angie."

"Oh Joan..." She paused, taking it all in. "I'm honored. That's just wonderful. Congratulations! How big is she?"

"Seven pounds even. And she's so beautiful, with light hair and brown eyes. She definitely resembles our side," she said. "And they let me stay awake for this one."

"My goodness, the boys are going to be thrilled. I can't wait to sink my chops into her!"

Joan laughed.

Ross tugged at the old lady's housedress. "Into who?"

Mama covered the phone's mouthpiece with her hand. "You have a sister," she whispered, adding a victorious grin.

Ross was speechless. His eyes glossed over, as he tried to figure out how it felt to have a baby sister. For more months than he could remember, he'd expected another brother.

"And the doctor says she's perfectly healthy," Joan reported on the other end.

Mama grabbed the crucifix that hung from her neck and kissed it. "Of course, she is. When are you coming home?"

"Tomorrow, I think."

"Okay. Get some rest. And tell Frank I said congratulations and thank you for naming her after me," Mama said.

"I will, Ma." She laughed. "He didn't have much say in naming this one, though. But he didn't argue it, either."

Mama laughed. "Here's Ross," she said and handed the phone to the boy.

Mama approached the kitchen table where Brian was sitting. "You have a baby sister," she told him. "Her name is Angie. Can you say Angie?"

"A...E."

"First shot, huh?" She wrapped him up in a bear hug.

He smiled, proudly. "A...E," he repeated.

After kissing his head, she said, "Well, I think we need to celebrate. You're a big brother now!" She looked at Ross, who was smiling on the phone. "Just like Ross."

Brian nodded, more excited about the details of the celebration than having a little sister.

Mama bent down to retrieve her baking pans from the cupboard under the counter.

Brian bounced around in his seat, excited with the anticipation of a sweet treat.

"What do you think you're doing just sitting there?" she asked, picking him up and lugging him off to the bathroom. "Let's go wash your hands. No more free rides for you in Mama's kitchen. You're going to help!"

"Yets!" he yelled, and squirmed with excitement in her arms.

As Mama passed Ross on the telephone, she planted a big kiss on his head. "Another grandbaby," she whispered, so as not to disturb his telephone conversation. "God is good."

As she stepped into the bathroom with Brian, she looked in the mirror and thought about it for a moment. *But I wonder if it's enough to save my daughter's failing marriage?*

# Chapter 10

*Late Summer 1981*

For two solid years, each family member took his or her turn helping Brian walk around the house – which usually meant dragging him by the arms. As he grew stronger, weekends were spent with Mama at the shore, with the old lady holding him in the salt water while he squirmed to be freed. And although everyone said it was much too early, Mama began spending hours with him at her kitchen table, tracing the alphabet and numbers from one to ten.

It was bordering on fall. Heidi and Steph ran into the house, panicked. Joan and Mama were sitting at the kitchen table, drinking Sanka and talking.

"Brian fell!" Steph yelled. "Brian just fell!"

Both women jumped up from the table and hurried for the door. "Is he hurt?" Joan asked, carrying Angie in her arms.

"No," Heidi panted, running to catch up.

Mama slowed down. "Then all you need to do is pick him up, brush him off and start again with him."

"We know, Mama," Steph said, as they reached the side of the house. "It's what happened before he fell that you need to see."

Ross stood behind Brian, holding his hands over his head. As the two women approached them, Ross whispered something into his brother's ear and then let go of his hands. "Go see Mom, Brian," he said, his voice cracking.

Both women froze in place and, for a moment, Brian did the same. Then, he wobbled once, steadied himself and with the biggest smile, he took three distinct steps before going down in the grass. His smile quickly curled into a pout and he began to cry.

Joan gasped. "Brian!" she hollered and hurried toward him.

"STOP!" Mama yelled out. "Joan, please stop."

Joan froze. She looked down at her crying son and then looked up at her mother with a stunned glare.

Mama's eyes softened. "He can do it, Joan. Let him do it." Mama then bent over and stared into Brian's eyes. "No more tears, Brian. You're a big boy. Now get up and walk."

Brian returned his stern grandmother's gaze and in that one moment, it was as if a sacred secret had been shared between them. Without another whimper, he pulled himself up to his knees. It took a few seconds before he could get his balance, but once he got to his feet, he just took off – one miraculous step after the other.

"Brian!" Joan screamed out again. In one sudden motion, she put Angie down and scooped up Brian once he finally went down. "Mommy's so proud of you. I love you so much!" She kissed his cheeks a half dozen times before turning him to face his grandmother. "Now, go walk to Mama," she whispered in his ear, the tears streaming down her face. "She's been waiting a long time to catch you."

Mama dropped to her brittle knees and spread her arms wide. "Come fly to Mama, little butterfly," she wept.

At nearly five years old, Brian placed one foot in front of the other until he'd made six solid steps. Mama caught him as he was going down. "Stupid doctor," she cried. "Stupid, stupid, stupid doctor!" Brian looked up from the safety of her arms and smiled. Mama collapsed to the ground with him, smothering him in kisses, hugs and tears. While Angie ran to them, Joan, Ross, Heidi and Steph joined them on the ground – crying, laughing and celebrating one of God's great miracles.

Steph said, "But the doctor said Brian would never..."

Mama kissed the crucifix around her neck and shook her head. "Doctors can't measure heart, faith, love or the strength of the human will – Brian's or any of ours." She wiped her eyes. "I told you all along...when Brian's ready, he'll walk. His heart will tell us when." She kissed the little boy. "And he picked today."

"I can't wait to tell Frank," Joan squealed, and rubbed noses with Brian. "You just wait 'til your daddy sees you strutting around."

After the little boy marched between Joan and Mama like some toy soldier, Mama sneaked off into the house and called Uncle Sal to tell him the news. Lowering her voice, she looked out the window to ensure that no one was eavesdropping. "Listen, Sal," she whispered, "I have an idea that I'm going to need your help with..."

~ ~ ~ ~ ~ ~ ~ ~

That night, kneeling on her pillow, Mama finished her prayers and spoke openly with God. "Father, I have no words for the many blessings you have bestowed upon this family. Today, I have witnessed a caterpillar become a butterfly and my life is now complete. Thank you is not enough." She blessed herself. "I love you – for all eternity."

~ ~ ~ ~ ~ ~ ~ ~

Three weeks to the day that Brian walked for the first time, Mama hosted a carnival in her backyard. She had invited everyone to a cookout but arranged a surprise carnival instead. Only Uncle Sal knew her secret.

She'd gone to the Five & Dime and purchased two carts filled with trinkets – stuffed animals, blow-up beach toys, posters, jump ropes, whiffle ball bats, hula hoops, Kewpie dolls, GI Joe action figures – everything she could find.

Uncle Sal's friend owned a catering company that loaned Mama the tents, five in all. The first was set up as a pavilion of sorts located right in the middle of the midway. Long rectangular tables were covered with colorful plastic cloths, with rows of folding chairs sitting beneath them. The other tents were used for carnival games, arranged in a circular fashion around the dining area.

Balloons and a giant banner that read *BRIAN'S FIRST STEPS* fluttered in the salty, autumn breeze. As adults showed up to "the cookout," Mama assigned stations. The ladies worked concession, while the gentlemen manned the game tents. A rented bounce house loomed in the corner of the yard, with pony rides on the other end. Circus music played over and over, driving the adults crazy. It was magical.

Mama had strung clotheslines within each game tent and hung a variety of toys by clothespins. Screaming kids ran from station to station, filling goodie bags.

For the first tent, Uncle Sal had cut out a block of wood and placed a large stuffed tiger on top of it. A hula hoop fit perfectly around the block, and if someone landed it, they won a large prize of their choice hanging from the clothesline. If they missed the mark, they still won a piece of candy or a smaller toy. No one could lose.

Steph rang the tiger three times, but only walked away with one prize – an inflatable shark. "This is for Brian...for the beach," she told Mama.

The old lady hugged her and plucked an inflatable dolphin from the same clothesline. "And this one's for you," she said, handing her the prize, "so two kind hearts can play together."

The second tent hosted a game that involved three softballs and an old rusted milk can. Neighborhood friends, Herbie and Arthur, ran the booth together, heckling anyone who passed by.

While she chewed on her bottom lip, Heidi tossed several dozen softballs. One bulging bag of candy later, she walked away with a giant stuffed turtle. "I'm going to name him Arthur," she announced.

Arthur raised his hands in victory and looked at Herbie. "She likes me more than you!" he declared.

Heidi laughed. Herbie pouted.

The next tent had five of Uncle Sal's Narragansett beer cans stacked in a pyramid, sitting atop a round plywood platform. Each player had three baseballs to knock all the gold cans off the platform and win a large prize.

With Ross' help, Brian stepped up, grabbed a ball and dropped it two feet in front of him. Mama watched closely, as Uncle Sal let the boy take a few giant steps forward. Brian grabbed a second ball and dropped it in front of him again. In one swift motion, Uncle Sal's arm flew out and swiped every last beer can off the shelf. "We have a winner!" he yelled, and as he reached for a stuffed animal, Mama approached – shaking her head.

"He can do it, Sal," she told her brother before looking at her grandson. "Isn't that right, Brian?"

The little boy grinned and picked up another ball, waiting for Uncle Sal to reset the cans.

Mama pointed at Uncle Sal and told Ross, "Don't worry about him. He's used to my tough love." Ross laughed at his older uncle.

Ten long minutes later, one of the balls somehow hit the shelf and miraculously knocked down one of the cans. While everyone held their breath, it rolled and teetered until finally falling onto the ground. "Yes!" Uncle Sal yelled out. Loud applause echoed over the carnival music.

Eyes filled with tears, Sal immediately looked to his sister. With a grin, she nodded her approval. "We have a winner here!" he screamed and handed Brian the coveted stuffed monkey.

As the proud boy walked away with Ross, Sal confessed to Mama, "It's the damndest thing, but I've never tried that hard for anything in my life... and it was only a cheap stuffed animal."

"And that's what makes Brian special," she explained. "Nothing in this world is cheap to him. He has to fight for everything he gets, and that makes everything priceless." She smiled. "Even a stuffed monkey."

The final tent simply hosted a dart board, three darts, and the adult who felt the most courageous at the time. Even though Frank wasn't thrilled about the massive celebration, he eventually came around and was happy to accept the dangerous duty for a good part of the day.

At the concession stand, the ladies grilled hot dogs, smothered in mustard, onions, and Mama's own Coney Island sauce. There were brown paper bags filled with peanuts and rows of plastic cups filled with freshly squeezed lemonade. They also handed out cotton candy and pink sugary popcorn donated by McRay's Clam Shack.

It wasn't long before the gossip began. "What do you think about Lady Diana marrying Prince Charles?" Joan asked Bev.

"If you ask me, she could do better."

They both laughed.

"And it looks like Iran may finally release those poor American hostages."

"Poor people," Bev agreed. "They've been held captive for over four hundred days now, right?"

"Those poor people," Joan said.

"Bob says we should blow Iran right off the map...except that gas prices are already at $1.25, so who knows how high they might go."

"I'm not sure we should blow anyone off the map," Joan said. "Poor Uncle Sal might have to trade in his Cadillac if gas goes up again," she joked.

They laughed some more and then filled an order for six hot dogs with the works.

Cousin Margaret, one of the older family members, turned to Mama and asked, "Why all this, Angela? It's not like..."

"Brian has defied all the odds," Mama interrupted, "so I can't imagine a better reason to celebrate." She scanned the yard to see everyone having the time of their lives. She nodded. "I don't want Brian – or anyone else in this family – to ever forget what he's accomplished...that God let him walk."

Everyone was invited – family, friends, the entire neighborhood. This wasn't all that unusual. It was a very loving community. Like one large family, each person was welcome into the other's house. If you weren't from the neighborhood, though, you'd be spotted from a mile out. *Who's that? Who'd they come to see?* everyone would wonder. And even though they'd shoot a smile, outsiders weren't entirely welcome. But this day was different.

A couple and their young son from an adjacent neighborhood walked by and stopped, the little boy pestering his parents to go inside the yard and play. Mama spotted them and approached. "Good afternoon," she greeted them.

"Afternoon," the father echoed. "How much for one of those pony rides?" he asked.

"Free," she replied with a smile. "The food, the games...it's all free. And you're welcome to stay for as long as you'd like."

The man and his wife nodded, appreciatively. "Thanks, Ma'am. What's the celebration for?"

"My grandson walked for the first time," she answered, with no further explanation.

The couple smiled and stepped into the yard, clearly confused over all the fuss. "What's the big deal?" the man whispered to his wife. "Sooner or later, all kids learn to walk."

# Chapter 11

*Early Fall 1982*

It was Wednesday night and the family was gathered in Mama's kitchen. While they broke bread, Joan waited for the competing conversations to die down before she made her announcement. "Frank and I have decided to enroll Brian in Meeting Street School for disabled children. He'll be starting on Monday."

"Wonderful," Mama said, while the rest of them agreed.

"Are you excited?" Aunt Bev asked Brian.

He shook his head, but said nothing. He clearly didn't like the sound of it.

Mama searched his face. "It'll be fine, sweetheart," she told him. "It's the best thing for you – you'll see. You're going to meet a bunch of new friends your own age and..." She stopped.

For the first time in his short life, Brian averted his eyes from Mama's penetrating gaze. He was clearly disturbed by this new idea called *school*.

~ ~ ~ ~ ~ ~ ~ ~

Dressed in a new matching outfit and his lunch box packed with his favorites – a bologna and cheese sandwich, and butterscotch pudding for dessert – Brian brushed his teeth, while Joan parted his hair to the side.

"Ready?" she asked, admiring his polished look.

He shook his head. "Nah go."

"You have to go, Brian," she said, nervously. "We have no choice, so please don't make this any harder than it has to be."

~ ~ ~ ~ ~ ~ ~ ~

Joan pulled the Oldsmobile into Meeting Street School's parking lot and shut off the engine. She turned to face the back seat. "This will be fun. Just wait and see."

Brian stared out the side window, never moving.

She got out of the car, walked around the back and opened his door. "Let's go," she said, trying to sound strong. "You're going to be late."

He reluctantly got out and followed his mother. As they crossed the front of the school, Brian noticed several children playing in the fenced concrete yard. She searched his face, hoping for a positive reaction. His face was set like marble.

Joan completed some final paperwork in the main office before Mrs. Martin addressed Brian. "You ready to go meet your teacher?" she asked.

He looked at his mother, his eyes filled with terror. "Nah go cool," he begged. "Nah go, Ma."

Joan looked at Mrs. Martin and half-shrugged. "My husband and I have been talking to Brian about school for the last couple weeks. He doesn't like the idea of me leaving him here alone."

Mrs. Martin smiled. It was a smile that said she'd dealt with this same situation many times before. "But he won't be alone," she promised, looking directly at Brian. "He'll have plenty of friends before he knows it."

Joan followed Mrs. Martin out of the room and into the long, yellow hallway.

With no where else to turn, Brian moped behind the women until they entered the classroom at the end of the hall. An older teacher with kind eyes stood up from behind her desk and greeted them. "There you are, Brian," she said. "I've been looking forward to meeting you. I'm Mrs. Ledwidge." With a nod, Mrs. Martin left the room.

Brian turned to his mother again, his eyes completely panicked. "Nah, Ma...nah cool!"

Joan took a deep breath and explained the situation to Mrs. Ledwidge.

While they discussed Brian, he continued to complain, his voice growing louder with each desperate plea. "Nah, Ma. Nah cool. Go now."

Joan finished filling the teacher in and took another deep breath. She grabbed Brian by the shoulders and kissed his forehead. "Okay sweetheart, Mrs. Ledwidge is going to take care of you now. I'll be back..."

"NAH!" he screamed, and immediately collapsed to the floor – where he sobbed terribly.

"Get up, Brian," Joan told him, her cheeks pink from embarrassment.

"NAH!" he screamed again, and threw his arms around her leg. She tried to push him off, but he was locked on tight. "NAH, MA!" he wailed, his body now convulsing from fear.

Joan stood paralyzed. She looked to Mrs. Ledwidge for help. The teacher bent down and spoke quietly to Brian, trying to soothe him. "It's okay, Brian. We're going to have fun today."

He screeched like a wounded animal sensing its death.

"Maybe we should try it again tomorrow?" Joan suggested over the screams.

Mrs. Ledwidge stood erect and shook her head. "That's not a good idea, Mrs. Mauretti," she said. "Trust me, this won't get any easier."

While Brian screamed and cried, Joan's eyes filled with tears. "I'm so sorry," she said, "but I don't think either one of us is ready for this today."

Mrs. Ledwidge shook her head again. "Mrs. Mauretti, please..." she began to protest, but Joan had already made her decision.

Joan bent down and stared into Brian's eyes. "Okay, sweetheart. Let's go home."

In an instant, Brian was up, wiping his eyes and scrambling for the door.

Joan drummed up the courage to look into Mrs. Ledwidge's eyes. "I'm sorry," she said again. "We'll try it again tomorrow."

Mrs. Ledwidge nodded once and then watched as Joan and Brian hurried out of the classroom.

~ ~ ~ ~ ~ ~ ~ ~

Joan didn't even have her coat off when she was on the telephone, explaining the school nightmare to

Mama. "It was just awful, Ma. I've never felt so bad for him. And now I don't know what to do. Frank and I are supposed to testify at the Congressional sub-committee in a few days." She sighed heavily. "Maybe we'll just take him with us and I'll bring him back to school next week."

"Nonsense!" Mama said. "I'll take him tomorrow."

"Oh Ma, I can't ask you to do that. You can't imagine how bad..."

"But you didn't ask," Mama interrupted. "I offered. Leave it to me, I'll get Brian settled in this week, while you give them hell in D.C."

"Right...D.C." Joan sighed again. "I don't know which one would be easier," she muttered, filled with anxiety.

"Easier?" Mama asked.

"Testifying in D.C. in front of all those people is not going to be an easy thing to do, you know."

"Joan, easy has never played a role when it's come to Brian's story. You need to find the courage to do the right thing. It may not help your son directly, but I'm sure it will help others from having to go through the same suffering."

Joan breathed deeply. "You're right, Ma." She chuckled. "You're always right."

Mama laughed. "Well, not always...but close."

"Are you sure you don't mind bringing Brian to school?"

"Don't you worry. I'm more than happy to give him a ride. You just have him ready to go. I'll be there at 7:30."

~ ~ ~ ~ ~ ~ ~ ~

The following morning, Mama pulled up to her daughter's house, just as Frank was pulling out of the driveway and heading off to work. He stopped in front of her car, leaned across the front seat and rolled down the passenger side window. "Thanks for doing this," he told Mama. "You might honestly be saving your daughter from a heart attack."

Mama reached into the window and patted his arm. "My pleasure," she said, and looked down at her watch. "Aren't you late for work?"

He nodded. "A little. But I couldn't leave Joan alone with him this morning."

"As bad as yesterday?" she asked.

"Maybe worse," he said, his face filled with worry.

Mama nodded. "No worries, Frank. I'll take care of it. Now go to work."

"Thank you," he said, and truly meant it.

She shot him a wink and then marched off toward the house like the veteran drill sergeant she was.

~ ~ ~ ~ ~ ~ ~ ~

Mama wasn't past the threshold when Brian came running, throwing himself into her arms. "Nah, Mama. Nah cool!" he yelled. His face was awash in tears and mucous.

Mama looked past him to find her daughter standing there, looking like she hadn't slept in a week. She pushed Brian away to an arm's length and grabbed his trembling shoulders. "You listen to me right now, little boy! You get your butt into that bathroom this instant and wash your face, brush your teeth and finish getting yourself ready for school!"

For a moment, he stopped howling and sobbing. He looked up at her, shocked by her firm touch and harsh tone.

"Now!" she yelled, and spun him on his heels to face the bathroom.

He looked back once, but didn't dare make a peep. Instead, he put his head down and started walking.

"How dare you put your mother through this!" she scolded, as she followed him into the bathroom. "Every boy and girl needs to go to school, and you're no better than any one of them."

Joan stood in the hallway – watching in awe as her mother barked orders and her son obeyed – and felt two hundred pounds slide off her shoulders.

~ ~ ~ ~ ~ ~ ~ ~

Mama took Brian by the hand, marched him into the school and straight down to his classroom. With a surprised look on her face, Mrs. Ledwidge stood to greet them. Mama extended her hand. "Good morning. I'm Angela DiMartino, Brian's disappointed grandmother. It's nice to meet you."

The woman smiled.

Mama gave the teacher a quick but thorough inventory of Brian's likes and dislikes, his quirks and eccentric ways. "Amongst his other gifts, Brian suffers with Obsessive Compulsive Disorder. Everything has to be just so. He gets very uneasy when things are out of place or off schedule. He lives a very safe and structured life, and it's tough to get him to try anything new."

Mrs. Ledwidge smiled at the obvious point.

"He's obsessively clean," Mama continued, "always washing his hands. And he's a true daydreamer, his mind traveling to places that I'm not even permitted to go. I usually allow him to take the trip."

Mrs. Ledwidge nodded.

"For reasons that reach beyond my understanding, he hates when people get lower than him. Whenever his brother wants to tease him, he crawls up to Brian who will always scream and lash out from fear. Just be aware of that when he's around the other kids."

Mrs. Ledwidge nodded again.

"When Brian gets really upset, he whines, hyperventilates, and paces. 'That's enough,' I tell him. 'That's enough now!' Only a firm tone will calm him." Mama paused for acknowledgement of this.

Mrs. Ledwidge nodded her understanding.

Mama returned the nod. "But when he's not terrified out of his mind, he's a real charmer and will do whatever he can to get his way. Please be firm with him."

"I will," Mrs. Ledwidge promised, grateful for the valuable insight.

Mama sighed heavy, satisfied that the information had been shared and understood. She concluded the conversation by handing the impressed woman a piece of paper with her telephone number scribbled on it. "If you need me to come back and pick him up, I will." She peered into her eyes. "But if you're willing to keep him, then he's all yours for the day."

As the teacher nodded, Mama bent down and kissed Brian's head. "Have a good day and listen to your teacher," she told him. "I'll be back to pick you up this afternoon."

"NAH!" he screamed and dove to the floor to grab her legs. But she had anticipated the move and side-stepped it like an experienced wrestler, leaving him huddled and crying on the floor. Mrs. Ledwidge quickly moved in and restrained him long enough for her to leave. Desperately, he reached for her, screaming, "NAH MAMA...NAH GO!"

Mama turned around and headed for the door, never once looking back.

"NAH MAMA...NAH GO!"

She heard his screams echo down the hallway and her eyes filled with tears. She grabbed her crucifix and kissed it. *Lord, please give me the strength to do what's right for this boy. I beg you – just give me the will to stay strong for him right now.*

"NAH MAMA...NAH GO!" he wailed out again.

She threw open the school's front door and hurried out. For the next hour, she sat in her car – praying and crying, all at the same time.

~ ~ ~ ~ ~ ~ ~ ~

Wednesday was just as bad, with Brian having a complete breakdown and Mama showering him with all the tough love she could muster. Thursday seemed a little bit better, but not much. On Friday, Mama walked Brian into his classroom for the last time. She told Mrs. Ledwidge, "Brian needs to apologize for his childish tantrums this week and..."

"Oh, that's not necessary," Mrs. Ledwidge interrupted, smiling at Brian. "We're making great progress."

Mama nudged him in the back. "Go on, Brian."

"Soy," he whispered.

"What's that?" Mama asked. "Your nice teacher didn't hear you."

"Soy," he said louder.

Mrs. Ledwidge smiled compassionately and bent down to grab his hand. "Apology accepted, Brian."

~ ~ ~ ~ ~ ~ ~ ~

First thing Saturday morning, Joan arrived at the cottage to pick up the boys. After smothering them with hugs and souvenirs from Washington D.C., she took a seat at the kitchen table with Mama. "So how did Brian do at school this week?" she asked, her brow folded in fearful anticipation.

Mama looked past Joan to find Brian standing in the doorway, eavesdropping. "Piece of cake," she said.

"Are you kidding me?" Joan asked, shocked.

Mama nodded. "He was a perfect angel," she fibbed. "Just wait and see how good he's going to do this week when you drop him off at school."

Brian smiled, and then disappeared into the living room.

"So tell me what happened in D.C.," Mama said.

Joan's smile told the story long before her words could. "It was a little rough going at first. I had to breathe through a terrible panic attack, but once I started testifying the anger took over and I gave them every detail of what Brian's been forced to go through...what we've all been through."

"Good for you. So what was the outcome?"

"Well, in the end, the FDA and Infant Formula Council both agreed that regulatory legislation is needed. One bill is expected to receive overwhelming approval in the House. Another is going before the Senate health subcommittee by the end of the month."

"That's wonderful," Mama said. "Just wonderful."

Joan nodded. "Syntex will be mandated to reformulate its products and will have to work with the FDA to ensure that they meet all nutrient guidelines. Once tested and FDA approved, they'll be allowed to put their formulas back on the market."

Mama shrugged, less impressed.

"The Senate health subcommittee will also establish – through the CDC – a registry of children who developed metabolic alkalosis as a result of using Neo Mulsoy formula...so at least all of the babies affected will be accounted for."

Mama stayed quiet for a few moments, digesting all that she'd just learned. "I'm proud of you, Joan," she said. "You've just made a positive difference in this world...even if it wasn't the easiest thing to do."

Joan nodded. "And through it all, those company attorneys couldn't have cared less about Brian, or any other baby that the formula poisoned. Can you imagine that?"

"Unfortunately, I can," Mama said, shaking her disgusted head. "It's all about the money these days. If they weren't trying to save money by taking the sodium out of the formula in the first place, Brian wouldn't have to fight so hard for every inch of his life."

~ ~ ~ ~ ~ ~ ~ ~

Due in part to Joan's emotional testimony, Congress finally passed the Infant Formula Act. The new act created a separate category of food designated as *infant formula*. It mandated that every infant formula on the market meet explicit standards of quality and safety, and contain all the essential nutrients infants need – including chloride – at specific levels. Under this act, the FDA required manufacturers to follow quality control procedures, analyze each batch of formula for required nutrients, test samples for stability during the shelf life of the product, code containers identifying each batch, and maintain and make records available to FDA inspectors. It was the first in a series of major legislative and regulatory steps taken to ensure the safety of infant formulas.

Ignoring Frank's lack of enthusiasm, Joan threw a party. She and the *Mothers of Neo Mulsoy Babies* – with Mama as their special guest – celebrated like they'd just witnessed the second coming of Christ.

# Chapter 12

## *Spring 1983*

Mama continued to take the kids on day trips that allowed her to teach them about the world, and more importantly, themselves.

A city rich in history and culture, Boston is one of the most popular destinations in the world and luckily for Mama and her brood, it was only sixty miles away from the cottage by the bay. She wanted to walk the decks of the USS Constitution, explore the historical landmarks along the Freedom Trail, and roam the streets of Beacon Hill with the kids, introducing them to the old world charm and international flavor of the state's capital.

They drove to North Quincy and took the train to the Bunker Hill Monument in Charlestown near the old Navy Yard.

Although he was much too big for it, Brian sat in his oversized stroller, drinking from a yellow sippy cup. Some woman began staring at him. "Do you want to take a picture?" Mama asked. "I can put on some lipstick if you want."

Brian pointed at the woman. "Pitcher?" he asked.

The woman scurried away, embarrassed.

Mama laughed in her usual roar, scaring the stranger even more.

As they walked along, Heidi commented, "Everyone stares at Brian. They must think..."

Mama stopped abruptly. "Never worry about what people think. God knows...and that's enough!" Her eyes softened and she lowered her tone. "Remember guys, caring little of what other people think of you will allow you the energy to focus on what you think of yourself." She shook her head and her tone rose again. "But never apologize for Brian. If people are uncomfortable around him, then it's too bad for them. It's their loss!"

As they walked on, the kids pondered her words and could feel the same protective love stir deep within them; seeds planted for a lifetime.

According to the plaque, the Bunker Hill Monument was the site of *The first battle of the American Revolution*. There were two hundred ninety-four steps to the top, where the views of Boston were supposed to be unmatched. "There's no way I can make it," Mama declared.

The USS Constitution was the oldest commissioned warship afloat in the country. Nicknamed "Old Ironsides" because cannonballs bounced off her thick oak sides, the fifty-two-gun frigate had never lost a battle. Mama willed her legs up the gangplank and was happy she did. Ross loved it.

They passed on the Whites of Their Eyes Museum and instead spent some time at the Boston Tea Party Ship. This replica ship hosted a costumed re-enactment of the colonial protest against taxation without representation. Mama and the kids cheered as Paul Revere and Sam Adams threw tea overboard into the Boston Harbor.

Mama then purchased five tickets for a two-hour tour on a San Francisco-style trolley. The bus was clean and the seats were padded. It was enough to make her smile. The tour offered free unlimited reboarding at any of their stops, but she had no plans to get off until they hit the Commons. With the windows open and the kids full of questions, they embarked on the Freedom Trail.

The trolley only stopped at prime historic and scenic areas of the city. As they passed Cobb's Hill Burial Ground, the guide said, "We're told that there've been some recent ghost sightings for anyone interested in investigating the old hallowed grounds."

Steph's eyes lit up, but Mama quickly poked out the flame with a shake of her curly head.

"But Mama..." she whined.

"Stay seated."

They passed the Old North Church to get to Paul Revere's House. "Built in 1680, it's the oldest wooden house remaining in Boston," the guide said. "Of course, the silversmith is best known for his ride to warn of the coming British."

Little Italy in the historical North End smelled like Mama's kitchen and the kids' mouths watered. Again, she shook her head. "Not today," she said. "We'll be back at Christmas."

Before long, they were at Faneuil Hall Marketplace, also known as Quincy Market. The guide picked up the microphone again. "In 1742, Quincy Market was a gift from merchant Peter Faneuil to be a town meeting place and public market. It was here in 1772 that Samuel Adams first suggested that the colonies unite against the British." The kids looked out of the trolley to find an upscale shopping mall, specializing in a diverse selection of foods. They all turned to Mama. She remained seated, with no intention of budging from her seat. None of them dared ask any longer.

At the Boston Massacre Memorial, a bronze figure of Crispus Atticus, the first to fall, represented revolution breaking the chains of tyranny.

From there, it was on to the Old State House, then the Old South Meeting House, and then to the Old Corner Bookstore.

"Everything's old around here," Steph said.

"And sore, too," Mama said with a wink.

The Granary Burial Grounds and King's Burial Ground each offered ghost tours and had the kids sulking as they passed. The Massachusetts State House put them near historic Beacon Hill. The narrow streets of this charming neighborhood were off limits to trolleys. Instead, costumed actors led tourists into the *heart of Boston* on a forty-five-minute walking tour. Mama said, "Sorry guys, but these old legs will never make it."

Though they didn't stop at the New England Aquarium or the Bull & Finch Pub – the inspiration for the television series, Cheers – they did end up in downtown Boston, where they jumped off the trolley and waited for the blood to flow back into Mama's cramped legs.

Heidi stared at the expensive clothes in one of the shop windows. Her eyes wide, she turned to Mama and asked, "You know what I want, Mama?"

"More than what you already have, I'm guessing," Mama replied.

The comment was sharp enough to break Heidi's hypnotic trance. Along with the others, she looked up at her grandmother.

Mama smiled. "If you don't always want or need something, then you already have everything you'll ever need, right?"

They half-shrugged, half-nodded.

She turned to Brian. "Right?"

"Yets," he replied.

With a grin, Mama glanced at the newest fashions hanging in the window and shook her head. "Besides, pretty book covers are nice, but it's the story inside that counts," she concluded, hoping they would remember the lessons and understand them someday when they were older.

Though the line wrapped around the corner, Chacarero's traditional Chilean sandwich was well worth the wait. It was homemade bread, split and stuffed with lemon and garlic-marinated chicken, steak tomatoes sliced thin, steamed green beans, a slice of Muenster cheese, avocado spread, salt, pepper and their secret hot sauce. Mama ordered two of the giant sandwiches to split with the kids. "I remember the first time your papa and I shared one of these sandwiches years ago," she told them. "I've never forgotten the taste."

As they ate, Steph said, "I still think about Papa a lot. I miss him."

"Me, too," Mama said between bites. "He was a good man who made sure we all knew how much he loved us."

"How did you know how much Papa loved you?" Heidi asked.

"Some years ago, when I threw out my back, your grandfather took care of my gardening, making sure the flowers still bloomed. I didn't find out until the fall that he'd also thrown out his back that spring. Now that's love." She smiled. "It's the little things that really do matter. He could make me smile when I was exhausted and he never once complained about my snoring." She smiled wider, clearly in love with her deceased husband. "I still feel him with me," she whispered.

Kneeling by the stroller, Ross looked from his brother to Mama. "And Brian?" he asked. "How can you tell how much Brian loves you?"

"Brian's different. He's like a puppy that'll lick your face, even after you've scolded him." Mama sighed, grinning at her little angel. "Brian's love is unconditional. He doesn't stay angry for more than a moment. He'll forgive you long before you'll ever forgive yourself and he'll love you hard – even on those terrible days when you don't have the energy to show him that you feel the same." She ruffled Ross' hair. "There isn't a day that goes by that your baby brother doesn't teach me about myself...and about real love."

Ross nodded, bent down and kissed his brother's cheek. "He is a special guy."

~ ~ ~ ~ ~ ~ ~ ~

Amongst the other tourists, Mama and the kids eventually flocked toward the famous Duck Boat tours.

As the tour began, the guide announced, "During the early days of World War II, the allies were faced with a tough tactical problem: How could they unload cargo and men from their ships in places where the dock facilities had been destroyed or simply didn't exist? The answer was to unload cargo directly over the beach. But how?

"The demands of war, along with technical know-how and old fashioned Yankee ingenuity combined to create the perfect solution: A vehicle that was half-boat and half-truck that could run on land and water. Code-named DUKW, the first *DUCK* was actually a GMC truck enclosed in a water-tight shell.

"It wasn't long before DUKWs were playing a crucial role in the war effort, aiding in the allied invasions of Sicily, islands in the Pacific, and the biggest invasion of all – the Normandy beaches on D-Day. In fact, more than forty percent of all over-beach supplies in Normandy were transported by DUKWs during the first four months. So today, you're not only having the ride of your life, you're riding on a proud part of American history."

Mama leaned toward the kids and explained, "My father – your great-grandfather – fought in Normandy and was wounded by the Germans three times. And he only missed a total of seven days worth of combat. Now that was a great man!"

While the girls nodded, Ross' eyes lit up with admiration and respect. Mama caught the look and grinned. *Oh boy*, she thought.

With a splash, the duck-boat drove into the Charles River. The kids squealed with excitement, while Mama held her mid-section and moaned. She'd forgotten her motion sickness pills. *The things I won't do for these kids*, she thought.

After all the children aboard had the opportunity to steer the boat, the ride down the river proved surprisingly smooth and enjoyable. Giant skyscrapers filled the skyline, while seagulls catching a free ride on the warm winds escorted them.

As the boat drove back onto land and parked, the kids unbuckled their seat belts and stood in a half-circle around Mama. The old lady looked pale and very tired. "You okay, Mama?" Steph asked.

Ignoring the nausea as well as the pain in her legs, Mama nodded. "Never been better," she said with a smile. "It was worth the trip."

On the way home, the subway train went underground and traveled through a long stretch of dark tunnel. Though Mama looked out the window, she couldn't see anything outside the train – only the reflection of those who shared the ride with her. She smiled. Heidi, Steph, Ross and Brian – *I couldn't have chosen four better people to share this journey with.*

The train rattled around a tight corner, nearly throwing Brian out of her lap. She tightened her grip around his waist and couldn't decide what she liked better – *going away on our little trips or coming home?*

~ ~ ~ ~ ~ ~ ~ ~

Even though she'd spent the day with Brian, at eight o'clock Mama kept to their nightly tradition. She picked up the telephone and dialed.

The telephone rang. Joan picked up. "Hello?"

"Hi, Joan. Where's my angel?"

"But you just dropped him off a little while ago," Joan said.

"Just put him on the phone, please. I have a few questions."

"Hold on. I'll get him." Joan covered the mouthpiece and yelled, "Brian, it's Mama...for you." For as long as Joan could remember, her mother called each and every night at eight o'clock and spent ten minutes on the phone with Brian. Although the old lady claimed it was only to stay in touch, Joan knew better. Her clever mother used the time to force Brian to verbally express himself, while increasing his vocabulary and practicing his sentence structure.

Brian hurried to the phone and grabbed it from his mother. "Allo?"

"Hi, sweetheart. How was your day today?" Mama asked.

"K, Mama. You door."

"I know I was there, love. But I want to know what you thought of our little adventure in Boston?"

There was a pause; Brian searching his thoughts. "Fun, Mama. Bode."

"That was a fun boat ride," she agreed. "So what did you like best about it?"

And no matter how much effort or time it took for him to articulate his thoughts, the questions just kept coming.

# Chapter 13

*Late Summer 1983*

The civil case – Mauretti vs. Syntex – proved far too draining for Joan, inviting one brutal panic attack after the other into her world. "I just can't do it anymore," she told Frank. "The stress of testifying and dragging Brian through this over and over is killing me."

He was livid – but no matter what he said, he couldn't convince her to hang on. The legal fight was the one thing he thought he could do for his son; the one thing he might be able to control and get right. *But Joan's taking that away from me, too.*

With the help of Attorney Russell McCarthy, they opted to settle out on behalf of Brian for a fraction of what they'd initially sought in damages. Frank bit his tongue so hard he nearly chewed it off.

Months later, Sheridan vs. Syntex was tried in Illinois. Before going to trial, Syntex offered three hundred fifty thousand dollars to the tiny plaintiff who was fed Neo Mulsoy and suffered brain injury resulting in learning disabilities. However, the family stuck in there and took the case to trial.

Within two weeks, *impairment of language and motor coordination* was proven on behalf of the defendant, an infant who suffered no greater losses than Brian.

At the trial, it was also revealed that Syntex's decision not to add salt to its formula – an essential nutrient for brain development – was prompted by economic considerations. They were trying to save money.

The Sheridan family won – the jury awarding twenty-seven million, with twenty-two million in punitive damages.

Frank read the court transcripts and couldn't sleep for weeks. *Stupid woman!* he repeated over and over in his mind, allowing years of bitterness and anger to poison him.

~ ~ ~ ~ ~ ~ ~ ~

Joan called Mama and told her about the terrible fights they were having over it.

Mama simply replied, "Money's the last thing in the world that will help Brian. All he needs is love and the support that comes from it."

~ ~ ~ ~ ~ ~ ~ ~

The arguments that were taking place once a month became weekly until Frank and Joan were screaming at each other at least once a day.

"That's just great," Frank hissed.

"If you don't like it, then there's the door!" Joan screamed, tired of her husband's constant insults.

"Nah...nah...nah..." Brian whined like a wounded animal. He placed his hand over his face, rocked back and forth and whined, "Nah...nah...nah..."

Joan and Frank both stopped, while Ross hurried to his brother's side. "Stop it!" he ordered. "You're hurting him! You're hurting all of us!"

Joan's eyes filled and she turned to Frank. "He's right. And I can't keep shipping these kids over to my mother's to avoid the drama. Before long, they'll be living there full-time."

"I know, Joan. It's my fault again," Frank barked, as he slammed the door on his way out of the house.

She quickly tended to Brian. While she began to soothe him, she thought, *Something has to be done, or we're going to lose our whole family over a marriage that pretty much ended years ago.*

~ ~ ~ ~ ~ ~ ~ ~

It was an ordinary Tuesday night when everything came to a head. Brian had made a terrible mess of himself at the dinner table and Frank began to clean him up like Brian was a helpless infant.

"Let him clean himself, Frank," Joan pleaded.

"Why? He'll just make even more of a mess." Frank finished the job and returned to his seat at the head of the table.

Joan looked at Brian for a long moment. He was a beautiful boy. Besides a vacant stare and the fact that he still sat in a high chair, he appeared no different from any other child. She then stared at her husband for a few minutes. "You still treat Brian like a cripple," she hissed. She knew that even with all they'd accomplished, Frank was still a non-believer. Although he loved his son, Brian was still helpless in her husband's eyes. "No one else in this family treats Brian like he's handicapped. In fact, it's just the opposite. Brian can't be treated like a victim, Frank. If he is, then he'll act like a victim. We need to set high expectations so he can strive toward them."

Frank smirked. "I wonder who you sound like now?"

"And I'm glad I do!" she replied. "It's taken me a long time to understand that everything my mother's ever said about Brian is true. Even with all the challenges and obstacles in front of him, she's teaching him to take responsibility for his words and his actions...for his life."

Enraged, Frank stood. "I'm done with all the preaching!" he screamed. "That's it!"

Joan turned to Ross and said, "Please take your brother and sister and go to your room and play. Mom and Dad need to talk."

Ross helped Brian out of his chair and then grabbed Angie. "Fine," he said and moped down the hall with the two little ones.

Joan turned her attention back to her husband. "That's it?" she asked, almost laughing. "I think we went past *IT* a long time ago, Frank."

"And you're happy with that?"

"As happy as you are, I suppose." She shook her head. "I don't give it a lot of thought, to be honest. There are so many other things that need..."

"And that's the problem right there, Joan! Everything else is more important than us...than our marriage."

"That's not true. This family is the most important thing in the world to me. It's just that some of us require more attention than others and you've never been able to handle that." Her eyes filled. "And let's be honest – at this point, you and I don't share a marriage. We share memories."

He opened his mouth, but couldn't respond. His eyes looked tormented. "It wasn't supposed to be like this," he finally muttered, his voice cracked.

"Or maybe it was?" she replied softly. "Either way, life is the way it is and all we can do is our best with it." She gazed into his eyes. "Our best, Frank."

His eyes were filling now. "But what if I have given my best? What if I don't have any more in me to give?"

He was right. In the deepest part of her heart, she knew he was right and it tore at her soul. She didn't reply.

With his head hung low, he said, "Remember when we used to meet at McRay's for clam cakes and walk the beach for hours? We'd talk about everything or nothing at all. It didn't matter back then. Life was easy. We were so in love." He looked up at her. "What happened, Joan?"

"Life," she whispered. "We grew up, accepted our fair share of responsibility and then we had children together – one, a disabled son who required all of our time and patience and energy." In spite of her husband's tortured face, she grinned. "And when I think about it, I wouldn't have had it any other way."

He tried to share her smile, but couldn't – nor could he agree with her and she knew it. She grabbed his hand and held it tight. They sat quietly together for longer than either of them could remember. Quite simply, it was their way of trying to retain a shred of dignity in what used to be a great and passionate love. "I'm so sorry," he said.

"I know, Frank. Me, too."

"Most days, I just can't take it."

"And I know that, too. But we can't keep fighting. It's worse than staying together just for the sake of staying together."

"I'm so sorry," he repeated, crying.

"It's going to be fine," she promised.

Tears streamed down his face, as Frank came to terms with their parting. Joan rubbed his back and tried to console him, but there were no tears left for her to give. She'd used them all up long ago. All she could feel now was an amazing sense of relief.

When she thought about it, their separation was inevitable. They'd hung in there for more than five years after Brian's birth. All of Joan's attention had been shifted to their son. Frank loved him, but Brian's needs were all-consuming, and he had finally admitted that it was too much for him to take.

~ ~ ~ ~ ~ ~ ~ ~

It was a cool fall morning when Joan and Frank formalized their separation. While the rest of the world went about their usual routines and commuted to work, Frank and Joan ascended the court stairs together to put an official end to their partnership as man and wife.

Ross, Brian and Angie sat at Mama's kitchen table, unaware of just how much their world was about to change.

"What does *divorce* mean, anyway?" Ross asked, trying to better understand what his parents were in the process of.

With Angie sitting on one leg and Brian perched on the other, Mama explained, "It means that there'll be no more fighting and that your dad will be living somewhere else from now on. Other than that, nothing else will change."

Ross searched her eyes to see if she was candy coating the truth.

"Both your mom and dad will love you just as much as they always have. You'll be taken care of – like you always have. You're a family...we're a family... and there's nothing on God's green Earth that's ever going to change that."

Ross peered into her eyes.

Mama raised her pinky. "I swear on it," she vowed.

Ross locked pinkies with her and then smiled. Brian followed suit. Angie just nodded, as if she understood.

~ ~ ~ ~ ~ ~ ~ ~

When Joan returned to the cottage, Ross met her at the door. "Hi sweetheart," she said.

"Where's Dad?" he asked, nervously.

Joan stepped through the door and took off her coat. Mama was standing at the stove, cooking – Angie clinging to her leg. Brian ran over to hug his mother. Through it all, Joan never broke eye contact with Ross. "Please take a seat," she told him, while Angie jumped into her mother's arms to listen.

Ross sat.

She sat alongside him and took his hand. "Dad went to work, Ross. He'll pick you guys up on Saturday."

Concern swam in the boy's eyes.

"Now you listen to me," she told him, "even though Dad won't be living with us anymore, we're still a family. And without all the arguing, we can become a close family again. Won't that be great?"

Ross looked at his grandmother, who shot him a wink. Her words had been confirmed. "Yes," he finally answered.

"Now take your brother and sister into the living room. I want to have a few words alone with Mama," she said.

"Why can't I stay?" Ross complained.

"Because you were just asked to leave," Mama barked.

Ross stood still. It only lasted a moment, but he didn't budge.

Mama took one step toward him. "This is an adult conversation and you're not welcome to join it until you've grown up and become an adult, understand?" He nodded. She pointed toward the living room. "Now do as you're told and don't let me ever see you question your mother again."

As he began to backpedal, he said, "I won't, Mama," and meant it.

Tenderness immediately replaced her scowl. "That's my boy," she said.

Brian and Angie followed, also getting the message.

~ ~ ~ ~ ~ ~ ~ ~

Before she ever opened her mouth, Joan began to cry. "Even though Angie's only four, it's a relief, Ma. I can finally give all of my attention back to the kids. And we can live in a house of peace again."

Mama nodded.

"Frank's agreed to take them on alternate weekends."

Again, Mama nodded, but held her tongue.

"There was no fighting over property or child support," Joan explained, her eyes leaking tears. "I'll stay in the house with the kids and Frank will find an apartment." She shrugged. "Who knows...by breaking up, we might have a real shot at being a happy, close knit family again." She rustled through her purse for a tissue.

Mama grabbed a crumpled ball of them from her housecoat pocket and handed it to her daughter. "Are you okay?"

"It's just so sad, Ma...to have gone through so much with another person; a partner that had been promised for life. And now I feel so detached, like we just put an end to a bad business deal." She blew her nose. "The whole thing lasted half the time that the wedding took and cost us three times as much."

Mama shook her head. "Well, it took longer than I thought."

Joan readjusted Angie in her lap and shrugged. "Actually, we went for lunch at a Cracker Barrel afterwards and discussed our own terms. Frank offered to take the kids for dinner every Tuesday and Thursday. Once he gets set up, they can sleep over his place every other weekend. He's just not sure he'll be able to..." She stopped, leery of her mother's harsh judgment.

"I'm sure Brian will love to see his dad on Tuesdays and Thursdays, but you need to keep your job so I'd be happy to have him stay with me every other weekend."

"That's exactly what I told him."

"And he's okay with that?"

"He was relieved." Joan stared off into space and shook her head. "He told me that he loves Brian with all his heart; it's just that he worries himself sick about being able to fulfill his needs. He really..."

"I know, Joan," Mama kindly interrupted, devoid of any judgment. She knew that Brian's best interest was what everyone had in mind and the boy spending time at the cottage was clearly best for everyone – especially Brian. "And you're absolutely right in what you told the kids, you know."

"What's that?"

"Now you guys can move forward as a family. And you'd better," she said, grinning, "because I pinky swore on it that you would."

For a moment, Joan gazed at her mother with the same skepticism that Ross had.

"What is it?" Mama asked.

"I'm just surprised, that's all. I thought you would have been dead-set against this divorce."

"Joan, flowers don't bloom in the shade, where it's dark and cold. Brian can't grow and make progress in a house of turmoil. None of the kids can. You made the right decision."

# Chapter 14

## Summer 1984

Protected by her wide-brimmed hat, Mama wore a one-piece bathing suit with a colorful sarong wrapped around her thick waist. Her late husband had made a cart that she piled beach chairs – hers and a smaller one for Brian – a cooler and Brian's sand toys atop, and pulled it down to the shore for the day.

As she and Brian walked through the neighborhood, she pointed out every detail. She lived two streets in from the shore, but it was a totally different community from those located right on the water. They were still considered beach properties, so one house sat right on top of the next; a strip of cottages with the wealthiest family at the end. They had a gazebo that they lit each night with little white lights. They also owned a private way that led down to the beach, posted: *NO TRESPASSERS*. She and Brian always used it and no one ever said a word about it.

There were several bird houses in each yard. Hydrangeas, honeysuckle and plum rose bushes grew everywhere; anything that could live in a mix of sand and soil. Some houses were decorated with maritime accents: life preservers, rope and oars. Mama never went for the colored buoys, lobster traps, or anchors, though.

Some neighbors had matching striped awnings, but she couldn't afford those. They also had planters hanging from their porch, but not Mama; she refused to allow anything to obstruct her view of the bay. Hammocks and rocking chairs sat on most porches or front yards. She went with the mismatched chairs on the porch, painted in different pastel colors.

She and Brian finally reached the marina filled with expensive toys. The docked boats had more money invested in fishing tackle than most folks did in their yards. Boats with such names as *Shark Bite, Happy Hobos, Sea Hag, Solitude* and *Unreel* sat idle, waiting to be played with.

At the pier, Mama spotted two old-timers, Herbie and Arthur, fishing together. Arthur wore a thread-bare sweater and boat shoes. Herbie had on a worn T-shirt with suspenders, faded khakis and Velcro sneakers. They were always on the pier, fishing and arguing about issues that had long passed as important. "You two should be married," she teased them. "You're never apart."

"He'd be damn lucky to have me," Arthur replied.

"We're going deer hunting," Herbie teased.

"I'll shoot you both first," she replied and laughed. "What trouble are you two up to today?"

Herbie shook his head. "Wasting time with Arthur."

Arthur rolled his eyes and cast his bait again.

"You guys?" Herbie asked.

"Brian's taking me to McRay's for some clam cakes. We're on a date."

Like some comical bobble head, Brian began nodding and giggling. "Yets," he confirmed. "Dot. Yets."

"You two wouldn't know what to do without each other," Mama concluded.

Herbie chuckled. "Some good company and a fair breeze is all you ever need in this life," he said, and then shrugged. "Well, at least there's a breeze today."

Mama laughed.

"*Some* type of company and a fair breeze," Arthur countered. "That's right."

Hand-in-hand, Mama and Brian passed the pier, waving back toward Herbie and Arthur.

~ ~ ~ ~ ~ ~ ~ ~

McRay's Clam Shack sat at the end of the pier. A row of telephone poles stuck out of the cement three feet, their tops painted red, white or blue. The sign out front read: *Closed for Hurricanes*. Established in 1895, Joy, and her sister, Louise, had owned it for twenty-two years.

There was a deck with round tables and umbrellas. The board signs above the windows read, *Frappes* (coffee frappes being the most popular), *French Fries, Hot Dogs, Cold Drinks, Burgers, Clam Chowder, Clam Cakes, Fried Clams*. When they took an order, they gave the customer a sea stone with a number painted on it. When they called over the PA system, customers checked their rocks and picked up their order from the window – no rock, no food.

The signs also advertised *Cotton Candy, Salt Water Taffy, Ice Cream, Fried Dough, Flavored Slush, Fried Seafood* and *Overstuffed Lobster Rolls*. There were also onion rings and chili-cheese fries available, served in candy cane striped cardboard containers. They made homemade fudge every day. Chocolate walnut and peanut butter were their two biggest sellers.

It was their hot dogs that were unique, though. They had a western dog with BBQ sauce & onion rings, a sweet & sour dog, and a PB (peanut butter) dog – which Mama never braved. They also had a slaw dog, a tarter sauce dog, a chili-cheese dog, a kraut dog and a bean dog.

They served hard packed ice cream – no soft serve – and their root beer floats were enormous. On the deck, a sign read, *Sit, Relax & Enjoy the View*.

On the beach – just at the base of the deck stairs – were two benches formed out of granite slabs. Both had sayings carved into their seats. The first read, *If you look to the horizon, the possibilities are endless.* When Mama took Brian to McRay's to share a dozen clam cakes, they usually sat on this bench. It was their favorite resting spot. The second granite slab read, *Sunsets are like looking through the gates of heaven*.

McRay's was most famous for their clam cakes. While other clam shacks peddled greasy golf balls, these folks actually packed chunks of clams into their fluffy, oversized cakes.

That afternoon, as a special treat, Joy and Louise offered Mama and Brian a tour and taught them how they made their salt-water taffy. "Altogether, we make thirty-six batches a day at one hundred and five pounds per batch or flavor. And it sometimes takes us sixteen hours a day. For years, folks have tried to get our recipe, but it's been well guarded," Louise boasted.

Brian threw his arm around her waist and walked with her on the tour.

"We start at five o'clock every morning when we have to disassemble the equipment and boil each part – due to peanut allergies," she continued. "We then reassemble all of it before the day gets started. The process is simple: We boil the equipment, re-assemble the parts, throw in our secret ingredients and then cook each batch, stirring it with a giant wooden spoon. We then put it on a water-cooled table and add food coloring. Once it's cooled, we lift it off the table using wide putty scrapers. We then carry the taffy to the stretch machine, which is situated where our customers can watch. From there, we place it on a marble table and ball it up like a loaf of bread, forming it in the shape of a snake and then feed it through the cutting machine, which also wraps the pieces in colored wax paper."

They sold it by the pound and you could mix and match. Taffy flavors included strawberry, peppermint stick, coffee, bubble gum and peanut butter – amongst others. After the generous tour, Mama bought a pound – half black licorice and the other half watermelon for Brian. She also purchased lunch – a dozen clam cakes, a small French fry and two soft drinks – and headed for the sand with her hungry date.

~ ~ ~ ~ ~ ~ ~ ~

After finishing most of their lunch, Mama and Brian sat in their beach chairs and gazed up at the beautiful, sapphire sky. A seagull sauntered over. With its sharp beak, it grabbed the paper bag half-filled with French fries and ran off twenty yards to safety. Mama spotted the thief and nudged Brian. "Watch this," she told him. The seagull flipped the bag into the air a few times until the fries fell out onto the sand where he quickly devoured the greasy lunch. "No good bandit," she murmured and laughed at the spectacle. Brian applauded the show. More seagulls swooped in to fight for their share. Brian squealed in delight, making Mama laugh from her belly.

Once the show was over, Mama and Brian sat quietly for a while, watching tiny white birds called terns hover above the water and reveal where the schools of fish were located. A dozen men took notice, casting their bait from atop the long jetty. As the terns dove into the ocean for fish, Brian cheered each time one of them reappeared with its lunch.

Eventually, Mama and Brian made their way to the water. Mama pulled up her waist scarf, grabbed Brian's hand and walked in knee-high, where they stood in a thick black cloud of krill. The microscopic shrimp tickled Brian's legs and he laughed aloud. She laughed right along with him.

When they had their fill, they headed back to their chairs. On the way, they stumbled upon a shiny white rock. Mama gasped and pointed it out, show-ing Brian. "Look at this, Brian. It's a lucky rock. Yup, that's a lucky rock, all right. And whoever has this rock has all the luck in the world."

Excited, he grabbed it and placed it into his swim trunks pocket. From that moment on, he wasn't about to go anywhere without his lucky rock.

~ ~ ~ ~ ~ ~ ~ ~

All summer, while the young folks tied floats to-gether, creating a massive raft to lounge on, Mama watched Brian explore the sand all the way to the first foot of water. Beach time was their quiet time. It was like going to church. When they were at the shore, sitting side-by-side in their beach chairs, it wasn't only acceptable to be silent and still, it was preferred – taking in God's great work before them. Mama had always been humbled by the water and taught Brian to respect the same. Other than the lap of the tide on the shore, the squawk of seagulls and the salty breezes that whistled off the rocks, there was usually nothing but sweet silence.

Mama took in all the peace she needed before heading back toward the water for Brian's swimming lesson. As he lay on his back with her gnarled hands beneath him, all she could hear was the wind and her grandson's heavy breathing.

"Skee, Mama," he said, panting.

"Scared?" she asked. "Oh no, sweetheart, there's nothing to be afraid of! Both me and the good Lord are right here with you. Nothing bad can happen. You have to believe that, Brian."

He reached up and touched her face. She bent down, so that he could kiss her on the cheek. "Aaah, I feel the flutter of angel's wings," she said, her eyes filling with tears. Their eyes locked and she could see all that he felt for her. "I love you, too," she whimpered. "Now no more stalling, lazy man," she teased him, a tear streaming down her face. She then turned him onto his belly to get the swimming lesson started.

As usual, Brian began splashing around for a few minutes. And then something different happened. His awkward moves were now keeping him afloat. It was half dead man's float, half-dog paddle, but he now knew when to turn his head to breathe. Mama slowly slid her hands out from under him and surrendered the best part of her soul to the bay. As he paddled around in a circle, she stood waist deep, crying like a baby and doing her best to give thanks in prayer. "Another one of your miracles, dear Lord," she whimpered. "How blessed we are." She clasped her hands together and raised them toward the sky. "Thank you again."

Brian was eight and a half – and he could swim now, too.

# Chapter 15

*Early Fall 1985*

Although Ross had been cursed with Mama's lack of height, he never once neglected his duty of looking out for his little brother.

The street light had just gone on when an over-sized neighborhood punk named Owen told him, "We chipped in and bought your brother a helmet, so when he..."

Before the sentence was complete, Ross was running full sprint at the buffoon. The boy's shocked eyes and drooping jaw didn't stop Ross from ramming into him, head first. He caught him square in the mid-section and knocked the air right out of him. The bully went down. Ross went down on top of him, scurried up to his chest and began punching him in the face. Right, left, right, left – both fists firing. Blood splayed. "Stop! Please stop!" the boy screamed for mercy. Right, left, right, left – Ross kept punching, never uttering a single word. He wasn't insane with rage, nor did he black out. He was simply defending a boy who couldn't protect himself; a boy whom he loved with every cell of his being – his little brother. Right, left, right, left – he pounded away.

Mary MacDonald, Mama's neighbor, pulled Ross off. His T-shirt was tie-dyed in blood. "Are you crazy, Ross?" she screamed. "What do you want to do...kill him?"

Ross never answered. He stood, wiped his bloodied hands on his pants and bent down until he was inches from Owen's face. "You ever say anything about Brian again and I swear to God, I'll beat you to a pulp. You got it?"

Owen nodded and went right on crying.

It took all of twenty minutes for word to spread and for the whole neighborhood to learn that little Ross had snapped and that Owen, the bully, had experienced his wrath.

Joan questioned him about it at Mama's kitchen table. "Tell me what happened?"

He told the truth – explaining what, how and why in every graphic detail.

"I understand why you did it," his mother said, "but you can't go around beating up people who are too ignorant to understand your brother. Besides, if you can't find a more peaceful way to deal with it, you'll be in trouble your whole life."

Mama grabbed Ross' face and winked at him. "That's my boy," she whispered.

~ ~ ~ ~ ~ ~ ~ ~

Not long after, another boy called Brian "a window licker." He never knew what happened before Ross was on him, punching him in the throat and ears – whatever made the punk bleed and scream for mercy. When the boy's friend jumped in to help, Ross fought him, too – like a cornered badger.

At the end of the ferocious beatings, Ross told them both, "My brother's not a window licker. Understand?"

The heckler rolled into the fetal position, moaning in pain. His friend gurgled once and nodded his bloodied head.

This fight earned Ross the reputation of being a tough guy, along with a secret trip to McRay's and two hours at the penny arcade with Mama.

When it came to his little brother, it was instinctive – no fear, no regret, no mercy. If someone picked on Brian, or the special school that he attended for children with mental disabilities, if they called him a name, or even looked at him with a judgmental smirk, then they would have to face Ross – the judge, jury and executioner.

~ ~ ~ ~ ~ ~ ~ ~

While Joan refused to condone the violence, Mama was less critical over Ross' willingness to protect his brother. "Ross can't keep reacting like this," Joan insisted. "He's going to get into some real trouble someday; trouble that he might not be able to get out of."

"I agree," Mama said. "That's why we need to teach Brian to stand up for himself."

"You're kidding, right?" Joan asked.

"I would be, if we lived in a world that was free of bullies and jerks."

"But Ma..."

"I'm not talking about boxing lessons, Joan. I'm talking about teaching him to speak up and defend himself." She nodded with conviction. "Brian has to learn that he doesn't need to feel like a victim just because some nasty person thinks it might be worth a laugh."

Joan nodded, finally understanding.

"I couldn't give a spit about someone who pokes fun at Brian," Mama said, "but I'm sure he doesn't feel that way when it happens. It has to hurt him the same way it would hurt any one of us."

~ ~ ~ ~ ~ ~ ~ ~

On the very next weekend, an ugly opportunity to teach presented itself. While playing outside in front of the cottage, one of the bigger neighborhood boys called Brian, "a retard."

He ran into the house, crying. Mama immediately grabbed him by the arm and dragged him back outside.

The punk was still sitting on his bicycle, laughing in the middle of a small circle of kids.

"Hey you," Mama yelled at him, "come here!"

He started to pedal away.

"Whoa!" she roared, "you're not going anywhere! You were a big, brave man just a few minutes ago, so stay right where you are." She nodded. "We'll come to you."

The rest of the gang scattered, leaving the bully to face the angry, old woman alone.

When he finally realized what was going on, Ross made a bee-line out of the cottage and charged straight for the boy on the bike.

Mama spun on her heels and yelled, "Get back in the house, Ross! This isn't your fight. It's Brian's."

Ross stopped short, frozen in confusion.

"Back in the house," she ordered, "NOW!"

Reluctantly, he did as he was told, glaring back at the punk with each step.

The bully was in shock, terrified about what might happen next.

Mama grabbed Brian's arm again – feeling the fear and shame coursing hard through his veins. Together, they marched right up to the kid on the bike. "What did you call him?" she asked, gesturing toward her quivering grandson.

The kid's Adam's apple bobbed up and down, but he never uttered a word.

"What was it?" she asked again, her voice nearing a scream.

"A...a...retard," he stuttered, his voice broken into pieces. He awaited the worse.

She turned to Brian. "Now how did that make you feel?" she asked.

"Bad," Brian mumbled, his eyes locked onto hers.

She placed her thumb and forefinger on his chin, pushing his face so that he had to look right at his bully. "Tell the punk," she said, "not me."

Brian sheepishly looked at the boy. "Bad," he said, his voice no more than a whisper.

The kid nodded and looked away.

Brian shook his head, the fear in his eyes turning to anger. "Bad...ponk you," he said, louder.

"I'm sorry," the kid muttered.

"Bad ponk!" Brian screamed, "BAD!" It was just loud enough for the rest of the fear and shame to leave him.

The kid put his head down, while Mama grabbed Brian's face once more. "Good for you," she told him, proudly. "Now get back in the house. I'll be along shortly."

With the weight of the world now off his shoulders, Brian grinned and did as he was told.

While the bully awaited the worse, Mama wrapped both of her arthritic hands around the bicycle's handlebars and warned him, "If I ever hear of you picking on Brian again, or making fun of him, I'm going to set his brother loose. You understand?"

The kid nodded.

"You'd better." She let the bike go and the punk pedaled off as fast as his legs would take him.

As Mama turned back to the house, she saw both Ross and Brian standing behind the screen door. Ross was glaring, pure rage shooting from his eyes. Brian was wearing his innocent smile again. She laughed aloud.

She wasn't one step past the threshold when she turned to Brian. "It doesn't really matter what other people think about you," she explained. "The only thing that matters is what you think and feel about yourself. Words are nothing more than words. If they don't bother you, then that's a good thing. But if someone's words do hurt your feelings, Brian, then you need to let them know and stand up for yourself. Understand?"

"Yets."

"Good."

Ross nodded. "And if you ever need help, you let me know," he hissed. "I got your back."

Mama smiled. "Yeah. That, too."

~ ~ ~ ~ ~ ~ ~ ~

A few weeks had passed when the distinct carnival sounds of an ice cream truck permeated the neighborhood. It was a late run for the truck – a final run of the season – and everyone knew it. "I sceam!" Brian yelled, hurrying to find Mama and her bulky pocket book. "I sceam!"

With two quarters in hand, he was the first one at the truck, scanning the same menu he'd seen a thousand times before. A long line quickly formed behind him. He didn't care. He would never rush such an important decision.

"Hurry up, dummy!" one of the bigger kids finally yelled.

Without hesitation, Brian spun on his heels and approached the older boy. "Bad," he yelled. "Ponk you!"

The heckler was taken aback, unsure of how to respond. To save face, he looked toward his friends and tried to laugh it off. No one else laughed.

Brian nodded, took his rightful place back in line and selected a rocket pop with a gum ball at the bottom. As he stepped away from the truck with his frozen prize, he scowled at the heckler, clearly feeling pretty good about himself.

At the very back of the line, Ross watched the entire episode in silence. Once Brian was back in the cottage and out of ear shot, he followed the heckler down the street. "Hey, wait a minute," he called after him. "I just need to talk to you for a minute."

"Oh no!" the kid shrieked. Dropping his ice cream sandwich, he took off running.

Ross took chase.

# Chapter 16

## *Spring 1986*

In 1968, though many experts were opposed to the idea at the time, Eunice Kennedy Shriver founded the Special Olympics because of her passionate belief that people with intellectual disabilities – young and old – could benefit from participating in competitive sports. She believed that the lessons learned through sports would translate into success in school, the workplace and the community. Above all, she wanted the families and neighbors of persons with intellectual disabilities to see what these athletes could accomplish, to take pride in their efforts, and to rejoice in their victories. The Special Olympics mission statement reflected all of these goals: *To provide year-round sports training and athletic competition in a variety of Olympic-type sports for individuals with intellectual disabilities by giving them continuing opportunities to develop physical fitness, demonstrate courage, experience joy, and participate in a sharing of gifts, skills, and friendship with their families, other Special Olympics athletes, and the community.*

For the first time in many of their lives, men and women with disabilities competed for the sheer joy of taking part – not for money, endorsements, national pride or personal glory. The entire program was destined to become a symbol of hope. To the athlete, the Special Olympics promised a lifetime of active participation in sports. To the many needed volunteers, it offered an experience that touched the heart and uplifted the spirit.

On July 20, 1968, the Special Olympics Torch – "The Flame of Hope" – was lit for the first time and one thousand athletes took part in sports competition in the Olympic tradition. It was a spark that would enlighten the world and bring joy and fulfillment to millions. Its flame would show the world the courage, character, dedication, and worth of persons with disabilities.

~ ~ ~ ~ ~ ~ ~ ~

Joan called the Rhode Island Chapter of the Special Olympics to see whether the organization might benefit Brian.

The friendly woman explained, "Ma'am, signing up your son may be the best decision you'll ever make. You'll be joining millions of people who not only support their athletes, but also find a strong support system for themselves. You'll be joining a network of people with similar concerns, questions and life experiences. You might even receive help finding medical expertise and community resources." She paused. "For many, the Special Olympics is a place of acceptance, respect and belonging – where you and your family can make friendships to last a lifetime."

"That's wonderful."

"Children with disabilities must be at least eight years old," the woman quickly replied.

"Oh," Joan said, "he's nine."

"Well, then he's eligible for training and competition right now...although he probably won't compete until next year."

"That's great!" she said. "How do we sign up?"

"I can take your information now and get a packet about upcoming events into the mail to you. Within two weeks, you'll receive a call from one of the coaches." After taking all the information, the woman asked, "Mrs. Mauretti, by any chance do you know what the Special Olympics Athlete Oath is?"

"I don't," Joan admitted.

"It's 'Let me win, but if I cannot win, let me be brave in the attempt.'"

"That's perfect – exactly what we're looking for," Joan said.

"And I've seen it inspire greatness," the woman concluded.

~ ~ ~ ~ ~ ~ ~ ~

One week to the day, a Special Olympics coach called Joan. "Mrs. Mauretti, I'm Lisa Cowen, Brian's Special Olympics coach. How are you?"

"I'm very well. Thank you for calling."

"No worries. I'm told that you're interested in signing up your son, Brian?"

"Yes. I was hoping for some information...some direction."

"Of course. Besides teaching your son to compete in whatever sporting events you choose, it's my priority to give each of my athletes an awareness of their own worth, ability, and capacity to grow. Essentially, my real job is to encourage confidence and self-esteem."

Right away, Joan could sense a deep level of sincere care and concern in the woman's voice. "That's wonderful," Joan replied, totally impressed with Lisa's enthusiasm.

"I'm required to attend a course offered by the Special Olympics every four years in order to remain certified as a coach. I also try to stay current on all the latest information and methodologies so I can help prepare my athletes – both physically and mentally."

"Wonderful," Joan repeated. "But I'm not sure which sports Brian might like."

"We could try them all, if you'd like," Lisa said. "Rhode Island Special Olympics provides year-round sports training and athletic competition for a few thousand children and adults with intellectual disabilities. We match age and ability on a sport-by-sport basis. Brian could try a variety of sports ranging from basketball to golf to figure skating. Whatever you choose, he'll improve his physical fitness, sharpen his skills, challenge the competition and have fun, too. We combine athletes with intellectual disabilities to promote equality and inclusion. It enables athletes to learn new sports, develop higher skills, and have new competition experiences. And on my teams, each athlete is guaranteed to play a valued role. As far as having fun, Brian will have an amazing opportunity to socialize with peers and form friendships – for life, we hope."

"That's exactly what we're looking for. What are the sports options?" Joan asked.

"Rhode Island hosts more than forty tournaments and competitions in twenty-four different sports. In the fall, we offer soccer, cross country running, basketball, and duck-pin bowling. In the winter, there's basketball again, as well as alpine skiing, Nordic skiing and snowshoeing, volleyball and bowling. Spring sports include aquatic time trials, cycling and power lifting. Summer sports include sailing, golf and softball."

"Wow, that's a lot to choose from...a lot to think about."

"Sure is, but there's no rush. Talk it over with Brian and your family, and feel free to call me back when you've decided. From there, we'll schedule a meet and greet for Brian and me to get to know each other. And regardless of what you decide, Mrs. Mauretti, trust that the type of sport matters much less than celebrating Brian's special gifts – whatever his ability may be. Whether it's basketball or swimming, my goal for him will remain the same – to contribute to his lifelong physical, social, and personal development."

"Thank you," Joan said, overjoyed with this stranger's willingness to make her son's life better.

"You're welcome," Lisa replied, sincerely.

~ ~ ~ ~ ~ ~ ~ ~

It was a rainy Tuesday evening when Lisa arrived at the house to meet Brian. The family had decided he would start off with softball and running for the warm weather months, and basketball for the rest of the year.

Blonde and blue-eyed, Lisa was middle-aged but looked younger. She explained, "I've never had a disabled child, but was inspired early on to help. I've been at it for years." Her dedication was obvious and, after spending ten minutes with Brian, her love for special children was even more transparent. Under Mama's vigilant watch, within the hour Lisa was officially inducted into the family.

The whole family stood witness as Brian raised his right hand and smiled at Lisa, while she recited the Special Olympics Athletic Code of Conduct.

"Sportsmanship: I will practice good sportsmanship. I will act in ways that bring respect to me, my coaches, my team and the Special Olympics. I will not use bad language. I will not swear or insult other persons. I will not fight with other athletes, coaches, volunteers or staff. Training and Competition: I will train regularly. I will learn and follow the rules of my sport. I will listen to my coaches and the officials and ask questions when I do not understand. I will always try my best during training, divisioning and competitions. I will not hold back in preliminary competition just to get into an easier finals competition division.

"Responsibility for My Actions: I will not make inappropriate or unwanted physical, verbal or sexual advances on others. I will not smoke in non-smoking areas. I will not drink alcohol or use illegal drugs at Special Olympics events. I will not take drugs for the purpose of improving my performance. I will obey all laws and Special Olympics rules, as well as the International Federation and National Federation Governing Body rules for my sports." She winked at him and continued, "I understand that if I do not obey this Code of Conduct, I will be subject to a range of consequences by my Program or a Games Organizing Committee for a World Games, up to and including not being allowed to participate." She paused. "Do you agree with this code, Brian?"

"He'd better," Mama blurted out. Everyone laughed.

"Yets," Brian said, with a nod.

Lisa smiled. "Good," she said and returned his hug. She put out her hand and he slapped her a high-five. "Now the fun begins."

She turned to Joan and Mama. "We'll start training this week and although Brian won't be ready to compete in the games next month, I'd like to have him come along and be my assistant, if that's okay?"

Both women beamed. Their boy had found a champion for a coach. Joan nodded her approval.

~ ~ ~ ~ ~ ~ ~ ~

Although he didn't officially compete the first year, for Brian and his proud family, it was an experience that would never be forgotten.

The Torch Run was a series of torch relays in which police, fire and correctional officers carried the "Flame of Hope" to the opening ceremonies of the Special Olympics Rhode Island State Summer Games, showing the community the true meaning of sport.

Logistically, there were five legs in the Torch Run. It began in Woonsocket and Glocester at about 10:00 a.m. and came together at the State House in Providence. The East Bay leg left from East Providence at 1:00 p.m. and continued through each of the towns on the East Bay. Mama was mending pants on her front porch when the torch came by her house. She dropped the mending and stood to cheer the runner on. As he waved back, a shiver traveled down her spine. For reasons unknown to her, she wept like a baby. *Something magical is underway,* she knew.

The East Bay leg converged with the Providence leg in South Kingstown, where runners from Westerly, Charlestown, and South Kingstown all met up for the final leg. As the sun went down, the final leg was a five mile run into URI's Meade Stadium, where the Mauretti family cheered until they couldn't speak.

~ ~ ~ ~ ~ ~ ~ ~

Throughout the competitions the following day, Brian never left Lisa's side. By the afternoon, though, he'd obviously grown tired of passing out water bottles and towels. During the final run meet, he looked up at Lisa and then took off alongside the competing athletes. While Lisa watched on, laughing, Brian sprinted with everything he had. And although he was much slower than the rest of the field, he didn't stop until he crossed the finish line. Joan, Mama, Frank and all the kids felt confused about how to react. Suddenly, the crowd erupted even louder. It was immediately obvious that at these special games, the applause didn't end until the last kid crossed the line – whether he was a qualified competitor or not. There were no disappointments and everyone was a winner. "If only all sports could teach the same," Mama said aloud.

Frank was seated beside Joan and Mama in the bleachers and never noticed that one of the officials kept looking over at Joan – and smiling.

The final event was a softball game, which included a throwing competition. After everyone had finished their throws and their distances had been marked, Lisa approached Brian and handed him the final ball of the day. The giant crowd cheered in support. Brian looked up at Lisa and smiled. The crowd grew silent. While Joan, Mama and Frank held their collective breath, Brian slowly approached the line and lifted the ball high into the air. For moment, he did nothing – and then he smiled wide. As if he were back at Mama's back yard carnival, he dropped the ball two feet in front of him where it rolled six more inches and died in the grass. The crowd exploded in cheers, and just as many laughs. Frank, Joan, Steph, Heidi and Ross shook their embarrassed heads. Mama and Angie chuckled. "Brat," Mama mumbled.

At the awards ceremony, Lisa helped Brian onto the podium where a Rhode Island State Trooper draped a gold medal around the boy's neck. "Son, you have captured the spirit of these games and have shared it with everyone. Thank you."

Brian nervously fidgeted with his mouth. "Weecome," he finally replied and the crowd applauded for the final time.

~ ~ ~ ~ ~ ~ ~ ~

At end of their huddled celebration, Frank kissed Brian, Ross and Angie, said goodbye to everyone and turned to walk away. John Doak, the admiring official, slowly approached and told Mama and Joan, "Congratulations. Brian's quite a boy. He made me laugh." John had a shaved head, green eyes and a thick Popeye neck with forearms to match. He was rough looking until he smiled and the sparkle in his eyes betrayed his gentle demeanor.

"Sorry," Joan muttered.

"No, not at all. It's a shame that more people don't have his heart." He gestured his head toward Frank, who was almost at the parking lot. "Your..."

"Ex-husband," she quickly told him.

"Oh," he replied with a smile, his eyebrows rising with the hope of a new possibility. And then he stood frozen for a moment, unable to speak. "Well then..." he finally managed, "congratulations again."

Blushing, Joan nodded her appreciation and watched him closely as he walked away.

John wasn't ten steps from Joan and Mama when he suddenly stopped, turned and walked back. As he approached Joan, he took a deep breath. "Please forgive me if I'm being too forward," he said, "but if I don't do this now, I may never have the chance again."

"What is it?" Joan asked, oblivious to the man's obvious intentions.

Standing off to the side, Mama cracked a wide smile.

"I realize we've just met and you have no idea who I am," John said, "but I was hoping you might consider having dinner with me some night?"

Joan was paralyzed from shock and couldn't react. Mama nudged her in the back. John caught it and grinned. The old lady was as subtle as a strong upper cut.

"Yes, I'd love to have dinner with you," Joan finally answered and began fishing around in her pocketbook for a pen to write down her telephone number.

He placed his hand on her arm. "That's okay. I can get your number from the district office," he said, and walked away smiling.

Joan looked at the kids. Brian was smiling from ear-to-ear, Ross was glaring at the stranger and Angie wore her usual pout.

~ ~ ~ ~ ~ ~ ~ ~

At eight o'clock, the telephone rang. Joan picked up. "Hi, Ma."

"Hi, Joan. Is my butterfly home?"

"He sure is. And he's been waiting for your call. I think he's excited to tell you something."

"Great, put him..."

"Allo," Brian answered in a winded voice.

"Hi, love. Your mom says you have something to tell me?"

"Yets, I mole no state..."

"Slow down, Brian. Take your time and think about your words. There's no rush, sweetheart."

He took a deep breath. "K." There was another thoughtful pause. "I wore mole."

"What, sweetheart? What's mole?"

"Mode...l," he pronounced slowly.

"Mode...l?" she repeated, trying to decipher Brian's newest word puzzle.

"Mode...l," he said again, exercising an equal amount of patience with his grandmother.

A bell went off in her head. "Oh, medal!" she blurted. "Your medal?"

"Yets," he answered, proudly.

"You're still wearing your medal, right?"

"Yets."

"And I bet you won't be taking it off anytime soon. Do you know how proud Mama is of you, Brian?"

"Yets Mama."

"You'd better," she said. "Now tell me everything about your day."

# Chapter 17

*Late Spring 1986*

Joan was nearly giddy with anticipation. "John's picking me up at 7:00," she told Mama.

"I'll be there to get the kids at 6:00," Mama confirmed, glancing up at the kitchen clock.

"You don't need to be here that early. Brian wants to be here when he picks me up." She paused. "You think that'll be okay?"

"It better be," Mama said. "If he wants more than one date, he's going to have to get used to Brian."

They both laughed.

"So you excited?" Mama asked, already knowing the answer.

"I am," Joan admitted. "It's just that..."

"What is it?"

"The kids are still young and...Brian..."

"It's a date, Joan...just a date. The kids are fine. Brian's fine."

~ ~ ~ ~ ~ ~ ~ ~

Joan didn't take long to get ready and was already pacing the kitchen floor when she spotted John's car pull into the driveway. She felt a squeal of excitement rise in her throat, but she held it back while she watched her date from the shadows. John walked around the passenger side of the car, opened the door and retrieved a bright bouquet of flowers. The squeal pushed higher, but she kept it down. John closed the car door and checked his appearance in the window. He fixed the collar on his sports coat and, turning toward the house, took a deep breath. "Ooooh," Joan squealed and melted deeper into the shadows like a nervous teenager. As she straightened out her dress, the doorbell rang.

Although she didn't mean to, she threw open the door. He was standing there, his smile beaming behind the flowers. "Come in," she said. As he stepped past the threshold, he handed her the bouquet. "Beautiful," she said and accepted his gift.

His eyes took her in and he smiled. "I'd say." He then noticed the entire family sitting on the couch, watching. He wasn't surprised – or at least he didn't show it.

"Ha Ja," Brian said, getting off the couch to offer a hug.

"Hi Brian. I didn't think you'd be here when I came to pick up your mom," he said, hugging him back, "but I'm glad you are. It's good to see you." He clearly meant it.

Mama offered her approval in a smile. Ross and Angie nodded their greetings.

"Hi guys," he said, his arm wrapped around Brian's shoulder.

While the small talk began, Joan headed toward the kitchen to place the fresh-cut stems into a vase of water. "Can I get you a drink?" she yelled from the kitchen.

"No, thank you," John yelled back. "I'll wait for the restaurant."

Joan hurried with the vase and when she returned to the living room, she found Mama standing there, holding her sweater. "I'll bring the kids to my house. I need to get a few things done and I can use Ross and Brian's strong backs." She looked at John. "You two go out and have some fun."

John thanked her and said good-bye to the kids. Ross and Angie all but ignored him, while Brian couldn't stop giving him high-fives.

As Mama shuffled Brian to the door, she waved Joan over to her. "Let's just plan on them sleeping over."

Joan nodded. "That's not a bad idea. Thanks."

"But give me a call when you get home. I want all the details," Mama whispered with a smile.

"I can't imagine there will be too many details to share from a first date," Joan whispered back.

Mama grinned again. "Oh, you never can tell." She turned back to the kids. "Let's go, guys."

While Angie and Ross gladly filed out of the house, Brian stood beside John and wouldn't take another step.

John chuckled. "Do you want to come with us?" he asked Brian.

Joan quickly shook her head. "Don't even suggest it," she said. "He wouldn't hesitate."

Mama agreed. "Brian already has a date tonight," she said, grabbing his arm and dragging him out the door. "And I don't like being stood up."

Both John and Joan laughed, as they watched Mama escort Brian to her car. "You have a beautiful family," John said, sincerely. "You're very lucky."

She nodded. "I know. I'm blessed."

Joan took a deep breath, locked the front door and embarked on the first date she'd had in years. When they reached the car, John opened the passenger side door and held it for her. She took pause, looked into his emerald eyes and smiled. She'd never really thought about it until this moment, but it had been years since anyone had held a door for her.

~ ~ ~ ~ ~ ~ ~ ~

At Mama's cottage, the kids learned that the only heavy lifting to be done involved their grandmother's massive meatballs – from fork to mouth. After the dinner mess was cleaned, she decided it was time to teach Brian how to play Parcheesi; how to count out the spaces he could move by the combined number he rolled on the dice.

While it came so easy for Ross and even Angie, Brian struggled. "Kent," he finally muttered, shaking his frustrated head.

Mama's head snapped around at him, as though he'd just called her a curse word. "What did you just say?" she asked.

Brian shook his head again. "Kent," he repeated. This time, it was nothing more than a whisper.

While Ross and Angie sat back to watch the show, Mama leaned in and shook her head. "Here we go again," she complained. "When will you kids ever learn – there's no such thing as *can't*?"

Brian looked at her, but said nothing.

She picked up the small cup, placed both dice into it and handed it back to him. "Roll them again," she said. "We have all night."

Brian poured the dice onto the game board, and rolled a combined eleven. Mama counted the black dots aloud and then showed him how to move his game piece eleven spaces. "Do you see?" she asked.

He looked at her, but remained silent.

She picked up the small cup again, placed both dice into it and handed it back to him. "Go ahead, roll them again," she said. "We have tomorrow night and the night after that and the night after that, if we need it – whatever it takes." She looked at him and shook her head. "Can't, huh?" she muttered. "Oh, I don't think so!"

Ross sighed heavily, stood and extended his hand to his baby sister. "Let's go watch some TV, Angie. This is going to take them a while."

~ ~ ~ ~ ~ ~ ~ ~

Ross and Angie had long since gone to bed when Mama relented and allowed Brian to do the same. "But we're going to start again tomorrow," she promised. "Don't you worry. You'll get it, sweetheart."

"K, Mama," he said and puckered his lips for a kiss.

She bent over him and laid one on him.

"Nigh, nigh, Mama," he said.

"Goodnight, Brian," she whispered, and pulled the covers under his chin.

~ ~ ~ ~ ~ ~ ~ ~

As she closed the bedroom door, the phone rang. She hobbled over to the kitchen to answer it. "Hello?"

"How are the kids?" Joan asked, trying to conceal her obvious excitement.

"Great. We played a few games of Parcheesi."

"Brian?"

"Sleeping like an angel. We had a good night – spent a few hours working on his terrible math skills."

Joan chuckled at her mother's endless tenacity.

"So, how was the date?" Mama asked.

"He took me to the Old Grist Mill, that fancy place on the river. Actually, it was really nice – comfortable, you know?"

Mama said nothing. She only listened.

"They had the best baked onion soup, with melted cheese crawling down the crock. John had the clam chowder. For an appetizer, he ordered us the lobster stuffed mushroom caps. And for our entrees, I took his advice and went with the baked stuffed jumbo shrimp. He ordered the surf and turf special. Through it all, I never stopped talking and he never stopped smiling. I didn't realize how long it's been since a man was truly interested in what I have to say."

"That's great. So did you find out anything about *him*?"

Joan laughed. "At one point, I actually apologized when I realized he hadn't spoken a word through the entire meal and I hadn't shut up. He told me, 'That's fine. I'll fill you in on our next date.'"

Mama chuckled. "That sly fox."

"Well, I did learn that he started volunteering for the Special Olympics to spend time with his nephew, Calvin, who suffered from Cerebral Palsy."

"Poor darlin'," Mama said.

"I know. John said that he passed away from pneumonia about a year ago."

Mama sighed. "And John's still volunteering, huh?"

"He said he took a break from the Special Olympics for two months, but couldn't quit; that he didn't want to miss out on any of that magic."

"That's all you learned?"

"He's also divorced."

Mama snickered, but didn't comment.

"After treating me to a waffle cone of butter pecan ice cream, he walked me to the front door like a true gentleman."

"That a boy," Mama teased. "You really had quite a night, didn't you?"

"It was a perfect night – the restaurant, the conversation, the meal...and especially him." She paused. "He's absolutely wonderful, but the kids..."

"Joan, it was your first date," Mama interrupted. "Why are you already over-analyzing this?"

"Are you serious? With Angie's age and Brian's needs, I didn't expect you to respond like this."

"You didn't, huh? And when have I ever said you were less important than anyone else in this family — to include your children? Besides, children are happiest when their parents are happy. If you won't do it for yourself, then do it for the kids."

"But..."

"No more buts, Joan. The kids will love him — even Angie — although she'll never show it." She chuckled. "...at least not for years."

Joan sighed heavily.

"He's a good man," Mama added. "If he weren't, you know I'd be the first to call it out."

Joan cleared her throat, but didn't utter a word.

"Anyway," Mama said, "follow your heart and let go of those doubts. It's about time you gave yourself a shot at being happy. Lord knows you deserve it."

"Thanks, Ma," Joan finished. "I'll come get the kids first thing in the morning."

"If you don't mind, make it tomorrow afternoon. I think Brian and I are making some real progress on his math skills. Besides, I'm trying that butternut squash ravioli recipe in a sage cream sauce and I need a guinea pig to test it before I put it out for the rest of the family."

"Of course. Who else would you test it on?" She chuckled. "Goodnight, Ma — and thank you."

"Goodnight."

# Chapter 18

## *Early Fall 1988*

Mama saw children as a mound of beautiful clay to be shaped and molded. It was her job to form and design. She was the artist and, as such, she took full responsibility for the final result. She didn't make excuses.

Although Brian began attending school to learn sign language, she spent more time expanding his vocabulary than most people spent sleeping. "Brian's curious about everything," she confirmed with Joan. "He's a real explorer and that's how we'll make progress." She nodded. "And I'm confident he'll live a good life because of it."

~ ~ ~ ~ ~ ~ ~ ~

Night after night, weekend after weekend, Mama and her "butterfly" talked each other's ears off.

"Steph and Heidi are going to spend next weekend with us," she told him.

"Ot and Biddy."

"Steph and Heidi," Mama repeated, tirelessly.

"Yets. Ot and Biddy," he countered. "Beat go?"

"Sure, we can go to the beach, but we need to get you a haircut first."

"Arquette nah!"

"You need a haircut," she told him.

There was a long pause. "Skee..."

"Scared of getting your hair cut? Don't be silly. You've gotten a hundred haircuts. I think you're just trying to get out of it, so we can get down to the beach earlier, right?"

He laughed. "Rin. A...E?"

"I'll ask your dad if Ross and Angie can join us this weekend. Maybe we'll sneak away for a little adventure?"

"Dodo?"

"No soda. You need to drink more milk!"

"No low me," he said, and began giggling.

"You little stinker. Of course I love you. That's why I want you to drink more milk, so you can grow up big and strong."

"Dodo hemmy."

"Well, milk makes me happy."

He laughed again. "K, Mama. Low Mama."

"And I love you, sweetheart."

"Nigh nigh, Mama."

"Goodnight, Brian."

~ ~ ~ ~ ~ ~ ~ ~

As Brian grew – just like any other kid – he developed his own likes and dislikes. He loved going out to eat; hot dogs and ice cream were his favorite. Every Tuesday, he ate out with his father and brother; they called it, "Boy's night out."

He called one dollar bills, "George's" – or something that sounded close to that – and liked them more than twenties. No matter what the gift was, if someone hid a few singles within the wrapping, Brian celebrated like he'd just discovered Captain Black Beard's treasure.

He loved watching baseball with Ross and always wore a Boston Red Sox baseball cap that he tossed onto his head like he was auditioning for the circus.

Heidi dragged him clothes shopping, modeling one outfit after the next for him. He was brutally honest, without being hurtful.

Steph loved art and taught Brian to share that love. If they were together, they were doodling, or painting – even creating giant murals on Mama's driveway with stubs of sidewalk chalk.

And Angie – Brian loved spending time with his little sister, regardless of what they did – and whether or not she felt the same.

~ ~ ~ ~ ~ ~ ~ ~

Brian arose at seven o'clock each day and turned into bed at 8:30 p.m. every night – after recapping his day with Mama. Although he loved his daily shower, for whatever reason, he hated brushing his teeth. Mama often interrogated him, "Did you brush yet, dragon breath?"

Brian usually lied, nodding that he had. But he was unable to look his grandmother in the eye.

She smelled his breath and cringed. "You fibber," she gently scolded.

He laughed. "Mama, kid you. No fib. Bush go now."

This very exchange went on for years.

~ ~ ~ ~ ~ ~ ~ ~

Brian loved school, which made Mama laugh – considering how it all began.

He loved the older cartoons like the Flintstones and Jetsons. And he liked wearing cologne, while claiming to have many girlfriends.

He hated costumes or any type of disguise. It scared him. Every Halloween, he'd hide out in the house and ask, "Done now?" again and again, hoping that the holiday had passed. "Tuckee tine?"

And Santa Claus was everywhere for Brian – which never changed as he got older. His innocence wouldn't allow him to question the existence of the jolly old elf. Each year, many photos were taken of Brian sleeping beside the aluminum foil manger beneath Mama's Christmas tree. "That's my angel," she boasted.

While the wall calendars were replaced – one after the next – he became a fixture at Mama's kitchen table. And without ever being asked, he liked to rub her back while she slaved over her giant pots and pans.

~ ~ ~ ~ ~ ~ ~ ~

During many of the adventures Mama and Brian shared, she often brought back something to plant in her flower garden as a souvenir. Besides collecting photos, she also built flowerbeds of memories. While on Cape Cod, someone gave her Cosmos to plant. In the Berkshires, another new friend gave her Hydrangeas.

When she described heaven to Brian, besides listing "music, angels and laughter," she also told him it was filled with flowers – "meadows and meadows of beautiful, sweet smelling flowers."

"Daze?" he asked.

She laughed. "Yes, sweetheart, there are daisies in heaven."

~ ~ ~ ~ ~ ~ ~ ~

It was early fall when Mama and Brian rented the movie The Champ, starring Jon Voigt and Ricky Schroeder. He cried, but only because he was so in tune with his grandmother's feelings – who wept like a baby.

After the movie, Brian asked, "Bonden me?"

Mama looked at him and shook her head. "Your birthday's not for a few months," she told him.

"Keekeemist?"

"Pretty soon, it'll be Christmas."

"Ho Ho Ho," he bellowed, smiling wide. "Taekrit god."

She smiled. "Santa Claus is good. But he's always watching, so you'd better make sure you're on your best behavior."

His face turned serious and he nodded. "Yets Mama. Much god."

She took a deep breath and sighed. "The Lord must think a lot of me to send me such an angel," she said aloud.

Wearing his finest smile, Brian stared out the cottage window for awhile and enjoyed the stillness. "Ate now Mama," he finally announced.

"You're hungry?"

"Yets."

"Do you want Mama to make you some ravioli?"

"Ate god."

"You like Mama's ravioli, huh?"

"Yets."

"You'd better," she joked and laughed loud enough to wake her deceased husband.

Brian laughed, too – hysterically.

They were quite the pair and anyone overhearing them would have thought that they were both insane.

# Chapter 19

## *Spring 1989*

Mama threw down her final hand. "Gin rummy!" she announced, and stood to stretch out her crooked back. "I expect to see you at church tomorrow," she told Steph, with a yawn. "No excuses."

"Yes, Mama," Steph said.

"Brian likes it when we're all together. And it's good for us to show him by example, so he can also grow in his faith."

Steph looked at the old woman like she had just arrived from Jupiter.

"What?" she asked. "You don't think Brian has faith in God?"

"I know he enjoys going to church with you every week, but really – how much does he understand?" Steph asked, already wondering whether she had misspoken. She awaited a scolding from her tiny grandmother.

Mama looked at her and laughed. "Believe me, Brian knows Jesus a lot better than any of us do. Think about it – he's a true child of God, sent here to teach us."

"Teach us?"

Mama nodded. "Unconditional love – just like the Lord has for each of us and what we should all aspire to."

Steph's eyes went cold and she looked away.

Mama caught it. "Stay the night," she told her granddaughter. "We can go to church together." She looked out the window. "Besides, the weather's getting worse."

"Okay," Steph said, and stood to get ready for bed.

Mama shook her head. "Why don't you stay up with me for a while, so we can talk." She shrugged. "Seeing as you're already sitting in my confessional..."

Steph reclaimed her seat.

"What is it?" Mama asked, cutting to the chase. "Something's eating you up inside. I can feel it."

The rain came down hard, lapping at Mama's windows. Steph looked out to see that everything had lost its outline. The need to express her feelings clawed at the inside of her throat. She tried to shape the words, but they just wouldn't come out. She then felt Mama's hand in hers. In the next breath, she confessed, "I'm gay."

"I'm happy, too," Mama replied with a grin.

"No, Mama. I'm actually *gay*. I knew I was different from the time I was a little girl. I..."

With her gnarled and leathery hands, she grabbed Steph's other hand and halted the rant. "You're not gay. You're perfect – exactly the way God made you."

Steph's eyes filled with tears. "But the church doesn't think..."

"Not my God," she insisted in an angry tone. "My God loves unconditionally. And because He loved me so much, He sent you to me. Don't ever label yourself, Stephanie. You're so much greater than a label. When you get right down to it, you are what's in your heart. And even if you wanted to, you would never be able to hide from God." She nodded. "Steph, there's nobody else like you in this whole universe, so don't you dare ever be anything but who you are!" She winked. "Besides, Brian wouldn't allow it."

Weeping in relief, Steph hurried around the table and hugged her tiny grandmother. "Do you have any idea how much I love you?"

"Some," she teased and kissed her forehead.

~ ~ ~ ~ ~ ~ ~ ~

The following morning, they went to church as they did each week, with Steph and Brian sitting by her side in the pew. Mama was a devout Catholic who believed in the ceremonies and traditions of the Roman Catholic Church.

Thirty minutes into the Mass, Father Benton called, "All the Lord's children to receive the body of Christ." While everyone else in the row stood, Steph remained seated. Mama noticed it, stopped and bent into her ear. "What's the matter?" she asked.

Steph thought about the penance she'd recently received for her terrible sin of being gay. Though reluctant at first, she quietly recounted the bad memory to Mama...

~ ~ ~ ~ ~ ~ ~ ~

Steph sat in a confessional booth and came clean with the priest. "I've known it since I was a kid," she admitted. "I'm gay."

Father Benton was quiet for a few moments before saying, "Child, I think you should spend some time searching your heart. And until you find your way back to the flock, I don't think it's appropriate for you to receive the Holy Eucharist. It really wouldn't be right."

Steph paid her penance that afternoon; ten Hail Mary's and ten Our Father's. Once she was done, she cried herself all the way to Aunt Joan's house.

Devastated over Father Benton's sinful judgment, she wept in Ross' bed. Hearing this, Brian climbed into bed with her and stroked her hair for hours while she cried. "K," he repeated. "K," he told her until exhaustion took over and she nodded off.

~ ~ ~ ~ ~ ~ ~ ~

Mama listened to the story and most of her blood went straight to her face. Her hands trembled from the rage that tore through her heart. She looked up at the altar and shook her head. While she reclaimed her seat, her eyes filled with tears. "Well, if you're not welcome at the good Lord's table, then neither am I!" she barked.

Others looked over. Steph slid down the pew. "Please, Mama. Please receive the body of Christ. I know what it means to you."

Disgusted, the old woman shook her head and remained seated. "I don't believe for a second that

Jesus would ever deny you a place at His table. It's the priest's prejudice, and I can't think of a greater sin." The last few words were nearly delivered in a yell.

Steph was horrified. It was important to Mama to receive the Holy Eucharist each week.

Mama shook her head again. In a much lower tone, she said, "I love the message down to my bones, but many of the messengers have lost their way. They can't clean up their own house, so they shouldn't be worried about ours." She turned to her bewildered granddaughter. "Stephanie, you listen to me right now! Be true to yourself – true to God. Unconditional love cannot allow room for prejudice, bigotry or hatred. All the love you feel for others; all that's pure inside of you – that's God. Believe in that to lead your way and light your path." She turned and glared at the altar. "And leave Father Benton to me. I'll take care of him!"

Steph didn't know whether to hug her grandmother or hide under the pew and conceal her burning cheeks. Instead, she looked at Brian.

"Mad Mama," he said with a grin and then went to his knees, continuing to mimic the old woman's every move.

~ ~ ~ ~ ~ ~ ~ ~

At the end of the ceremony, Mama stood and straightened out her Sunday's best. "Wait with Brian outside," she told Steph. "I'm going to talk to Father Benton for a few minutes."

"No, Mama," Steph pleaded. "Please don't."

Mama shook her head. "This isn't only about you, Stephanie. I need to see if he thinks that Brian's unwelcome at the Lord's table, too."

"Oh, God," Steph muttered.

Brian grinned. "Mad Mama," he said again.

~ ~ ~ ~ ~ ~ ~ ~

On the ride home, Mama remained quiet. Steph finally broke the silence. "If I'd had a choice, Mama, I wouldn't have chosen this life. No one in their right mind would choose this much adversity."

Mama looked in the rear-view mirror at Brian and snickered.

As they reached her driveway, Mama parked the car, shut off the ignition and turned to her grand-daughter. "You are who God made you to be, so have the courage to be that person. The church doesn't believe in unconditional love, but God does – or at least my God does." She shook her disgusted head. "People who preach fear or hatred do not speak for God. There's no greater conflict of interest. 'God detests this and God abhors that' – and then they'll say, 'He's a just and merciful God who loves unconditionally.' You can't have both, though, can you?" She looked toward the backseat again and winked at Brian. "And being different doesn't mean you're wrong, or bad." She looked back into Steph's eyes. "Don't you ever be anyone other than yourself, okay?"

"Okay," Steph replied and hugged her grandmother. "I won't." As they climbed out of the car, Steph asked, "So what did Father Benton say?"

"About what?" Mama asked, fighting back her smirk.

"About Brian being welcome at the Lord's table?"

"Father Benton — in all his ignorance — was unsure whether Brian would be able to truly comprehend the church's seven sacraments." The smirk won out and overtook her face. "So I convinced him to shepherd the boy...personally." She chuckled. "Brian starts one-on-one catechism with Father Benson next week."

"That's great," Steph said.

"Sure is. And he'll be receiving the Holy Eucharist with you before he knows it."

"With *me?*"

"Of course! It's the Lord's table, Stephanie — not Father Benton's."

## Chapter 20

*Early Winter 1989*

Without complaint, Heidi tagged along with Mama to Brian's weekly Special Olympics basketball practice. On the ride, Mama spoke in hushed tones so that Brian wouldn't hear her from the back seat. "I'm worried about him," the old lady whispered, taking a peek into the rearview mirror.

Heidi looked over her shoulder. Brian was staring out the side window, wearing his usual carefree smile. "Why?" Heidi asked, louder than Mama liked.

"Because your cousin's a smart boy in his own right, and I recently noticed that for the first time in his life, he's starting to realize he's *different* from other people." She shook her head, and lowered her tone even more. Heidi leaned in closer to hear. "We just need to watch him and make sure he doesn't feel bad about being different, that's all."

Heidi nodded and then looked over her shoulder once more. Brian appeared no less than overjoyed to be who he was.

~ ~ ~ ~ ~ ~ ~ ~

On the basketball court, while Brian and his friends ran around in circles trying to learn the game, Mama and Heidi sat in the bleachers cheering him on. At one point, he actually scored a basket. Mama screamed out, "Great job, Brian!" Heidi continued to stare off into space, completely lost in her thoughts.

"A penny for your thoughts," Mama told her.

Heidi shook her head. "It'll take more than that, I think."

"You'd be surprised," Mama teased. "Let's hear it."

Heidi turned, so that she was completely facing her grandmother. "I met this boy, Peter Larkin. He's the football quarterback at my school and he asked me to the dance last week."

"I don't see a problem so far," Mama said.

"Well, he has dark brown eyes that are two shades lighter than his skin." She paused, waiting for Mama's reaction.

The old woman never flinched. "So he's *different* from you. So what? White, black, green – what difference should it make?" she asked. "Is he good to you? Would Brian like him?"

Heidi nodded, her smile taking up most of her pretty face.

Mama shared her smile. "Then I like him, too. Did you go?" she asked.

"I did...and had the time of my life, Mama."

"So what could be wrong?"

"Dad wasn't as understanding – to say the least."

"What happened?"

"I finally found the courage to tell him and he shot out of his recliner like an angry wild man. 'Oh, I don't think so!' he kept screaming. 'You'd better find one of your own kind.'"

Mama put her arm around Heidi and pointed toward Brian. He was playing with his tall, black friend – Jerome. "We're not born knowing bigotry or racism. It's something we learn along the way... well, some of us anyway." She shook her head. "I'll make you a deal. You leave your father to me. Your grandfather helped break him, so I'll help fix him. For your part, just keep a close eye on your cousin for me. Feeling different can sometimes make you feel bad. When you see it in him, make sure you correct him. He needs to understand that we're all different."

"Deal," Heidi promised, and they sealed it with locked pinky fingers.

~ ~ ~ ~ ~ ~ ~ ~

Two nights later, Bob sat alongside his mother and watched Brian struggle to hone his crude basketball skills. Without wasting a moment, the old woman went right after him. "Your father, God rest his soul, instilled some real ignorance in you. True love is color blind, Bob. The soul doesn't see color. It sees another soul. I thought I taught you better than that?"

He was still distraught over the news. "You don't understand, Ma. I have one daughter who's a lesbian and another who likes black men."

"A black man," she corrected him. "And what you have are two beautiful daughters, Bob."

"I didn't say otherwise."

"Then what are you saying?"

He shook his head.

"We are who God designed us to be. And if you can't tell, each one of us is different from the other." She pointed toward Brian. "After all these years, you should at least understand that." She placed her wrinkled hand on his knee. "You and Bev did a great job raising the girls, but they're their own people now. I know you love them and they know it too. Just don't be foolish and put conditions on that love."

"But..."

"But nothing!" Mama snapped. "You'd better dig your head out of your backside, or you're going to lose them both." She shook her head. "Passing judgment over your girls is like scratching an itch with poison ivy. It just doesn't make sense and it's not going to help anyone."

He shook his head again and watched as Brian and Jerome walked down the court, their arms slung over each others shoulders. "You're right," he said. "I guess we are all different."

~ ~ ~ ~ ~ ~ ~ ~

It was a miserable, rainy afternoon when Mama sat in Dr. Grady's office, waiting for the oncologist's prognosis. Seated on the edge of his desk, the man fingered through her thick medical folder and offered her a sympathetic smile. "Unfortunately, the biopsy came back malignant, so we need to begin treatment as soon as possible." He offered a supportive smile and prepared to answer the usual panicky questions.

Nearly indifferent over the devastating news, Mama sighed heavily. "Well, we'd better get on it then," she said, matter-of-factly. "Brian's making too much progress for me to check out just yet."

"Brian?" the man asked, surprised over her nonchalant reaction.

"My grandson," she answered. "Long story...I was just thinking aloud."

"Oh, okay then. We'll start chemo therapy tomorrow," he said, relieved she'd taken the news so well. "Depending on where we get with that, we may have to consider radiation down the road."

"Whatever we need to do, doc," she said. "I need more time."

He nodded – as if he understood.

*And I'll need some real help from a higher power*, she thought.

~ ~ ~ ~ ~ ~ ~ ~

The following night, Mama had just finished her ten minute conversation with Brian. She was watching a rerun of The Andy Griffith Show when Aunt Bee's voice became fuzzy and distant. She fought to stay with the nice, old woman, but it was no use. Her eyes grew heavy and she drifted off. She began snoring...

~ ~ ~ ~ ~ ~ ~ ~

Mama was gardening at the side of the cottage near St. Jude's statue when Jesus walked up the driveway and approached her. With a smile, He extended His gentle hand. "Are you ready?" He asked.

Filled with an inexplicable peace, she nodded. "I am," she vowed, "but he's not." She pointed at Brian who was playing in the front yard.

Jesus looked at Brian and glowed with love. Smiling, He nodded once and walked away.

Giggling like a child, Mama stuck her hands back into the cool, moist earth and planted more daisies.

~ ~ ~ ~ ~ ~ ~ ~

Mama awoke with a gasp and grabbed for one of her legs. It throbbed with the cancer that was rotting it away. *I'd be gone for sure, if Brian didn't still need me,* she thought and was certain of it. *Looks like me and this pain are going to become real close friends for a while.*

Although she'd been diagnosed with cancer and was now living with intense physical pain, she had no intention of burdening her family with it. *There are more important things for them to focus on*, she decided.

~ ~ ~ ~ ~ ~ ~ ~

With no time to waste, Mama began reading even more to Brian and Angie. She finished book after book and even a few travel brochures of Italy. "... through one enchanting hill town after another, past miles and miles of classic vineyards and silvery olive groves, discover Renaissance cities full of art treasures and savor the relaxation. Close your eyes and feel one of those lovely balmy summer evenings, the heady perfume of rosemary and jasmine hanging in the air. Open your eyes and be mesmerized by the sheer spectacle that is a Tuscan sunset. Visit the vineyards; rows upon rows of lush green vines that give way to the rolling hillsides and single ranks of dark-green cypress trees. Travel the meandering sandy roads that lead to rust-colored farmhouses and moss-covered castles, rounded hilltops claimed by romantic towns, elegant gardens, rich in sculptured fountains..."

Brian and Angie loved sharing their grandmother's dream with her.

There were also countless hours of illegible scribbling and traveling outside the lines, requiring the need for a saint's patience. She went to the Five and Dime store once a month to buy school books for Brian and Angie – kindergarten for him and more advanced for her – and they burned through them as fast as she put them out.

~ ~ ~ ~ ~ ~ ~ ~

As they had for countless Saturday nights, Mama and Brian sat at the kitchen table working on his writing skills. The table was covered with crayons, colored markers and pencils. There were stencils of different size fonts and reams of multi-colored construction paper.

Methodical and structured, Mama began their routine by writing certain letters on the paper and then instructing Brian to trace her work. Once they'd run through the alphabet a few times, she had him use the stencils by himself. A half hour through that routine, it was time for his evening snack. While he ate his Cornflake cookies and drank his milk, he'd watch closely as she spelled out simple words like *BRIAN, MOM, DAD, MAMA, ROSS, ANGIE*. Once Brian finished his snack and got cleaned up,

Mama allowed him some free time to practice his letters or doodle – whatever he wished.

She washed the last of the dishes and turned back toward the table. "Why don't you finish up, Brian? It's almost time for bed."

Strangely, he didn't reply. Instead, his eyes stayed focused on his work. She draped the dish towel over her shoulder and approached the kitchen table. "What's got you so quiet...?" she began to ask and froze when she saw it.

In free hand, Brian had written *M A M* in big red letters on a sheet of yellow construction paper. She stood back a few feet and watched in awe, as he penned the last letter of his masterpiece – *A*.

Bursting into joyful tears, she threw her arms around his shoulders and squeezed him tight. "Oh Brian..." she wept.

He handed her the precious gift. "Mama you," he said with the proudest smile.

She grabbed it, held it up to her face and read it over and over. "Mama. Mama. Mama." She bent down and hugged him again. "Oh thank you, my sweet boy. It's the best gift I've ever gotten. Thank you so much."

Brian was twelve years old.

~ ~ ~ ~ ~ ~ ~ ~

As she tucked him into bed, she said, "Goodnight, Brian."

"Mama nigh," he said and closed his eyes.

She closed the door and returned to the kitchen table. She picked up Brian's work and read it again.

"Mama." A fresh tear tumbled down her wrinkled cheek. "Stupid doctors," she mumbled. "What do they know?" She grabbed the crucifix that hung from her neck and kissed it.

~ ~ ~ ~ ~ ~ ~ ~

Within two days, Brian's masterpiece was professionally matted and framed. Mama hung it in the living room, where she could look at it every day from her gray armchair. It was her most cherished possession; the centerpiece amongst all of the framed family photos.

# Chapter 21

## *Winter 1989*

Angie peeked out from the thick curtain. The auditorium was packed with spectators. Her heart beat hard in her ears and she began hyperventilating. She never imagined such incredible pressure at a fifth grade spelling bee. The thought of stepping out in front of the crowd was overwhelming. *You can do this*, she affirmed in her head. *You've been waiting for this moment for a long time.*

The red velvet curtain parted. She took a deep breath and stepped out onto the stage. The applause was deafening. She felt her face heat up. She spotted her mom, Brian and Ross seated in the second row. *Dad's working, as usual*, she thought. *And Mama must be really sick. She'd never miss this.*

Joan waved proudly. Angie was thrilled to get some of her mother's undivided attention. Ross was slumped in his seat, clearly wanting to be anywhere but there. Brian, on the other hand, was squirming with excitement. He waved at her in his usual dramatic way. Reluctantly, she half waved back, hoping against all hope that he would stop. He didn't.

Before introducing the five contestants, Mr. McKee, her teacher and host, thanked the crowd for attending. Angie looked over at Charlie Kai – aka, "the brainiac." He'd been her greatest nemesis since the first grade. He smiled at her. It was fake. She returned the same to him.

In the audience, Brian was so excited to see his little sister on the stage that he began yelling her name. "A...E. A...E." He was so animated that some people in the audience began laughing. Others sighed over the love he openly displayed for his little sister. Seeing this, Angie shook her head. *As usual, Brian's getting all the attention again!*

Ignoring her anger, she focused hard. The first few rounds went quickly, burning away the chaff. Within a half hour, Angie was a finalist. Just as she'd expected, it was just her and "the brainiac."

Mr. McKee turned to Charlie. "Spell erroneous," he said.

For the first time in the competition, Charlie hesitated, bringing hope to Angie's quest. "Could you please use it in a sentence?" the boy asked.

Mr. McKee nodded. "The witness' testimony was discovered to be erroneous and the case was dropped."

Charlie nodded, but Angie could tell he'd only been buying time. Slowly, he began, "E.R.O.N.E.O.U.S," he said, "Erroneous."

Mr. McKee shook his head. "Sorry, that's incorrect." He flipped the next index card and turned to Angie. "Spell Poinsettia."

Adrenaline shot through Angie's veins and she nearly squealed with joy when she heard the word. She'd learned how to spell it during one of Mama's

Christmas visits to Little Italy. She glanced over at the brainiac and grinned.

Mr. McKee detected her hesitation and asked, "Would you like me to use it in a sentence, Angie?"

She shook her head. "No, thank you," she replied. "Poinsettia... P.O.I.N.S.E.T.T.I.A," she recited with confidence.

Mr. McKee palmed the index cards and stood. "That's correct," he announced with a big smile. "Congratulations!"

The applause was deafening. Angie beamed with pride.

At the brief awards ceremony, Angie received her tall, golden trophy. When she turned to meet her moment of glory, Brian began screaming, "A...E. A...E. A...E!" Again, the crowd released a collective sigh. She couldn't help it. Her ears burned red with anger.

In the lobby after the ceremony, Brian ran to his little sister and wrapped his arms around her. Instinctively, she pushed him away. Joan's nostrils flared, but she bit her tongue in front of the thick crowd. "We'll talk about this later," Joan hissed under her breath.

Ross glared at Angie and shook his head.

Angie returned his stare and never looked away. She was just as furious.

~ ~ ~ ~ ~ ~ ~ ~

In the car, both mother and daughter were steaming mad. No sooner had her door slammed shut when

Angie screamed, "BRIAN...BRIAN...BRIAN...IT'S ALWAYS ABOUT BRIAN!"

"Angie, that's not true at all," Joan said. She really wanted to speak with her daughter, but knew that Angie was too angry to listen.

"You know, I try to understand," Angie blurted. "I know he has problems and that he needs lots of help, but he's not the only kid in this family." She wiped her eyes and looked at Brian – who was now staring out the side window. "Sometimes, I need help, too." Angie loved Brian very much. Yet with all the time and attention he took up from everyone, she couldn't help but feel a deep resentment toward him. She was sick of standing in the shadows where it was so cold and lonely. She was the baby of the family but had never felt like it. From day one, she'd missed out on all the perks that went with the title and she carried the animosity for it.

Joan began to cry.

Angie shook her head. "And then you wonder why I like to go over to Dad's house on the weekends!"

From Joan's sorrow, anger instantly reared its head. The comment was hurtful and totally uncalled for. "Oh Angie, I know you're hurt, but there's no reason to be mean. You were raised better than that."

"You're so ridiculous," Ross added, his voice now deep and authoritative. But he left it at that when his mother shot him a look of warning.

Interrupted by the occasional sob, the ride home was traveled in silence – except for Brian's one comment. He placed his hand on his little sister's shoulder and whispered, "K, A...E." He patted her shoulder again. "K." After that, even he had the good sense to keep quiet.

~ ~ ~ ~ ~ ~ ~ ~

It was exactly eight o'clock when the telephone called out. "Hi Ma," Joan answered.

"Hi Joan. Where's the boss?"

"Hold on. I'll get him."

Mama didn't wait long.

"Allo Mama," Brian answered in a tired voice.

"My goodness, someone's sleepy tonight."

"Too nigh nigh," he yawned.

"You sound tired. You must have played hard today?"

"Fun Rin, A...E...long."

"So you, Ross and Angie had fun all day. That's good. I talked to your sister a little while ago. She won the spelling bee. Lord, I wish I could have been there. That must have been wonderful to watch."

"Yets." They spoke for a few more minutes when Brian blurted, "Pee pee."

"Okay, if you have to use the bathroom, you go ahead. Make sure you wash your hands, though, okay?"

"Yets." He yawned. "Low Mama."

"Love you, too. And make sure you brush your teeth before you go to bed, okay?"

"Nah," he answered, and began giggling.

"What's that?" she asked, trying to sound stern.

"K. I bush, Mama."

"Promise?"

"Yets. Nigh nigh, Mama."

"Goodnight, Brian."

~ ~ ~ ~ ~ ~ ~ ~

The following night, John brought Joan to the Old Grist Mill Tavern. Built in 1745, it was a rare relic of Pre-Revolutionary New England designed to grind the grain raised by nearby colonial farmers. It was also the location of their first date.

As they crossed a thick planked bridge suspended above a short waterfall, they paused to watch an older couple feeding a family of mallards.

Framed in dark wood and decorated in country antiques, the place was candle lit. A low ceiling with exposed beams led to Colonial-paned windows that faced the waterfall. It was the best table in the place and, as he accepted his menu, John nodded his appreciation toward the hostess. The place was packed, with only one empty table – right beside theirs.

They sat in high-back burgundy leather chairs at a white linen table and scanned the menus.

"How romantic," Joan said.

John looked up from his menu at her.

"It's the exact same table we had on our first date," she explained.

"It is?" he asked, playing stupid.

Joan shook her head and returned to her menu. "You really like this place, huh?"

He half-shrugged. "It's the best place I know."

As if he'd just redeemed himself, she placed her hand on his. "Then thank you for bringing me here again."

A seasoned waitress with salt-and-pepper hair and a full mid-section placed a basket of warm bread in the center of the table. "Can I get you folks some drinks to start?"

Joan pulled her hand away and returned to the menu. "I think I'd like a glass of the Pinot Grigio, please."

The woman nodded. "Sir?"

"Sam Adams Boston lager, please."

As she headed for the long bar, John turned to Joan and smiled. Without any warning, he pushed his chair aside and went straight to one knee. "Marry me," he blurted, opening the black velvet ring box, "and make me the happiest man..."

Joan was taken aback – thrilled and terrified, all at once. "Oh John, I love you so much. I do. But the kids...and Brian's still..."

"You know, I thought you might respond like that," he said, stopping her in mid-sentence. Smiling, he stood and waved his hand over his head, like he was trying to flag down a cab in Times Square.

Joan thought she might fall out of her chair. As if they were marching in the Thanksgiving Day Parade, Ross, Brian, Angie and Mama made their way through the crowded dining room over to the empty table located beside theirs. As she tried to take it all in, John pushed the two tables together.

"What is...?" she began to ask.

Everyone took their seats, while Brian approached John and hugged him – as if nothing was out of the ordinary. "Hi Ja," he said.

"Hi buddy. Thanks for joining us," John told him.

Brian smiled and then approached his mother. "Hi Ma," he said, bending down to kiss her.

"Hi sweetheart," she said, still in shock. She looked over at her mother for an explanation. Mama grinned behind a chunk of bread she was already chewing on. She managed a wink. Joan looked back to John for an explanation.

His eyes filled with joyful tears and he went to one knee again. "Joan, from the moment we met, I understood that being with you would be a package deal...that it could never be about just you and me." He looked at the kids and nodded. "And I couldn't have been happier."

Ross and Angie returned the nod.

He looked past the kids to Mama – who was still chewing on a buttered dinner roll. "So I asked them all to join us tonight," he said, "because I realize that this is a family decision, as it should be." He cleared his throat. "So, will you guys have me?"

Past her hazy tears, Joan watched as Ross nodded his approval. "As long as you treat her right, I'm okay with it," he warned, displaying his usual protective approach. "She deserves to be treated well."

"I couldn't agree more, Ross," John said, "and I promise to do just that." He looked at Angie.

Angie followed her brother's lead, and also nodded. "Yeah, that's fine," she said, without complaint or fanfare – a by-product of her age.

As far as Brian, he was dancing in his seat, clearly overjoyed that they were all together. He jumped into John's arms and gave him a big hug – which he would have done anyway, regardless of the subject at hand.

It made Joan's heart flutter. She finally looked toward the toughest of the bunch – Mama.

The old lady smiled wide. "Joan, if this night doesn't prove to you what John is all about, then you've lost touch with reality altogether."

Everyone laughed.

"Like I always say, flowers only grow in a stable, nurturing environment," she said, placing Brian's hand into hers. "And I can't imagine anything but sunshine between you two."

Joan pulled John to his feet and stood to meet his kiss. "I would love to be your wife," she whispered, and kissed him again.

"I'm the luckiest man alive," he said, holding her tight. "...the luckiest man alive!"

The entire family applauded, each taking turns congratulating the newly engaged couple.

Mama gave the last squeeze. "Can we eat now?" she finally asked. "I'm starving."

~ ~ ~ ~ ~ ~ ~ ~

At the end of the night, John and Joan stole a moment alone.

"Happy?" he asked, tickling her ear with his whisper.

"More than I could ever explain," she admitted, and then studied his face for a moment. "You realize what you're taking on, right?"

"I do."

"They can all be tough at times, but Brian is all-consuming."

He smiled and repeated, "I do."

She pulled him closer and kissed him. "I'm going to love being your wife."

They kissed for a long while.

When they came up for air, Joan asked, "What do you think about a small ceremony in my mother's garden?"

He nodded. "Just family?"

She smiled. "Yes."

"Sounds perfect...but I've heard about your mother's back yard celebrations." He grinned. "No pony rides, right?"

She slapped his arm. "Not if you don't want them. But Brian won't be happy," she teased.

# Chapter 22

*Summer 1990*

It was late June when Joan and John exchanged vows in Mama's back yard sanctuary.

As promised, it was a small event, with only close family in attendance. Simple chandeliers illuminated the interior of the lily white tent, while seasonal flowers and greens decorated the homemade chapel.

The Justice of the Peace was a kind-looking woman who presided over the wedding with the same care that Mama put into the catering.

"Do you take this man to be your husband?" she asked Joan.

"I do," she answered, swimming in John's eyes.

"Do you take this woman to be your wife?" she asked John, smiling.

"I do," he answered, locked within the same gaze.

"Then I pronounce you husband and wife."

And that's all it took to get a kiss. Once they came up for air, Brian jumped in the middle of them to get his share of affection. Everyone applauded – even Angie.

An acoustic guitarist serenaded them during the reception. After Mama had stuffed everyone with more meatballs and manicotti than they could eat, John extended his hand to Angie and asked, "Can I have this dance?"

With a subtle smile, she took his hand.

Joan was thrilled. She looked over at Ross. "It's important that you guys accept John because you three mean..."

Ross grabbed her hand. "And you mean the world to us, Ma," he interrupted, "and you deserve to be happy. It's about time." He shrugged. "He's a good guy and he's been great with Brian and Angie. I think even Dad likes him." He grinned.

She laughed.

"If he wasn't a good guy, I would have taken care of it a long time ago," Ross concluded.

Joan slapped his arms and laughed. "Stop it," she said.

He gave her a kiss on the cheek. Little did she know – he wasn't kidding. He led her onto the portable parquet floor where the family danced the rest of the night away. It seemed to last all of three winks.

Before the final dance, John slipped out of the tent and quickly returned, holding the reins of the largest pony Joan had ever seen. "I figured that Brian and Angie might enjoy a midnight ride," he said with a smile.

Joan's eyes leaked from joy, while Mama hugged her new son-in-law. "I knew you were a keeper from the moment I met you," she told him. "And so did Brian."

While Angie stood back, pretending she didn't want to ride, Brian jumped into the pony's brown leather saddle and began giggling from excitement.

"Yee haw!" Uncle Bob yelled to him.

"Hee yaw," he yelled back. And with John holding the reins, he hit the dusty trail.

~ ~ ~ ~ ~ ~ ~ ~

Joan and John were on the final days of their honeymoon in the Berkshires when Brian contracted meningitis and had to be hospitalized. Frank immediately responded, but Mama told him, "Go to work, Frank, and provide for your family. I have all the time in the world. I'll stay with him."

"Did you call Joan?" he asked.

"Got in touch with her this morning. They're on the road, coming home now."

"Okay. Ross and Angie are already staying with me, so..."

"So everything's fine," she told him. "We're family, Frank. That's how it works!"

He searched her eyes for condemnation or even sarcasm, but there wasn't a hint of either. All he saw was genuine compassion and concern. His body tingled. "Thank you," he said, and hugged her for the first time in years.

She squeezed him back. "You're welcome."

Right away, the head nurse warned the family, "Anyone entering the room must wear a mask because if you contract the virus as an adult, it could mean a death sentence."

Mama shook her head. "Brian hates masks," she said. "They terrify him." The old lady never hesitated. She marched right past the nurse and into the room where she began tending to Brian – no mask, no gloves, no robe. To her, the idea of frightening him was so much worse than the risk of contracting the terrible virus – or even death.

"Skee, Mama," he whimpered. He'd been alone in the room, with nothing but the beep of his heart monitor, and his eyes betrayed the terrible anxiety that it had caused.

"Don't you dare be scared," she told him, making herself comfortable by his side. "Both me and the good Lord are right here with you."

He smiled – his fear evaporating into thin air. If Mama said it was okay, then it was okay. There was never any reason to believe otherwise.

In time, his body recovered from his latest ailment and he was released to return home. In appreciation for all that the hospital staff had done for her fragile "butterfly," Mama began donating money to the hospital in Brian's name.

~ ~ ~ ~ ~ ~ ~ ~

During his first weekend back at the cottage, Mama forced Brian outdoors to take in the fresh air. On their slow walk, they came upon a fruit and vegetable stand on the side of the road that still worked on the honor system. It sold fresh corn, homemade strawberry preserves, beautiful sunflowers, and the sweetest cherry tomatoes. A coffee can was set up to receive the money. Mama dropped in a five, grabbed a jar of preserves and two sunflowers – one for each of them.

A few miles up the road, they spotted a lemonade stand with two kids trying their hand at business. In no hurry, they stopped and quenched their thirst.

"God," Brian told the kids, as he chugged the sweet drink.

They looked up at Mama in confusion.

She winked. "He thinks it's good," she translated, and finished her cup.

The two slowly wandered down one of the long dirt lanes where they ended up blueberry picking. "We're going to make your favorite pie tonight," she told him, as they filled the small cardboard basket.

"Booby?"

She laughed. "Yes, blueberry."

~ ~ ~ ~ ~ ~ ~ ~

It had taken many years and countless bumps and bruises, but by the very end of that fateful summer, Brian finally learned how to ride a bicycle. Mama had been relentless in her pursuit. Most people thought this final feat was ridiculous, but as Uncle Sal put it, "It's almost as if her mission isn't complete unless the two of them can figure out this last piece of the puzzle."

With Mama's advanced age and failing health, Frank couldn't sit back any longer and let her tackle this daunting task alone. "I'll be over on Saturday morning with a new helmet for Brian," he told her on the phone. "And we'll teach him how to ride."

Trial and error was a painful process and equally exhausting for Frank. With his bright helmet strapped tight, Brian sat on the bicycle seat and gripped both handlebars.

"Ready?" Frank asked him.

Brian nodded. His eyes focused ahead; his tongue licked his bottom lip in total concentration.

Frank pushed him a few feet, let him go and started yelling, "Pedal, Brian! Pedal!" All the while, he ran beside the bike, laboring to breathe. Mama watched on from her chair – most of the time, with one eye closed.

It was the same every time: Frank let him go and Brian would coast half the distance of the yard, bobble a few times and then go down in the grass. While Frank grabbed for both his knees and panted for air, Brian pushed the bike off of himself and got back up. He grabbed the handlebars and pulled it up, got on it and then waited for his sweaty, red-faced father to give him another push. Although Brian was covered in grass stains and both of his elbows were skinned, he'd stopped crying after the first week.

Mama cheered them on. "He's getting it, Frank," she yelled every time they started over. "He's catching on. I can see it."

Her words and the evidence before them were in total contradiction. Frank shook his head and snickered. "Is this entire process meant more for me and my lack of patience than for Brian learning a new skill?" he asked himself under his breath.

But they never quit – either one of them. Saturday after Saturday, it was as though Frank spent the long, aggravating hours as much for the stubborn, old lady as for his son.

It took several consecutive weekends. The leaves were starting to turn colors when all of it just clicked. The bicycle's handlebars were slightly bent and the paint was nearly scraped off the frame – the name *Schwinn* barely recognizable. Frank's lungs burned as badly as his legs, which felt like they were now made of gelatin.

It was already getting dark. As determined as ever, Brian sat on the bicycle seat and held both handlebars.

"Ready?" Frank asked him.

Brian nodded. "Yets, Dah."

Frank pushed him a few feet, let him go and yelled, "Pedal, Brian! Pedal…"

And he did. He swerved and wobbled on the bike, but somehow kept it balanced on two wheels.

"Brakes!" Frank yelled when his son reached the edge of the yard.

As he'd been taught many times, Brian pushed back on the pedals until the bike came to a stop. He then leaned on one leg. The bike stood upright with him still sitting on it – now smiling.

Frank couldn't hold back. He went to his knees and began to cry. "He did it," he yelled to Mama, wiping his eyes. "He finally did it!"

"You sure did, Frank," Mama replied, her proud eyes leaking onto her wrinkled face. "And you should be very proud."

~ ~ ~ ~ ~ ~ ~ ~

In celebration, the three of them walked over to Back Door Donuts. It was a small shop three streets over that filled the neighborhood with the undeniable smell of cinnamon. For the locals, they opened from 8:30 p.m. until midnight. Mama and her two sidekicks stepped up to the back door to order apple fritters and cinnamon rolls the size of hubcaps. The rules were posted and if you wanted service, you needed to follow each one of them: *No pushing, no screaming, be respectful to the neighbors (they're sleeping); no screeching, no wrestling, no cursing.*

It took all of the energy that Frank had left to convince Mama that it was his treat.

"Fine," she finally conceded. "But I usually get a dozen to go, so don't complain."

They both laughed, and took turns congratulating Brian with hugs.

~ ~ ~ ~ ~ ~ ~ ~

Besides day trips, Mama never actually went anywhere – not even Italy. And although she never spent any real money on herself, she always had a few bucks to help someone else. Most of the time, it was offered without ever being asked. She recycled cans and bottles, and saved the change for the Special Olympics, as well as St. Jude's Children's Hospital.

Even for a woman in her seventies, she refused to sit still. She was afraid that if she ever sat in the chair long enough, her heart would rust and stop pumping. But by fall, it was becoming much more difficult to move about. She'd occasionally let out

an involuntary moan, but she never actually complained about the physical pain. "What is it, Mama?"
they'd ask. For the family's sake, she blamed the
aches on bad circulation in her legs, showing off her
tight stockings as evidence.

~ ~ ~ ~ ~ ~ ~ ~

It was eight o'clock. Joan was on the telephone when
it clicked. She told John, "Hold on a second, babe.
It's my mother calling in for Brian."

"No problem. Take it," he said.

"Okay, just hold a second." Joan clicked over.
"Hi, Ma."

"Hello, Joan. Where's my boy?"

"Can you wait one second? John's up in Maine on
business. I have him on the other line and I need to
say goodnight to him."

"Just tell him I need ten minutes before Brian
heads to bed for the night. The phone is all his for
the rest of the night."

"I'll let him know," Joan said. She clicked over.
"Babe, I'll call you back in ten minutes. My mother
has a scheduled telephone date with my son."

He laughed. "That's fine. But don't forget to call
me back."

"Not a chance," she promised. Clicking the
phone over one last time, Joan covered the mouthpiece and yelled, "Brian, it's your girlfriend."

Laughing, Brian hurried to the phone and
grabbed it from his mother. "I, Mama."

"Hello, my love. How are you tonight?"

"K. You?"

"I'm good. Thank you for asking. So tell me about your day, sweetheart..."

~ ~ ~ ~ ~ ~ ~ ~

Days turned into weeks that threatened to become months. Each of the kids was becoming a young adult that Mama and the rest of the family could be insanely proud of.

It was a frigid afternoon – the bay winds beating hard on Mama's windows – when Ross said his good-byes to set out for the Army. Depressed over his decision to leave, Mama lay in bed, refusing to get up. *Where did all the years go?* she wondered, looking up at her eldest grandchild. She just couldn't bring herself to say goodbye to him.

As if in worship, Ross kneeled by her bedside. "I've wanted to join the military since I was a little boy," he told her – as if she hadn't known all these years. "I feel bad about leaving Brian behind, but I know he's in good hands." He smiled at her. "I'll be back before you know it," he vowed, kissing her tear-stained cheek. "And I'll be safe, Mama. I prom-ise. I'll be home soon."

*But I may not be here,* she thought. She shook her sad head and peered into his eyes. "Just go. But know that I love you and that I always will."

No one knew she had been fighting cancer with every ounce of her strength and that it was now winning.

# Chapter 23

*Winter 1991*

The TV hummed like white noise in the background. Mama was just about to doze off in her chair when she noticed Brian pacing the living room floor, nervously. She opened both eyes and watched closely for a few minutes. Brian looked at the TV, wrung his hands together and paced across the floor. When he got to the other side, he looked back at the TV, wrung his hands again and began a new lap. Mama studied the TV and the truth immediately hit her. The news channel was airing some graphic footage of the war; soldiers fighting in a cloud of smoke – God-awful explosions competing with human screams.

*Brian senses danger,* she realized. *He's worried about his brother.* She shot out of the chair like a hellfire missile. Brian jumped. "Sorry, sweetheart," she said. "You're worried about your brother, aren't you?"

He looked toward the TV and wrung his hands. "Rin," he whispered. "Bad."

"He's okay," Mama reassured him. "Your brother's a tough cookie. And he's doing a very honorable thing over there by standing up for people who can't stand up for themselves."

Brian nodded. "Rin," he said again, his eyes filling with sorrowful tears.

Mama hurried to hug him. "I know, sweetheart. I miss him, too." She thought for a moment. "So what do you think we should do?"

He looked at her, his face blank.

"What would you do if Ross was here? What would you tell him?"

He hugged Mama to show her. "Low Rin," he said. The longing in his voice brought goose bumps.

She began rubbing his back. "How 'bout we do something nice for Ross? Something to let him know we're thinking about him?"

Brian nodded. "Rin," he said, "Low Rin."

"And he loves you, too – very much."

Brian nodded.

"So let's put a package together for him, a care package to let him know that our spirits are with him. What do you say?"

For the first time, Brian smiled.

"Use your words, Brian."

"Yets."

"Okay, you draw him a nice picture and I'll write him a letter...from the two of us. Then we'll throw in a big batch of Cornflake cookies and a few other sweet surprises. Sound like a plan?"

"Cook, cook. Me, Mama."

"Yes, you can have some, too. But let's get some work done first."

Brian hurried for his colored construction paper and crayons.

~ ~ ~ ~ ~ ~ ~ ~

They packed the last batch of cookies into the cardboard box and sealed it tight with tape. As Mama started cleaning the kitchen, Brian sat back down at the table and began drawing again.

Mama thought it peculiar. "We've just packed three beautiful pictures for your brother. I think that's enough, sweetheart."

He looked up at her, smiled and then continued drawing.

"Is it for Ross?" she asked, taking a break from scraping down the dirty cookie sheet.

He put his crayon down, stood and walked into the living room – gesturing that she follow him. "Go, Mama," he said. She did. He pointed at the TV.

"Another picture for Ross?" she asked again, confused.

He shook his head and pointed at different spots on the television screen. "Moe bad."

"Oh," she said, the reality of her grandson's compassion sending a strong pulse of heat through her chest. "You're drawing pictures for the other soldiers that are with Ross, aren't you? For the troops?"

"Yets," he said proudly, and turned on his heels to return to his artwork.

"Good for you," Mama said. "They're going to love them."

In each new drawing, Brian wrote, *Is Ok*.

"What are you telling them?" she asked him, forever making him exercise his vocabulary.

"K," he said.

"You mean, *It's OK* – like everything's going to be okay, right?"

He looked up from his work and grinned. "K," he repeated.

"You stinker, that's it!" she said, and pulled him up from the table. "Enough work for now," she said, hobbling off toward the living room. "Let's dance!"

~ ~ ~ ~ ~ ~ ~ ~

It was amazing – and terrifying – how a few months could feel like years, and change a life forever.

It was hotter than hell, which seemed appropriate given the surroundings. Operation Desert Storm was a surreal experience; being placed in such a foreign environment. The surroundings were so alien that even the air in the desert felt different. The only beauty was found in the night sky. The same stars that twinkled over Narragansett Bay sparkled just as brightly in the Arabian Desert, and it brought the only peace Ross could find. Many nights, when he sat alone with his insomnia, he set his eyes upon them and found just enough peace to keep going.

He missed Brian and Angie something awful, but he knew his life would never be the same again. It was as if the door to innocence had been slammed closed, never to be opened again.

Sitting on the hood of his Humvee, he stared up at the stars and thought back to the days of innocence...

~ ~ ~ ~ ~ ~ ~ ~

He envisioned Mama's cottage. On the street, at the edge of her yard, there was a *Deer Crossing* sign.

Someone had painted a little red Rudolph nose on it and Mama knew that it was one of her grandbabies who did it. Publicly, she was opposed to the vandalism. Secretly, though, everyone knew she appreciated the creativity.

He pictured Mama talking on the phone, lying on a carpet runner in the kitchen – stretched out just like a cat.

In the summer, it was cool in the cottage. The windows were always open to collect the salty breezes. He could see himself, his brother, and his cousins drinking Kool-Aid from jelly jars on her front porch.

In the winter, Mama had a big fluffy down comforter that the kids would get lost under.

On the living room walls, Brian's smiling face beamed in most of the framed photos. There was a couch, a matching loveseat and Mama's gray leather armchair where she drank her Sanka and watched her shows – and she really loved her afternoon shows. She was a guest at Luke and Laura's wedding, as well as at a thousand other events. Afternoons – or the soap operas that filled them – were her guilty pleasure. Even Brian knew the characters and story lines. As far as the heinous looking armchair, she couldn't part with it. As long as they still made duct tape in gray, she could match the color in any repair.

Ross' breathing finally reached a peaceful rhythm and he drifted off even deeper...

Filled with sun catchers, there was always something cooking in Mama's kitchen. For a portly woman, she never actually sat and ate. She was a grazer who snacked all day long. She had bad arthritis in her hands that curled them like dry autumn leaves. And although she insisted she was five feet tall, she would have to be on the tips of her toes, standing on the crest of a hill to reach that height. She joked that she'd "shrunk in her old age" and that it was God's cruel joke because she didn't have a whole lot of height to give up. Still, she was a giant of a woman.

Mama slept on a high mattress wearing a foam head-wrap – like a queen's crown – to keep her hair shaped the way she liked it. She loved babies and they loved her. Her soft mid-section was like a giant pillow. If she were guilty of anything, she did too much for the people she loved.

She loved Dean Martin, Frank Sinatra – the whole Rat Pack. Her favorite song was *Summer Wind* by Old Blue Eyes. She was a tough, no-nonsense woman. Whenever she was questioned about her own health, she said, "Don't worry about me." The love her family felt for her was immeasurable and the environment she created for them was heaven...

~ ~ ~ ~ ~ ~ ~ ~

Ross shook his sorrowful head. *Heaven – I should be so lucky,* he thought. For the first time since he could remember, he began to cry. Reaching into his pants cargo pocket, he took out a pen and some paper, and began to share his soul:

Dear Mama & Brian,

I hope this letter finds you both well. Thank you so much for the package and your encouraging letter. My squad loved the almond cookies and biscotti, although I tucked away the Cornflake cookies just for me. Brian, you're the only person in the world I'd ever share those with.

And Brian, I can't thank you enough for the drawings you sent me. They mean the world to me, brother. I look at them every day. Those pictures have really kept me going. I've started a scrapbook (just like one of Mama's). You've definitely done a lot of drawing since I've been in the Gulf. It's weird, but there are times when I can actually feel you standing right beside me – though I'm grateful you're a world away from here.

Mama, I'd be lying if I didn't admit it's been a tough ride over here. I pray more now – for forgiveness, for protection, but most of all that God's listening. If you've taught me anything, it's that any wound can be healed – no matter how deep it is. Some guys see a hopeless future before them, but I know better – thanks to what you and Brian have shown me.

I can't wait to see you all again and spend the weekend down the bay like we used to. I wouldn't want much – just the whole family to be there, a large pan of your raviolis in red gravy and for the day to end with one of your famous hugs. Please keep the letters and drawings coming. They keep me connected to the real world.

And please kiss Ma and Angie for me. I miss them a lot, too.

All My Love, Always,
Rin

Even though she was on the other side of the globe, Mama could still read between the lines. There were so many things – terrible things – that Ross hadn't written. She could feel it in her heart and it ached. She grabbed her crucifix and kissed it. *Walk with him, Lord,* she prayed. *Protect our boy with an army of your angels.*

In the meantime, Mama fought her own internal battle – with cancer. She ignored the sharp pains in her legs, read the letter to Brian for the third time and folded it up "I think it's time for a visit to the old country," she said, and wiped her eyes. "We'll go tomorrow."

Brian nodded and allowed his tears to air dry.

~ ~ ~ ~ ~ ~ ~ ~

Although Steph and Heidi had grown old enough to make their own holiday plans, Angie was with her dad and Ross was off serving his country, Brian was still happy to visit Little Italy with Mama at Christmas. The old woman smelled strongly of citrus from the gallons of Jean Nate bath splash she'd received as gifts through the years.

On the train, Mama read to Brian from one of her old, tattered brochures of Italy. "Tuscany is a charmed land, located in the heart of central Italy. Renowned for its food and wine, it is also home to exceptional beaches, villas, gardens, and some of the world's most beautiful landscapes. The back roads head into rolling hills, through fortified medieval villages. A treasure hunt of great meals, fine wines, medieval villages, castles, and Renaissance palaces, Tuscany is interspersed with magical gardens, gentle country walks, spectacular views, art and architecture. Perched high on a hilltop, lush acres produce high quality olive oil and some of Tuscany's finest red wine..." She looked at Brian and kissed his face. "Someday," she whispered.

"Yets. Soebay."

~ ~ ~ ~ ~ ~ ~ ~

As they walked along Hanover Street, large decanters of olive oil and strings of garlic cloves and red peppers decorated shop windows. On one corner, there was a sports club for the gentlemen. On the next, there was a Laundromat for the ladies. Beneath shop canopies, people spoke in a wonderful hybrid of English and Italian slang, their hands flying about to punctuate each point. The air was filled with old world music and the smells of fresh bread and garlic. Mama inhaled deeply, still teaching her grandson to do the same.

On old, broken down legs, Mama made her annual Christmas dinner donation and then escorted Brian toward the statue of the Virgin Mother. She kneeled on the concrete and offered her prayers. Brian kneeled beside her and mimicked her every movement. As if on cue, they blessed themselves at the same time. Brian looked at her and smiled, proud that he'd gotten the timing right. She returned the smile and kissed his head before he helped her to her feet. "God is good," she told him.

"God God," he answered, making her chuckle.

As Mama and Brian passed a restaurant, a violinist with a bushy white moustache and dressed in a red velvet vest waved at them. Everyone knew Mama, which meant that everyone knew Brian. He received more freebies – sweets, gelato, decaffeinated cappuccinos, and even goodies to take home – than a celebrity athlete. He was embraced by an entire community that he only visited a few times a year.

Mama and Brian patiently waited in line at Mike's Pastry Shop.

A little boy and his mom stood in front of them. Suddenly, the boy screamed, "I want a cupcake now!" While his mother spun to stop him, he stomped both his feet.

"Stop it, Robby. We have to wait our turn," the mother halfheartedly scolded.

"NOW!" the boy screeched, flipping out even more at the woman's unwillingness to meet his immediate demands. "NOW! NOW! NOW!"

Not nearly as embarrassed as she should have been, the woman looked back at Mama and shrugged.

"Sometimes a swift kick in the backside will straighten 'em right out," Mama suggested with a wink.

The stranger glared at her. "I think you should mind your own business, lady," she hissed.

Mama took a step toward the woman. "And I think you should mind your son's business so nobody else has to."

The woman started to reply, but the words got stuck in her throat. Instead, she huffed once, grabbed the spoiled brat by the arm and dragged him out of the busy shop.

Mama shook her head and looked at Brian. "I tell ya, sometimes I'm glad I'm close to the end. This world is changing fast and not for the better."

"Cook cook?" Brian asked. "Pease cook, Mama."

She smiled. "Of course you can have a cookie, sweetheart. With those manners, how could I say no?"

Julia, Mike's wife, greeted Mama and Brian with a smile. "What can I get for you, Mrs. DiMartino?"

"Let me have a half dozen cannoli with powdered sugar, two dozen mixed biscotti, and a half dozen custard cups." She felt a tug at her jacket and looked up to find a big pair of hopeful eyes peering down at her. She nodded. "And Brian can choose one thing – whatever he wants."

His eyes filled with joy. "Cook cook!" he ordered.

Julia nodded. "A cookie it is." She smiled. "Good choice, Brian." She leaned over the counter and whispered in his ear. "And I'll throw in a few extra for you."

Mama laughed.

As Julia boxed Mama's goodies, she asked, "When are we going to get the recipe for those famous Christmas Butterballs?"

"Just as soon as I get the recipe for Mike's cannoli," she answered. Heaven could be found in the taste of Mike's cannoli and nowhere else in the world – no matter how far a sweet tooth like Mama's was willing to travel.

Julia smirked at the clever comeback, but only shrugged in reply, ending the playful banter. She tied the three pink boxes with white string and gave Mama her change. "Have a great holiday, Mrs. DiMartino."

Mama nodded. "Merry Christmas, and send my love to Mike."

~ ~ ~ ~ ~ ~ ~ ~

For the first time, Mama's legs would not allow her to make it to the end of Hanover Street; to the quaint restaurant where she'd been raised. Her eyes filled with sorrowful tears. *My legs are done.* Leaning on Brian, they headed back toward the train when a man called out, "*Viva Italia*."

"*Viva* America," Mama replied. She loved her heritage, but was adamant about being respectful to America and the incredible blessings it had afforded her family.

~ ~ ~ ~ ~ ~ ~ ~

After tucking Brian in for the night, Mama sat in her chair, thinking about the little boy in the pastry shop. *Things sure have changed*, she thought, *and things were so much better when I was a kid…*

Childhood in Little Italy was a real dream and although it wasn't actually rigid, there was an expectation that all children would show the utmost respect to their elders – no exceptions. Some fathers might have been heavy-handed and some mothers were definitely subservient, but that wasn't Mama's family. She grew up in satin and bows, dressed like a doll and treated like a princess, and there was always a silver dollar from Uncle Carmine which he delivered like a professional magician…

~ ~ ~ ~ ~ ~ ~ ~

The telephone rang. Mama was removed from her memories and picked up. "Hello?"

It was Frank. "Hi," he said. "I hope I'm not calling too late."

"It's never too late," she told him.

He paused for a moment. "If you don't mind," he said, "I'd like to take Brian this weekend…and maybe start alternating weekends with you after that."

Mama could tell right away that this request wasn't made out of guilt or a sense of obligation, but from a real desire or need. It had taken years, but he now had everything he needed to properly provide for his son. She smiled. "That sounds just fine, Frank."

# Chapter 24

## *Spring 1992*

Heidi and Peter had just finished stuffing themselves with Mama's chicken mozzarella over ziti. The old lady had insisted on cooking an impromptu dinner to celebrate their engagement. The conversation bounced from topic to topic until it ended up at its usual destination – Brian.

As Heidi helped clear the table, she said, "I'm still so amazed at all the progress Brian's made."

"He sure has, but there's still more work to be done."

"More work?"

Mama half-shrugged, concern etched in her face. "Brian struggles with confidence and self-esteem. I need to find experiences to build him up – things for him to take pride in."

Heidi and Peter looked at each other and exchanged big smiles.

Mama caught it. "What is it?" she asked.

"You tell her," Heidi told her new fiancée.

Peter smiled. "It's actually kind of ironic that we're talking about this. Heidi and I have been talking about how to get Brian involved in the wedding – I mean, really involved."

Heidi stepped behind him and put her hands on his shoulders.

"I'd like to ask Brian to be my best man," he finally announced.

Mama kept her eyes locked on his and said, "Brian has the best sense of character I know, and he loved you right away, Peter." She slowly stood, walked around the table, grabbed his head with both her hands and kissed his forehead. "If you weren't already family – which you have been for some time now – this would seal it for me." She peered into his eyes again. "Thank you, sweetheart."

~ ~ ~ ~ ~ ~ ~ ~

Glen Manor was a Chateaux-inspired Manor House. Built in 1920 from the plans of a French castle, it was situated on the Sakonnet River with a view of Tiverton and Little Compton on the opposite shore. Heidi fell in love with the waterfront location and the stone terrace, but when she saw the flower garden out back, she knew her childhood dreams were about to come true.

It was an unseasonably warm May afternoon. Rows of white folding chairs lined the garden lawn, facing the Sakonnet River. Bob surveyed the land. The expansive river and formal gardens that led out to the red-clay cliffs provided the perfect backdrop for his princess to be wed. He turned to Peter, his future son-in-law, and smiled. Approaching the young man, he said, "If it were any other man standing before me today, I would be asking him – no, telling him – to take good care of my daughter. But not you. I already know that you will."

"Yes, sir, I will. You have my word."

Bob placed his hand on Peter's shoulder. "I know. And you have my sincerest apology, son."

"Sir?"

"Before I'd even met you, I misjudged you – and harshly. You would think that being around Brian all these years, I would have already learned, but..." He shook his head at his own foolishness. "Anyway, I was ignorant and I'm grateful you gave me a chance to learn."

Peter was at a complete loss for words.

"Will you forgive me?" Bob asked.

"Already did...a long time ago," Peter managed, past the lump in his throat.

Bob's eyes filled and he hugged the decent man that stood before him. "I'm so happy Heidi picked you," he whispered. "Welcome to our family."

Peter's eyes filled, too, and he returned the embrace. Looking sharp in his black tuxedo, Brian walked over and hugged them both.

Seated in the front row, Mama watched the entire exchange and nodded with pride. "Looks like your Uncle Bob has finally grown up," she told Angie. "And that your brother still refuses to miss out on a hug."

Angie laughed.

~ ~ ~ ~ ~ ~ ~ ~

Beneath a pink rose-covered gazebo – and with Brian by their side – Heidi and Peter exchanged vows.

Filled with nerves, Brian fumbled with the rings. Peter all but stopped the ceremony to patiently assist him. Mama's eyes filled. The deep love the young couple felt for each other was so pure and transparent that both families quietly wept. The preacher pronounced them man and wife, and they kissed. Bob clapped almost as loud as Brian – who'd been previously warned by Mama not to join in on the couple's first kiss.

The reception was held just across the manicured lawn. In rhythm with the tide, a harp and piano duet played softly beneath the striped awning of a stoned archway terrace. The smell of fresh-cut grass competed with the warm salty breezes. Neatly dressed servers carried trays of hors d'oeuvres and colorful glasses of wine, while guests offered their congratulations to the newly married couple before mingling in small groups. Everyone was dressed lightly in the hope of a warm evening breeze. The photographer made his rounds and shot roll after roll of film. Bottles of wine were emptied before the sun went down and the night's first stars gradually appeared. Guests were gently ushered into the manor for dinner.

Inside the manor, there was a lovely circular staircase, huge fireplaces and quaint sitting rooms lit by hurricane lamps. Just inside the library, a bar was set up. French blue linens complemented the baroque interior. The dining room walls opened to the terrace where small candlelit tables with white linen cloths surrounded the perimeter. Seasonal floral centerpieces and tiny silver picture-frame Christmas ornaments were placed on each table; special details that promised an unforgettable night. It was absolutely gorgeous, with perfect views of the water and landscaped grounds.

To a room full of raised glasses, Brian fought past his choking fear of public speaking and offered a brief but heartfelt toast. "To Biddy and Pa," the best man said. "Low you." The entire room sighed. "Low you," he repeated, making sure everyone had received his message.

Mama looked at Joan and grinned. "We should have invited Brian's pediatricians to see this," she whispered.

Joan slapped her arm and laughed. She was overwhelmed with pride.

And Brian – he was as proud as a bride's father, strutting around in his black tuxedo. The photographer shot pictures all night – hundreds of them – with Brian at the center of most. Heidi and Peter went out of their way to make the celebration as much Brian's as it was theirs. Even Peter's family embraced him throughout the night. Mama and Joan were overjoyed.

Dinner was served in the elegant dining room where guests ate surrounded by the romantic details of the French chateau. The catered food was a mix of Italian favorites and soul food.

It was a magical night; two different cultures brought together to celebrate a deep and beautiful love. To the eye, it looked like a chess board – black and white intermingled. The room was filled with love; the coming together of two families.

After dinner, an enormous set of doors were opened to reveal a ballroom with giant beveled mirrors, crystal chandeliers and French blue-satin window dressings. Soft music wafted on the sea breezes and carried the guests into the exquisite room. As they made their way in, Peter approached the small musical ensemble and picked up an acoustic guitar that was leaning against an empty chair. He slung the strap over his shoulder and turned to face his expectant audience. "This is my first gift to my wife – a song that I wrote but decided not to share with her until tonight." While the crowd sighed, he gestured for Heidi to sit before him in the empty chair. "It's called *Mi Bella*...My Beautiful."

From the moment his fingers strummed the guitar strings, the crowd fought back the tears that both Peter and Heidi let go freely. Mama grabbed a tissue from her pocketbook, wiped her eyes and turned to Steph. "Your sister's life will be filled with love," she whispered. "God bless them both."

Overwhelmed with emotion, the new groom was unable to sing the final verse. It didn't matter. The guitar spoke for his soul, and the room swayed until the last note rang out. For a moment, there was silence – and then Brian clapped.

The rest of the night was a tasteful mix of tradition and the couple's own style. It was elegant and classy, without being stuffy. When it was time to cut the wedding cake, they fed each other pieces of the cake in front of a mob of flashing cameras, but it wasn't a formal white cake. It was carrot cake – Heidi's favorite. Brian waited behind Peter for his turn.

While the crowd cheered them on, Heidi fed her happy cousin a generous piece.

For their first dance as husband and wife, Peter had researched an old Italian tradition where the newly married couple got wrapped in silk ribbons until they were bound together as one. He wanted to surprise Heidi with this. Mama, Brian and the clan were more than happy to oblige his considerate request.

For the father and daughter dance, Heidi chose *Summer Wind* by old Blue Eyes. With the salty breeze blowing the curtains back, it was perfect. "I love you, sweetheart," Bob sobbed into her ear. "And I'm so happy for the both of you."

"I love you, too," Heidi wept. "We both do." She smiled. "And thank you for all of this, Daddy...for this amazing day."

"My pleasure," he said, moving her around the floor. "It's my honor."

Once all the traditions had been met, the live musicians were replaced by a D.J. The lights came down, the volume went up and the party began. Everyone danced. Even Mama swayed for a few moments with her handsome escort – Brian.

During one of the slow songs, Heidi stole her cousin away. As they danced, she remembered when she was a kid; the doctors saying that Brian would never walk and the devastation the whole family felt. "And now here we are – dancing," she thought aloud.

As if he could read her thoughts, Brian smiled at her.

She leaned into his ear. "I'm so proud of you, Brian," she whispered. "You've proven that even the impossible is possible. And you've given each one of us the courage we needed to be our true selves and to live our lives to the fullest." Her eyes filled. "Thank you for that."

He pushed away and peered into her eyes. "Weecome, Biddy." He smiled again. "Low, Biddy."

"And I love you, too," she told him, before planting a big kiss on his cheek.

~ ~ ~ ~ ~ ~ ~ ~

Although Mama was thrilled to take part in the celebration, it didn't take long for her legs to surrender. After trading her Cornflake cookie recipe for Peter's grandmother's pecan pie recipe, she approached Heidi and Peter on the dance floor. They stopped in mid-dance and faced her. She grabbed each of their faces and smiled. "I wish you all the love that I've known in my life," she yelled over the music, and then kissed them both.

"Thank you for sharing this night with us, Mama," Heidi said. "I know you haven't felt well..."

Mama shook her curly gray head. "Girl, I wouldn't have missed this for all the stardust in the sky."

She then looked into Peter's eyes. "Thank you again," she said. "I'll never forget that proud smile on Brian's face when he stood at your side today."

Peter hugged her. "There isn't anything I wouldn't do for him," he promised.

Mama kissed him. "And from what I've seen, that's a mutual thing. Brian loves you very much."

As if on cue, Brian wrapped his arms around them both and gave a long, hard squeeze. Heidi jumped into the pile for a group hug.

Mama scanned the young couple's eyes. "You hold onto each and never let go, okay?"

As Mama and Brian broke away, Peter pulled Heidi closer to him. They both nodded. Mama winked, grabbed Brian's hand and hobbled away.

On the terrace outside, Mama took Brian's hand. "You did real good tonight," she told him. "You should be very proud of yourself."

He gushed with pride. "Yets, Mama."

Mama pointed up at the sky. The moon was full and lit the night. "Luna bella," she said, nodding. "These are the nights we live for, my boy."

~ ~ ~ ~ ~ ~ ~ ~

Back at the cottage, Mama took three pills and washed them down with a tumbler of water. She limped to her chair and flopped down into it. She reached for her legs and tried to rub out the spikes that hammered into her brittle bones. The cancer felt like termites eating their way through an old, dry rotted shed. "Oh, Lord, please ease my pain tonight. It's something awful."

The Lawrence Welk rerun hadn't even released its first wave of bubbles when both the pills and the prayer took effect. She breathed deeply and drifted off. Her snoring could have woken the dead...

~ ~ ~ ~ ~ ~ ~ ~

Mama opened her eyes to a vast expanse of rich, rolling countryside dotted with cypress trees. In the distance, there were several grazing sheep, but the shepherd was nowhere in sight. Beyond them, at the outskirts of a silvery olive grove, she could barely make out a small house. It appeared to be made of stone. *Or maybe it's stucco?* she wondered. *It's the color of melted creamsicles.* On each side of it, there were small groves of trees. *Fruit – fig and pear,* she guessed. The sun was warm on her back and a slight breeze tickled her neck. It felt like the first day of spring; everything was green and rich and bursting with life. Shielding her eyes from the sun, she looked up at the bluest sky she'd ever seen. A few puffy clouds floated above. Besides the wind, only her breathing could be heard – slow, relaxed, and in perfect rhythm with the beat of her heart. Another scan of the hills revealed no human life. Yet, she felt anything but alone. She smiled.

Looking to her left, for the first time she noticed two straight rows of tall, green cypress trees lining a red clay roadway, the sun illuminating its natural path. Streams of light danced upon the path, auditioning for her attention. Without a thought, she turned and started for the path, an old Italian song coming to mind. "*Viva Tuscany,*" she started humming aloud, her smile growing wider.

As she followed the path, an old man dressed in soiled work clothes and a worn soft hat was whistling. He worked on his hands and knees, weeding out the base of an ancient stone wall. She approached. He looked up and smiled. His face was tan and weathered; his eyes, kind and aqua blue. "*Ciao, Bella,*" he called out.

"*Ciao, Signor,*" she replied.

He tipped his hat and smiled again. Without another word, he returned to his work and his whistling. Mama journeyed on.

At the end of the path, she came upon a field of daisies that looked like it went on forever. Butterflies and doves joined her as she walked, the breeze carrying them all toward something better. In a clearing, she stopped to watch a doe and her fawn prancing about. The scene brought so much joy that she laughed aloud. For whatever reason, it felt like a sign – though she couldn't understand what it might be. She took three steps forward when she looked up again to discover that she'd just entered the outskirts of a small Italian village. "It's Italy!" she gasped. "I've finally made it to Italy!" Afternoon had just turned to dusk.

Her young, healthy legs carried her on adrenaline and curiosity. At the edge of the small villa, she walked past an outdoor market that was closing for the day. Men and women packed up boxes of their baked goods – bread, cakes and biscuits. There was also an inventory of cheeses, cookbooks, coffee, kitchenware, pasta, oils, vinegars and wine. There was lots of red wine. "*Buona Sera, Bella,*" a copper-faced man called out.

"*Buona Sera, Signor,*" she replied and hurried toward the center of town, wondering why this was the second stranger to address her by her childhood nickname.

The tiny villa was a menagerie of cobblestone streets and intimate cafes. It was so wonderfully congested that it appeared each building was no more than an addition of the one before it. The smell of espresso filled the sweet spring air, challenged by the salami and cheese that hung in nearby shops. White, twinkling lights – strung from tree to tree – illuminated a smile on every face. Some waved at her as she walked by. She returned the gesture, oddly grateful that her presence had not gone unnoticed. The old cathedral called out to its faithful, its bells echoing through the granite square. As she approached the stone statues of angels and saints, two old women sang in Italian, a soft breeze carrying their notes toward the heavens. Love was all around – everywhere – and the world was perfect. She took a seat at the fountain in the middle of the square and scanned every inch that surrounded her: the architecture of the ancient provincial buildings was breathtaking, food peddlers and lovers protected beneath the terraces that overlooked the villa; balconies that were filled with terracotta pots of roses, wildflowers, and tiny pear trees. The faint scents of lemon and thyme wafted on the breeze. And then she heard the sound of water. She stood and looked back. *It's not the fountain*, she knew. *It's the ocean – the tide coming in and out.*

Drawn by its call, she hurried through the square and made her way down a narrow alley that led out to a long, wooden dock. She could see cobalt and turquoise dancing on everything. She squinted to see the Italian port filled with sailors mending fishing nets and singing about the day's great catch. *It's everything I ever thought it would be...everything I ever told Brian about and more.* With the taste of salt on her tongue, she licked her lips and picked up the pace. *This feels like heaven...*

~ ~ ~ ~ ~ ~ ~ ~

Mama awakened and sat motionless in her gray chair. At peace, she looked around the room until disappointment crept into her heart. And then – in one sudden surge – the pain came rushing back. It felt like cleavers being tossed into her hips and legs. She cried out and struggled to free herself from the chair. "Where are those painkillers?" she asked aloud. "Dear God, where are they?"

# Chapter 25

## *Winter 1993*

Angie was enraged and could no longer contain it. "Sure, you're tough on me, but for as long as I can remember, you've let the doctors push you around when it comes to Brian!" she screamed at her mother.

Joan was furious with her daughter for the sharp tongue and constant negativity, but Angie was right. She'd always been intimidated by the doctors and their orders for Brian. "I've done the best I could," she snapped back. "We're not all as tough as you, Angie."

Angie stared out the passenger window. "Well, at least I wouldn't have let Dad quit on this family," she muttered.

Before she could finish, Joan grabbed her arm and gave it a squeeze until she had Angie's undivided attention. "You listen to me, little girl. You want to pick on me, then that's one thing – but your dad's not even here to defend himself." Joan pulled the van over to the side of the road and threw the shifter into park. "And for the record, your dad never quit on this family. He's been there for you kids every step of the way, and has done the best he's known how. Don't you dare..."

Angie's shoulders started to shudder and the tears began to break. "I'm sorry," she whimpered. "I shouldn't have said that."

Joan pulled Angie to her and let the girl sob. "I know you're angry about a lot of things, sweetheart, but you need to let it go. The person you're really hurting is yourself."

Angie continued to cry for awhile. When she'd finally composed herself, she nodded once, gave her mom a final squeeze and said, "But you are a push-over when it comes to Brian's doctors."

Joan laughed. "I'll make you a deal then. I'll try to be tougher, if you..."

"If I'm not so angry all the time, right?"

Joan smiled. "Deal?"

"Okay," Angie said and returned to her seat.

"Good," Joan sighed, and pulled back onto the road. "Now, let's go root for your brother."

~ ~ ~ ~ ~ ~ ~ ~

The gymnasium was packed; family and friends in attendance to cheer for their heroes. Lisa rallied her basketball team into a close huddle. Dressed in red and gold, Brian, their leader, placed his hand into the middle. "Go, go now."

Ricky remained seated on the bench.

Brian waved him over. "Now Ra."

The boy jumped up and hurried into the circle. He placed his hand on top of the sweaty pile.

Lisa smiled. "Okay, gentlemen, this is what we've been practicing for all year. I expect you to do your best, but can anyone tell me what the most important thing is?"

Jerome – a tall, skinny teen with thick eyeglasses – raised his hand and yelled out, "FUN! FUN! FUN!"

Lisa gave him a high-five. "You're absolutely right, buddy! The main thing out there is for all of you to have fun." She searched each of their smiling faces and nodded. "Okay then, let's hear it on three. One...two...three..."

"Go Tee!" everyone yelled. Brian pulled his socks up to his knees and ran out onto the court, leading his squad into battle. The crowd roared.

On the polished parquet floor, Brian took his place in the center of the court and faced his opponent. They shared a smile and an awkward handshake. John, the referee, addressed both teams. "Let's have fun today, boys, and I expect fair play. You all know the rules, right?" Everyone nodded. He smiled, placed the whistle into his mouth and gave it a blast of air. Brian and the opposing center crouched, ready to leap. After a pregnant pause, John tossed the ball into the air. To the cheers of the crowd, Brian tipped the ball back to his teammate, Victor. The game had begun.

Victor bounced the ball a few times before traveling halfway down the court, the ball never touching the floor. John overlooked the blatant traveling violation.

Victor threw the ball to Jerome, who treated it like a hot potato, quickly tossing it to Brian, who was already positioned under the basket. Amidst a gaggle of lanky arms and sharp elbows, Brian threw the ball straight up. It hit the front of the rim, ricocheted off the back rim and then dropped through the net. The crowd erupted. The first two points registered on the scoreboard. As if nothing had happened, Brian trotted down the court to set his team up into its long-practiced defense.

For two periods of eight minutes each, both teams battled valiantly, while the crowd celebrated each basket and every miss. There were numerous timeouts taken for water breaks. At halftime, as loud music pulsated through the gymnasium and a half dozen cheerleaders with disabilities took the floor, Lisa used the extended opportunity to offer one of her famous pep talks. "You're doing great, guys! Keep up the energy and just keep taking your shots."

"Win us?" Brian asked.

"It doesn't matter," Lisa replied. "We're up by three baskets, but the score doesn't matter. We still have a whole half to go and anything can happen. Just play hard and..."

"FUN! FUN!" the team screamed.

At the end of the halftime break, Brian placed his hand into the middle.

They all joined in. Lisa smiled. "Let's hear it on three," she said. "One...two...three..."

"Go Tee!" everyone yelled – or something like it.

Smiling, Brian ran toward one of the cheerleaders and gave her a hug. She was happy to return the affection. In the stands, Joan looked at Mama and rolled her eyes. Mama chuckled. "I told ya. He's a ladies' man."

"Sure, but I think he just violated the Special Olympics Code of Conduct."

Mama laughed. "Well, at least he's not drinking alcohol."

Joan rolled her eyes again and joined her mother in laughter.

"Okay, Romeo," Lisa yelled from the bench. "Get your mind back in the game." Everyone within earshot laughed. Brian threw his coach a thumbs-up and got back into his crouch. John threw the ball into the air and the game resumed.

As they played, fans from both sides called out from the stands, "Come on, Bobby," and "We love you, Georgie." Even both coaches cheered on the other team's players. Brian hit three shots in a row, the ball arcing high toward the gym rafters each time. The gym echoed with applause, while the team celebrated on the court after every score. John – as the referee – struggled not to cheer along with them.

Returning on defense after his third consecutive basket, Brian watched as Joey, one of the boys on the other team, struggled once again to get the ball in.

Brian grabbed the rebound and to everyone's amazement, handed the ball back to Joey. "Ja, Ja, go," he yelled.

The boy tossed the ball back up, but missed the rim completely. Determined, Brian went back up with a vengeance, fighting his own teammate, Jerome, for the rebound. Brian won and stuffed the ball back into Joey's midsection. "Ja, Ja, go."

Realizing what was going on, the crowd went silent and got to its collective feet. Mama and Joan looked down the bleachers to Lisa for an explanation. The coach could only shrug, her eyes misting over.

Against his entire team, Brian fought like a wolverine on the boards, while Joey tried and tried to sink a basket – but couldn't get one to fall.

The ball finally landed in Jerome's hands. He turned and charged up the court. By the time he reached mid-court, though, Brian had chased him down and stolen the ball from him. Prepared to overcome any obstacle before him, Brian made his way back to Joey and handed him the ball. "Go, Ja Ja. Go!" he yelled.

While the entire audience held its breath, Joey launched the ball back into the air. It bounced once and then twice off the rim until finally falling through the net. Elated, Brian raised Joey's arm in victory. The crowd went wild. Overwhelmed with all the magic and love that filled the moment, Lisa took a seat on the bench and wept. John stood motionless on the floor, matching her tears.

Grinning, Mama looked at her daughter and snickered, "And they said he wouldn't walk. That's my butterfly...my beautiful butterfly." Weeping in joy, Joan hugged her mother, while the old woman removed a set of rosary beads from her jacket pocket. "Hail Mary, full of grace," she whispered, "the Lord is with thee..."

Before an ear-piercing crowd, the kids finished the game. The score didn't matter. Parents and friends swarmed both teams and congratulated them. While celebrating with Brian, Angie spotted a boy in a wheelchair on the opposite end of the court; he was having trouble shooting the basketball. She broke out of her family circle and approached the boy to help him. Mama caught it and slapped Joan's arm to watch. "Look at that." She shook her head. "Seems like Brian's taught her, too. It's amazing how fast she's grown."

Nodding, Joan beamed with pride. "Angie's going to do great things. I just know it."

~ ~ ~ ~ ~ ~ ~ ~ ~

After the medal ceremony, Mama suggested an impromptu celebration at the East Side Grille. "On my dime," she insisted. No one argued. The East Side Grille served the best barbecued ribs and cornbread in town.

Steph and her new girlfriend, Lauren, were at the bar ordering pitchers of soda when they overheard two men making fun of someone. "What a retard!" the older of them commented.

In a million years, Steph would never have dreamed of opening her mouth. But there was something inside her that just wouldn't let it go. "Retard? That's a real intelligent word, don't you think?" she asked, shocking herself even more than Lauren.

The guy looked up from his beer, sized the two girls up and muttered, "Whatever, dike."

Steph's blood rose. She wrapped her arm around Lauren and kept it there. "Another intelligent label," she snapped. "You must be a college professor, right?"

"Why don't you two go get a room," the older one chimed in.

"Why? Do you think there'd be something wrong with that?"

"No, I think that's exactly what God intended – man with man, woman with woman," he answered, sarcastically. "This way here, we can finally stop reproducing and bring the whole travesty to an end."

"What a hateful thing to say," Steph countered in a tone that betrayed more sympathy than anger.

"I prefer the term *traditional*."

"Yeah, okay, Archie Bunker," Lauren jumped in.

"As long as you people don't bother me, do whatever you want. I don't care," he finally surrendered.

"You *people*?" Steph asked, and then looked at Lauren. "There's that big brain working overtime again."

With a dismissive snicker, Lauren grabbed both pitchers of soda, while Steph paid the tab. As they turned from the bar, they spotted Brian standing there, staring at the two ignorant men – who were staring back at him.

"Bad!" Brian barked. He stepped up to the bar until he was inches from them. "Pitcher, ponk?" he asked.

For a moment, they were clearly at a loss. When the younger one opened his mouth to respond, Brian put his hand up – palm out – indicating that the conversation was already over.

Both men were stunned, and silenced.

As if they'd just come to an agreement, Brian nodded once. He then wrapped his arms around both girls. "Go now," he said, escorting them away.

Steph and Lauren looked back and shot the men a smile – whose mouths were still hung open in shock.

~ ~ ~ ~ ~ ~ ~ ~

Not ten feet from the bar, Lauren turned to Steph and laughed. "What the hell got into you?" she asked.

Giddy, Steph shrugged. "I don't know. I just couldn't let it go."

"I'm proud of you," Lauren said, and hugged Brian. "Both of you."

"For what?" Steph asked.

"For having the courage to argue and defend our love."

Steph shook her head and chuckled. "I've watched my grandmother and this guy..." She squeezed Brian's hand. "...stand up against the most brutal challenges and still hold their heads up high. I'm never hiding from anything again, I swear it."

Brian looked at her and smiled, proudly.

Lauren kissed her cheek. "Good for you," she said.

Brian glanced at Lauren and pointed to his cheek. She kissed it. He giggled.

Wearing giant smiles, all three rejoined Brian's victory dinner.

~ ~ ~ ~ ~ ~ ~ ~

While they ate and celebrated, John explained, "The Special Olympics is funded through corporate and individual gifts, but days like today could never happen without lots of other fundraising efforts."

"Like what?" Heidi asked, her fingers covered in barbecue sauce.

"There are several major events hosted annually – like the Recycle for Gold vehicle donation program and the Sports Celebrity Carnival." He shrugged. "But to be honest, most of the funds are raised at smaller, family-run events like spaghetti dinners, motorcycle runs, bowl-a-thons – things like that."

Heidi nodded twice, but her mind had already drifted far away. Watching this, Mama ignored her throbbing legs and smiled. She could read each one of her grandbabies like an old, favorite book.

As the waitress cleared the tables, Heidi announced, "As much as I've dreaded telling you all, Peter and I are moving to New York City in a few weeks."

"What?" Steph gasped.

Heidi's eyes filled. "We have to," she explained. "If I'm ever going to make a name in the fashion industry, I need to be working in Manhattan. I hate the idea of being away from the family, but..." She looked at Mama.

With each set of eyes upon her, the old matriarch rose and approached her broken-hearted granddaughter. "Wherever your heart is, then that's where you *must* be," she said, and kissed her forehead. It was the only blessing needed.

# Chapter 26

*Early Spring 1994*

Mama hung up the telephone and told Brian, "Go next door and help Mrs. MacDonald. She just called and needs a hand moving some boxes into the cellar."

He shook his head. "Nah, Mama. Nigh nigh," he said, not budging from his permanent throne at the kitchen table.

Her head snapped back at him. "What's that?" she asked, her tone sharp. "You're too tired to help someone?"

He nodded. "Yets."

Mama flipped out. "There are folks who need help in this world and whenever we can, we're going to help them!" she roared.

"But Mama..." Angie started, trying to come to her older brother's defense.

"But Mama, nothing!" she said. "Brian has an obligation. He was diagnosed to be a vegetable. Instead, the good Lord saw fit to make him a walking inspiration." She looked directly at Brian. "No matter how big or small the task, he needs to give back. We all do. I asked God for some pretty serious miracles on the day that Brian was diagnosed, and God came through. The way I see it, there's a heavy debt owed and there's no way I can pay it off all by myself."

"K, Mama," Brian said. "K." He got up from the table and quickly made his way to Mrs. MacDonald's house across the street.

~ ~ ~ ~ ~ ~ ~ ~

Angie filled her two older cousins in on the scene in Mama's kitchen. Two days later, Heidi called her grandmother. "Mama, Steph and I talked and we've come up with an idea to help pay back some of your debt, and hopefully get Brian more involved in his community."

"That's wonderful!" Mama said. "I'm all ears."

"We'd like to host a comedy fundraiser event to benefit the St. Jude's Research Hospital in your name, and Special Olympics in Brian's name."

Overwhelmed with unexpected emotion, Mama held her tongue – fearing that she would burst out in tears.

Heidi explained, "Peter and I will put off New York for a few weeks. This will take a lot of planning." She began reading from her list. "We're going to need four or five comedians, raffle prizes for a Chinese raffle, a Grande raffle and a silent auction. We're also going to need a hall to host this thing and some snacks because Steph doesn't think we should serve a sit-down meal. It'll cost too much to feed two hundred people."

"Two hundred people?" Mama asked.

"No such word as *can't*," Heidi teased, echoing her grandmother's age-old mantra.

"Amen to that, sweetheart!"

~ ~ ~ ~ ~ ~ ~ ~

Heidi was right. The preparation was immense. With a little less than three weeks to put it all together, she secured the St. John's Club in East Greenwich. The manager said they could use it free-of-charge, just as long as it was on a night in the middle of the week. The last Thursday of the month was selected.

Next, Heidi secured letters of intent from the St. Jude's Children's Research Hospital and the Rhode Island Special Olympics. She then made over three hundred phone calls and sent out even more emails and letters to solicit donations for raffle and auction items, as well as for snack food.

Steph called the local supermarket and scheduled two dates to "shake a can" to cover all expenses. Brian spent two full Saturdays with his sister and cousins, soliciting donations. They raised nearly one thousand dollars – or enough to fund the entire show. "Every penny we earn from the ticket sales will now go straight to the charities, Brian," Angie explained to him. "You really did a great job!"

Brian smiled wide. "Mama say," he told his sister, requesting that Angie share the good news with their grandmother.

~ ~ ~ ~ ~ ~ ~ ~

Heidi contacted the local printer and talked him into donating the tickets to be used for the seats and raffles. At work, Steph created signage for everything; tent cards for reserved seating, flyers to be placed under one seat per table for another fun give-away, and table cards for the Chinese Raffle items.

The Chinese Raffle was guaranteed to be the highlight. With fifty items to win, there would be a labeled cup for each prize. Each person could purchase twenty tickets for ten dollars and then place as many tickets as they wanted within the prize cup that they hoped to win. While some folks might place one ticket into twenty different cups, others would place all twenty tickets into one cup – greatly increasing their chances of winning that one prize.

Heidi then drafted up a press release to promote the event and faxed it out to every local media venue:

~ FOR IMMEDIATE RELEASE ~

Laughter & Miracles Comedy Night Benefit for St. Jude's Children's Research Hospital & the Rhode Island Special Olympics

Friends of St. Jude's Children's Research Hospital & the Rhode Island Special Olympics will be hosting the first annual "Laughter & Miracles" Comedy Night at St. John's Club in East Greenwich, RI on Thursday, March 26th.

Four hilarious stand-up comics will take the stage to make the audience laugh themselves all the way to their wallets and purses. The doors will open at 6:30 p.m., the show starts at

8:00 p.m., and for a minimum donation of $25.00, we promise a night to
remember.

East Greenwich 's own funny man, as
well as one of the hottest, up-and-
coming comics in the industry, Denis
Donovan, will be hosting the event.

Comedian Frank Santorelli, who
played Georgie the bartender on the
Sopranos, will be taking the stage. He
has appeared on "Las Vegas," "Law
& Order" and "The Conan O'Brien
Show." His stand-up act has been
dubbed "high spirited... exuberant...
hilarious."

Comic Chris Tabb has appeared on
BET's Comic View, NESN's Comedy
All-Stars, opened nationally around
the country for Mo'Nique, and is one
of the fastest rising stars in Boston
Comedy.

The show's headliner, "the Wild Man
of Comedy," Kevin Knox, will cap
off the magical night with a set that
he's perfected on stages from Cana-
da to the Cayman Islands. Recently
returned from a regular engagement
at the Tropicana Hotel in Las Vegas,

Kevin has been called a "high energy bag of fun" by the Boston Globe.

Door prizes, a silent auction and a Chinese raffle promise restaurant gift certificates, sports memorabilia, and tickets to the best amusements and shows throughout New England. All proceeds from Laughter and Miracles will benefit St. Jude's Children's Research Hospital & the Rhode Island Special Olympics, and the children they serve.

If you would like to purchase a ticket(s), please contact Heidi or Peter Larkin at 401-555-1717.

Once Heidi, Steph and their enthusiastic volunteers completed the preparation, they realized that ticket sales would be the true test.

Nervous and excited, Heidi turned in early the night before the big event. The telephone rang. Peter came into the room. "It's for you," he said, smiling. "It's Mama."

She jumped out of bed. "Hello?"

"Hi, sweetheart," Mama said. "I wanted to tell you that I'm not feeling well, so I won't be able to make it tomorrow. I'll call your sister to tell her."

"Are you okay?" Heidi asked, concerned.

"No worries. It's nothing that won't pass. I just wanted to let you know how proud I am of you, and that you can swing by and pick up your donation whenever you want."

Heidi's eyes filled. Mama's words had more power than anyone she'd ever known. "You don't have to do that, Mama."

"And you don't have to do everything that you're doing – though I'd be lying if I said I wasn't happy about it. And more importantly, thank you again for reminding Brian that he needs to think about others before himself. He's been telling me every night about all the things he's been doing to help sick kids."

"That's great, Mama. Truthfully, it's been an amazing experience for all of us to give back like this." She paused. "You sure you're okay? Do you need anything?"

"I'll be as right as rain, sweetheart. Good luck tomorrow, and know that I love you very much."

Heidi pushed the lump down into her throat. "Love you, too, Mama. Feel better soon." Heidi hung up the phone and looked at Peter.

"What's wrong?" he asked.

She shook her head. "Maybe it's nothing...but she'd have to be real sick to miss this benefit."

~ ~ ~ ~ ~ ~ ~ ~

The following morning, Heidi, Steph and the family – Brian, Angie, Lauren, Peter, Joan, Frank, John – met at Bob and Bev's house so they could all go out for brunch before setting up the hall. When they got to Roger's Spa on the corner, each of them ordered their meal and then shared the current details of their lives. As they finished eating, Heidi began to hand out assignments. "Uncle Frank and Brian, can you please pick up the balloons? Aunt Joan and Uncle John, can you please pick up the pastries from the local high school's culinary arts program? Then meet the rest of us at the hall."

As they walked out of the restaurant, Steph put her arm around her sister and asked, "You think we're ready for this incredible night?"

"God, I hope so," she sighed and tried to shrug off the intense pressure that pushed down on her shoulders.

They headed out to East Greenwich. When they got there, the hall was completely desolate. They had to arrange all the tables and chairs to fit like a perfect puzzle. Everyone had a role. Some set up tables and chairs, while others laid out tablecloths, put out raffle items and snacks on the tables, or began to keep track of the money. The silent auction table was set up, while banners and balloons were also put out.

No sooner had the family finished their work and changed their clothes when a noisy crowd stampeded into the hall. Although there was no need to turn away anyone at the door, it was a sold out show, with two hundred fifty people filling the seats – each one eagerly waiting to laugh.

Heidi took the microphone and, standing beside Steph and Brian, made the night's first announcement. "From the bottom of our hearts, my sister, my cousin and I want to thank each and every one of you for offering your support. Without people like you, these wonderful organizations would never be able to help all the children that they do."

Brian raised his hands and applauded the audience. They happily returned it to him.

Heidi added, "So, please have a great time tonight, allow yourself to be generous and know that for some kids who have faced unspeakable obstacles, you've just made all the difference in the world."

The hall echoed with applause, with Brian clapping the loudest.

Steph grabbed the microphone and said, "So without further ado, let's get on with the show. If you don't laugh tonight, you might want to consider medication."

With the help of a busy cash bar, people laughed for the first time and the sisters felt a few pounds slip off their shoulders.

Denis Donovan took the stage and from the first word out of his mouth, people were rolling in the aisles. The comedy was sensational and the crowd roared for two straight hours.

But even when the jokes ended, the night did not. People had really gotten into the Chinese raffle, putting all the tickets they bought into the cups of the prizes they wanted to win. The more coveted prizes included a weekend get-away for two on Cape Cod, several rounds of golf and three private vineyard tours.

Steph called out the numbers drawn, while Brian handed out prizes to fifty lucky winners. Heidi then took the stage one last time and announced, "It's with incredible gratitude that I can announce our grand total – to be split between the Rhode Island

Special Olympics and the St. Jude's Hospital – is eleven thousand, one hundred fifty-seven dollars."

There was enormous applause – most of it coming from the family table. When the roar of the crowd died down, Brian grabbed the microphone and faced the audience. "Ten you," he said, extending his heartfelt appreciation to the crowd. "Ten you...much."

For a moment, a respectful silence blanketed the enormous room.

Steph wrapped her arm around her cousin, leaned into the microphone and said, "Brian speaks for our entire family, as we want to thank you all for coming out tonight and supporting these two incredible causes. There have been many local businesses that stepped up and have pledged their support. Amongst them are Hutchins & Sons Enterprises, Rodriguez Home Maintenance, Express Printing, North Attleboro Patrolman's Union and members of the Massachusetts Department of Correction."

Everyone applauded.

Heidi said, "We also need to acknowledge the folks who volunteered their time and effort, and made the Laughter & Miracles Comedy Benefit a reality, as well as my cousin Brian and my grandmother for inspiring this event." Overwhelmed with emotion, she looked toward the family table, knowing that the old lady would be absent. *She has to be feeling just awful to miss this*, she thought.

"Lastly, we'd like to thank The Mauretti Family, Brad Cowen, Stephanie Grossi, Victor DeSousa, Allen Correiro, Tommy Rodrigues, Kevin Aguiar,

Bobby Leite – and, of course, Denis Donovan, and his cast of comedians. I want to thank them all and let them know that they each get a few months off... because Laughter & Miracles II is only a year away!"

With a final laugh, the hall emptied out.

~ ~ ~ ~ ~ ~ ~ ~

It was late. After placing calls to Steph and Brian, Mama called Heidi.

"We raised over eleven thousand dollars!" Heidi reported in a hoarse voice.

"I heard. That's wonderful! I couldn't go to sleep without congratulating each of you, sweetheart," Mama said.

"Thanks, Mama."

"No, Heidi – thank you. I can't tell you how proud I am," she said. "You're really making a difference in this world." Her voice cracked with emotion. "I just got off the phone with Brian and I don't know if he's told you yet, but he said that he wants to start volunteering with the Special Olympics...helping to train the younger kids."

Instantly, Heidi choked up and for a moment, she couldn't speak. Those simple words made every hour of effort worthwhile.

"You and your sister planted a seed inside of him, Heidi, and who knows how big this will grow... how many people it will touch."

~ ~ ~ ~ ~ ~ ~ ~

Once Mama finished her prayers, she checked the temperature on the heating pads and slowly slid into bed. Like a woman in heavy labor, she breathed through the pain and meditated on releasing it from her body. "I feel good," she affirmed, "I feel good. I feel good. I feel..."

~ ~ ~ ~ ~ ~ ~ ~

The taste of salt air was strong on her lips and tongue. In the late afternoon sun, Mama walked closer toward the shore to discover that the fishermen mending nets were now pale and paunchy, and that the nets were now two fishing poles entangled in each other's lines. The tanned and weathered Italian sailors were gone, replaced by Herbie and Arthur. She laughed when she saw them. They were too busy arguing to take notice.

"You're an idiot," Herbie told Arthur. "And no one knows it better than you."

"I'm the idiot? You cast your line over mine and I'm the idiot? No wonder no one else'll fish with ya."

"That's crap and you know it. No one else will fish with me because I'm always sitting on the side of the village idiot."

Chuckling, Mama walked past them and shook her head. "Evenin', boys," she called out.

They looked up for a second and tipped their hats to her. "Evenin' Mama," they said in unison before returning to their endless quarrel.

She strolled through the neighborhood. Most houses were painted in driftwood gray with white trim. A narrow wooden placard was attached to each house, names like *Rainbow's End* and *Serenity* labeling each stop. Amidst the seagulls, American flags took up the skyline, popping in the sea winds. Driveways of crushed, bleached-white seashells led to wrap around porches and faded cedar shingles. In one yard, an open fire pit was surrounded by abandoned Adirondack chairs.

On pain-free legs, she walked on to enjoy the laughter of children at play. A baseball game played on some radio; the Boston Red Sox rallying to win. A sprinkler head spit a steady mist of water into the salty air. Mesquite briquettes and barbecued meat challenged the smell of that same salt air. People who worked in their yards appeared just as happy as the couples who walked by, holding hands. As she reached the shore, she took in the small bay that was protected from the elements. When other folks on the coast got beaten up in bad weather, those here were as safe as a baby in her mother's bosom. A row of red and yellow sea kayaks – stacked upright, side-by-side and leaning on each other – led to the concrete stairs down to the sand. She looked at the posted sign, *No Dogs Allowed,* and chuckled. *No one's ever paid attention to that,* she thought.

Taking one deep breath after the next, she walked along the beach. Broken shells and stones as smooth as glass lay ahead of her, while a set of temporary footprints lay behind. She paused at a massive chunk of battered driftwood and leaned against it. There was a fifteen-degree difference in temperature at the water and, with a constant breeze, it couldn't have been any more comfortable. The water lapped at the shore, creating a natural rhythm. *Mother Nature's lullaby*, she thought. A few yards up the beach, white overturned skiffs led to an abandoned catamaran with its sails down. Turning toward the water, she gazed at the fleet of small motor and flat bottom boats -- all moored or anchored, slowly drifting in circles. And then she spotted the two beach chairs — one big and one small — sitting side-by-side. Overwhelmed with an inexplicable sense of joy, she laughed aloud.

The sunset was miraculous and she took a seat in the larger beach chair to watch the water color masterpiece come to life. Purple, orange and pink faded together, creating a color that Crayola had not yet duplicated. Hypnotized by the raw beauty, she lost any sense of time; any real sense of herself. It was the greatest blessing she'd ever known.

The evening breeze brought a million stars that twinkled above. The tide continued to run in rhythm with her breathing. She'd never known such peace and she cherished it. Suddenly, she noticed that the pretty beach house at the end of their little world was lit up with tiny white lights that framed a gazebo. She squinted and discovered a couple locked in a passionate embrace. *Love is the best excuse for living,* she thought. *It might just be the only excuse...*

~ ~ ~ ~ ~ ~ ~ ~

Mama awakened in a cold sweat, her body curled up in the fetal position. She struggled to straighten out her legs, but couldn't. She reached for the nightstand three times before she knocked the bottle of pills onto the bed. With deformed and frozen fingers, she somehow managed to twist off the cap, palm a few and jam them into her mouth. Without water, she choked them down. She rolled over on her back and lay there, the tears streaming down her face. She stared up at the crucifix that hung over the doorway. "Why couldn't you just let me stay?" she asked. "Please Lord...please bring me home. I can't take this pain anymore." She sobbed like a baby, weeping right up until the medication took its full effect and paralyzed her senses.

# Chapter 27

*Fall 1994*

No longer able to keep her secret, Mama finally told everyone about her dream of Jesus. "The same week that I learned I had cancer, I had a dream that I was gardening at the side of the cottage near St. Jude's statue when Jesus walked up the driveway and approached me. With a smile, He extended His hand. 'Are you ready?' He asked. I was filled with such an amazing peace. I told Him, 'I am, but Brian's not.'" Joyful tears streamed down her face. "Jesus looked at Brian and glowed with such love. He nodded once and walked away. That's when I knew I was dying, but that everything was going to be all right."

Though the family had suspected long ago, the shock and terror still took hold.

Against her will – and some serious debate – Mama was admitted into the hospital for more tests and some much-needed treatment.

~ ~ ~ ~ ~ ~ ~

While Bob and John took their shift at the hospital with Mama, the rest of the family gathered at her cottage. As they all talked and laughed, Joan made two trays of her mother's famous spinach pies, covering them with dish towels and letting them cool on a plastic tablecloth on Mama's bed. By her side, Bev tried her hand at the old lady's ravioli and red gravy. It tasted almost as good, but something was definitely missing.

Seated at Mama's old kitchen table, the grand-kids looked through one photo album after the next. Yellow, dog-eared pages filled the cracked, fake leather books. Steph took note of the dates marked on each binding and shook her head. "Mama has the organizational skills of an accountant," she noted.

Heidi agreed. "And, she's been into scrapbook-ing long before it was a popular pastime."

They all agreed.

"It seems so strange to be in the cottage without Mama here," Steph said. "Every time I smell dryer sheets, Jean Nate or garlic, I'm reminded that I'm not alone...that she's always with me."

Lauren wrapped her arms around Steph's shoulders and held her close.

"I've decided to cut my hair and donate it to young cancer patients," Steph announced. "I can finally cut my hair without Mom complaining," she teased.

Bev took a break from the stove and joined Lauren to hug her good-hearted daughter.

Angie sat beside Brian, pawing through the photo albums – marveling over the hundreds of memories. Placing her hands on her shoulders, Aunt Bev asked her, "So your mom tells me that you already know what you want to major in in college. A little early to make that decision, isn't it?"

She shook her head. "Not really. I want Social Work, with a concentration on disabled children and their families." She grinned. "I want to make sure that the families ask the right questions and get the right answers."

Everyone chuckled at the irony.

Angie shrugged. "I don't want to see anyone go through what my mother's had to go through. If I can help in any way, then that's what I want to do." Her mind wandered as she thought about all the sacrifices the entire family had made; all the time and attention that had to be focused on her disabled brother. She remembered the day her father left the house; she recalled watching her submissive mother cave in to dominant men and more educated people who thought they knew what was best for Brian, even when they didn't. She knew her reputation as the negative one in the family was a direct result of being angry about growing up in that environment. Now she wanted to turn that negative attitude into something positive.

Joan joined the clan at the table and asked Heidi and Peter, "Are you guys enjoying New York?"

"We are," Heidi answered. "We miss being around the family all the time, of course, but it's the best thing for my career." She stared at one of the pictures in the photo album and her eyes filled. It was a picture of Mama and all the grandkids on one of their many summer adventures. Brian was sitting on Mama's lap, kissing her cheek while she smiled at the camera. "We'll be up for the holidays and as much as we can during the summer."

"And for the comedy fundraiser in March?" Ross asked, home on leave from the Army.

She nodded, her eyes still peeled on the hazy photo. "Absolutely. I'd never want to let Mama down." Peter hugged her.

Ross looked at his wife, Isabella, and rubbed her swollen belly. She hugged him.

"You guys pick a name yet?" Joan asked him.

He smiled. "Christopher," he answered. "Christopher Jude." He looked at his brother Brian and took a deep breath. "...after Mama's two favorite saints."

The entire room sighed.

Angie hugged her big brother Brian, but quickly pushed him away and shot him a disgusted look. "Dragon breath," she said.

Everyone laughed – except her.

"Did you brush your teeth today?" she asked him.

He shook his head.

"Use your words!" she demanded in a harsh tone.

"Nah," he said, dropping his gaze from her.

"What? You know better, Brian. Mama would have your neck if she were here. Now go to the bathroom and get cleaned up – face, hands, teeth, and use the electric shaver that Dad got you," she ordered.

"Yets, A...E," he acknowledged, searching for approval in her sharp eyes.

With a nod, she smiled at him, letting him know she wasn't angry.

He hugged her before hurrying off to the bath-room to do as he was told.

Angie turned to face the others. They were all smiling.

"If I didn't know better," Heidi said, "I'd swear I just witnessed Mama's torch for Brian being official-ly handed to you."

Angie smiled, proudly. "Even if Mama is in the hospital, Brian needs to move forward, not back."

"But what about your reputation?" Steph teased. "What will people think?"

Angie shrugged, and then smiled wider. "God knows...and that's enough."

~ ~ ~ ~ ~ ~ ~ ~

As the family prepared to leave the cottage, Brian spotted a deer standing on Mama's front lawn. It was a doe, looking out over the bay. "Mama!" he squealed and everyone came running out to the porch to see.

Once the deer left, the family decided to do the same. Joan was the last one out. With a smile, she shut off the lights and stepped out of the cottage.

~ ~ ~ ~ ~ ~ ~ ~

At five minutes before eight o'clock, Brian headed for the telephone and waited.

The phone rang. It was Mama, sneaking a call from the hospital.

He picked up the receiver. "Allo Mama," he said, without hearing her voice.

"Hello sweetheart," she whispered. "How was your day today?"

"K. You?"

She chuckled. "Better than yesterday, thanks. Now tell me about your day."

He'd planted daisies in the yard, pot and all, and told his grandmother about his gift to her. "Daze you."

"Yes, I know, sweetheart. John told me they're beautiful. Thank you so much for doing that for me, Brian."

"Mama weecome."

~ ~ ~ ~ ~ ~ ~ ~

The following afternoon, Angie approached the auditorium's lectern to deliver her scholarship-winning essay. She cleared her throat and said, "The person I admire most is my grandmother; the woman I was named after. Angela Isabelle DiMartino – or Mama, as most of us know her – has lived a life that could breathe inspiration into the coldest heart. Just a simple smile or one kind word from her can make someone trudge on – no matter how bad things seem. She gives of herself with such conviction and unconditional love that you know you're a better person just by being in her presence, and you strive every day to become a fraction of who she is. And although she makes sure that each one of us feels special, there has never been any question that her favorite has always been my brother, Brian.

"From the moment my family received the devastating news about my brother Brian's terrible disabilities, Mama's primary mission was to instill independence in him. He has been her purpose in life and before she'll allow herself to move on, he'll need to be able to do for himself. The way she sees it, they're both in it together."

Most of the audience had no real context to understand the depth of love that their classmate was presenting, but they still slid to the edge of their seats to hear more.

"When the doctor said that Brian wouldn't walk, Mama said that he would – and he did." She looked up, struggling to hold back the tears. "When the doctor said that Brian wouldn't talk, Mama promised that he would – and he did. Sure, there are some people who might have trouble understanding my brother, but he communicates as plain as day to every one of us in the family. And we can each thank Mama for opening that channel."

There was a long pause, enough for Angie to settle herself. "The doctor swore that Brian would never swim, write his name or ride a bike, but that poor man had never met anyone like Mama."

There were a few chuckles. A woman from the rear of the room yelled out, "Amen." Everyone looked back. It was Angie's mother – Joan. Angie smiled when she saw her.

"Angela DiMartino – Mama – has never won a gold medal or a trophy of any kind, but I challenge you to find another human being who could match her stamina or willpower. Her name has never appeared in the newspaper or her face on TV, but the depth of her patience and compassion is the stuff that true legends are made of. And Mama may never be proclaimed a saint, but there hasn't been a soul that's walked this Earth who's had more faith in God and the miracles He can deliver – and deliver, they both have."

There was a final pause. Angie struggled against her emotions to finish. She looked up to find her mother smiling the proudest smile. It was all she needed to go on. "Every time I look at my brother, Brian, I see my grandmother's faith and work, and I know that unconditional love is both possible and eternal." She took a deep breath. "The person I admire most is Angela DiMartino – Mama."

To a small round of applause, she stepped out from behind the lectern and walked straight into her mother's embrace. The room fell silent.

## Chapter 28

*Late Fall 1994*

Mama was sent home. Evidently, there was nothing that could be done for her in the hospital that couldn't be done at the cottage – not to mention, the hospital staff had quickly grown tired of arguing with her.

With Angie and Steph snuggled up against her in bed, Mama handed out a few more nuggets of wisdom. "You need to have a relationship with God, Steph."

"You're worried about saving my soul?" Steph asked, surprised.

"Lord no – I've known your soul since you came into this world and I've never known anyone kinder or more considerate. No, what I'm talking about is finding a faith that allows you to finally know that you're not alone in this world...that it doesn't have to be such a difficult walk all the time. I'm not talking about religion. I'm talking about faith." She looked down at Angie and kissed her forehead.

Steph grinned. "When we were kids, I remember you trying to explain faith to us. You said that Brian was a single ray of light. I've never forgotten that."

She grabbed Steph's hand. "Sweetheart, we're each a single ray of light in this world. That's how we know the Lord is always with us." Nodding, she gave Angie a squeeze to be sure she was also listening.

While Angie hugged her back, Steph half-shrugged. "But religion..."

"We're not talking about religion," Mama interrupted, her eyes growing distant. She smiled, her gaze returning to Steph. "God's always with you, you know." She tightened her grip. "And there's no shadow large enough to conceal your light, Steph. Never forget that."

That night, Brian took his turn on the edge of Mama's bed, holding her hand. She gazed into his gentle eyes and took an inventory of the eighteen year old: *He has the mentality of a mischievous little boy, innocent and loving. He's completely reliant upon the kindness of those around him and remains a walking test to all mankind. Fortunately, he's surrounded by those who love and support him. He's lovable and likes most people, especially the girls. Although I've tried to teach him better social skills and introduce him to the handshake, it's clearly too impersonal for him. He's a gift from God. Even when Frank and Joan got divorced, he kept the family together. He never gets angry. Even if someone loses their patience and yells at him, he never gets upset with them. He possesses the loyalty of a cocker spaniel.*

*He can walk – and run and skip and jump. He can't sleep unless he has his warm glass of Ovaltine and is tucked into bed. Fortunately, Angie is happy to see to it now.*

*He can talk. Though he speaks like a stroke victim in bits and bytes, he's also learned sign language. His dialect is always going to be a work in progress. His vocabulary is minimal and choppy, but the family understands him well – and that's enough.*

*He can write and draw. Although it's from a child's perspective, he can still create.*

*He can ride a bike. It isn't pretty to watch, but he's learned to ride.*

*He can swim – like a beautiful fish.*

*He's generous. Every Christmas, he makes his own gifts for the family and they're always the most cherished. And he loves going out on field trips, a tradition that I've passed down to him. He knows everyone and everyone seems to know him. He waves at everyone until they wave back – which only happens a few times before they end up introducing themselves and a friendship is born. He's very sensitive to other people's feelings and is instinctive about sorrow. Many folks even cry on his shoulder without having to explain why, or him needing to know. He laughs a lot and invites everyone to join him....* Wiping her eyes, Mama smiled. *He's going to be okay*, she thought. *My butterfly will be just fine.*

~ ~ ~ ~ ~ ~ ~ ~

A few weeks later, Mama looked like a frail child lying in bed, barely holding on to her to life on Earth. With Bob, Bev, Joan and John standing guard, she took only enough medication to manage the pain while still being able to carry on a logical conversation. "Brian's with Frank?" she asked Joan.

"Yes, Ma. Brian's fine. You need to stop worrying about him. He's grown now and..."

Mama tried to laugh. "I doubt that'll ever happen," she slurred. "Brian's Mama's boy and he stole my heart the day he was born."

"I know, Ma. He loves you, too."

"Have Frank bring him over. I'd like him to stay the night."

"But Ma, you're not feeling well."

The old lady smiled. "You're right, so call Frank and tell him to bring me my medicine."

Joan looked up at John and gestured for him to make the call. He quickly left the room.

Mama tried to pull herself up into a seated position. She barely moved. "When I pass...and don't worry, it won't be tonight." She grinned. "It's not my time yet."

Glances of relief were exchanged all around.

"But when I do, don't you dare cry for me," she told her grown children at her bedside. "I've missed my ma and papa for too many years now. I can't wait to hug my mom again; to smell her neck and feel her arms wrapped around me. I also can't wait to dance with your grandfather and watch the sun rise upon his face again. And sit around with my aunts and uncles and share stories of what we did down here on Earth. Just wait until I tell them how special you all are and how blessed I was the day God sent each of you to our family; of all the love that we've shared. Nope, don't you dare cry for me. If you want to shed a few tears for the short time that we'll be apart, go right ahead...but know in your heart that I'm exactly where the good Lord wants me to be; exactly where

I need to be. And also, know that my spirit is with you – always."

Tears streamed down their faces. "You need to get some rest," Bob told her.

She took a deep breath and smiled. "Where's Brian?"

"On his way," John answered from the doorway.

She nodded. "Good. Maybe I'll just take a little nap while we wait." Within seconds, she was snoring.

~ ~ ~ ~ ~ ~ ~ ~ ~

Strings of small white Christmas lights were wrapped around the trees that sprang up from the holes in the concrete. Giant wreaths were hung on street lamps that lined both sides of the street. Mama felt a squeal of joy start from her diaphragm and rush out of her mouth. It was the old neighborhood and it was the holidays. *How wonderful!*

She nearly skipped down the street, taking in every magical detail. The cracks in the cobblestone trapped the melted snow and the light of the moon. Brick-faced brownstones covered in creeping ivy were protected behind ornamental wrought iron gates. Arched doorways, with heavy wooden doors and brass pineapple knockers, concealed a mix of English and Italian conversations. There was a warm light glowing from behind the lacey curtains in each apartment window; a sense of family, of be-longing; of real community. With a quick glance into any of those windows, she could figure out much of what was being said, as most folks talked with their hands. There were no great mysteries here anyway.

Old men talked about soccer, while old women talked about old men.

Flying the red, white, and green flag of the old country, corner shops and quaint restaurants were interspersed amongst the apartment houses. She took notice of the hanging balls of cheese and sticks of salami in fine black netting. Her mouth watered.

She rounded the corner and a dozen pigeons took flight. She was at The Mall, a small park with a statue of the Virgin Mary at its center. She genuflected, blessed herself and crossed the street.

She peered into one of the café windows. There was an old man sipping espresso at a tiny round table. He smiled when he saw her. She waved to him.

She moved on and passed a fancy restaurant with its white linen tablecloths and candle-lit feasts. Wine bottles lay horizontal, corks out, on rows and rows of mahogany racks. Oil paintings of the old country hung over the tables and half-filled decanters were the center pieces. The ambiance was just as important as the aromas that filled the place. She inhaled deeply. "Mmmm...pasta with red gravy," she purred.

Hand-in-hand, a young couple strolled past her, unaware she was even there. The restaurant door swung open, releasing the nostalgic sounds of a whining violin and the crooning of a spirited tenor.

Mama forged on and reached the pearl of the neighborhood. There were a couple of decadent pastry shops on the street – *but Mike's is the best,* she thought. They carried any sweet you could imagine, including the devious monstrosity called the Lobster

Claw – filled with real whipped cream and raspberry jam. You had to be nice to the ladies behind the counter, though, because there was no posted price list and prices differed every time you went in. A gentleman dressed in his pajamas sipped an espresso and enjoyed the evening paper at a small café table just outside.

Beyond the bridal shop at the end of the street where young girls would go to gawk and dream of the future, she spotted the apartment where she'd been born and raised. It was right above Lucia's, her uncle's family-style Italian eatery that boasted the biggest and best raviolis in Little Italy.

Sleigh bells called out in the distance and she noticed that it was starting to snow again, but she didn't feel cold. The closer she got to her uncle's restaurant, the louder the singing became. *Sounds like there's a big celebration being thrown...but for who?* she wondered. A warm glow pulsated from the windows and every step toward it seemed to lighten her troubles. People were definitely singing, and the smell of burnt caramel filled the air. "Mama's Christmas custard!" she blurted out and started running for the place on young, pain-free legs.

When she reached the door, she threw it open and was faced with a hundred friendly faces. Family members and friends who had long passed away greeted her, as she made her way through the crowded room. She was overwhelmed with love. With each kiss and hug, the crowd parted and she sensed she was being drawn to a force much bigger than herself. A Christmas tree blinking in the corner had an aluminum foil manger beneath it. She giggled. Then, when Uncle Bob and Aunt Lucille stepped aside, she saw her mama and papa seated at a table for three, waiting for her. She started to cry and hurried to them.

"Bella," her father cried. "Oh, my Bella."

She reached for her papa and they fell into each other's arms. Kissing his cheek, she turned to find her mother waiting, her arms opened wide.

"Welcome home, Angela," the woman said.

Mama jumped into her arms. "I love you so much," she cried.

The woman wept like a child, holding her daughter in her arms and swaying with her like they had on the day she was born. "I missed you so..."

Suddenly, Mama looked into her mother's eyes. "I don't want to wake up, Ma," she pleaded like a child. "There's too much pain."

Her mother smiled. "Just a little longer and then you'll be home to stay."

Holding her mother close, she didn't want to think about returning to the pain.

"Heaven is our reality," her mother explained. "It's life on Earth that's the dream." She kissed her forehead. "But you need to go back now."

"But Ma..."

"Just for a little while longer, Angela. Your work is not done yet."

~ ~ ~ ~ ~ ~ ~ ~

Mama awoke to find only Brian seated beside her on the bed. There was no longer any delay in response from the cancer. Like searing fire pokers, pitch forks pierced her body, tearing at both flesh and bone. "My pills," she managed past the nauseating waves of physical torment. Brian grabbed all of the bottles and dumped them on top of her. She fumbled for the right amber-colored tube, finally removed the cap and choked down two.

Awaiting the effects of the medication, she panted like an overweight dog in the summer heat. Brian never left her side. Instead, he grabbed her hand and panted along with her. "K, Mama," he reassured her between breaths. "K."

The pain was inhuman – unlike anything she could have ever imagined. As the large white pills fought for leverage, she tried to quiet her labored breathing. Brian did the same. She struggled to offer him a smile, unsure of whether she had pulled it off.

"K, Mama," he promised again, rubbing her back. "K, now."

She nodded. "Oh Brian, what are you going to do...when Mama's gone?" she asked, still gasping for air. Tears filled her eyes. "When I'm not around... any more?"

Without hesitation, he stood and left the room. Within seconds, he returned and took his rightful place beside her again. Smiling, he reached into the pocket of his robe and pulled out the old lady's portable telephone. He placed it into her hands. "Mama tuck, nigh nigh," he said.

She was certain that she'd managed the smile this time. "I bet we will still talk every night...won't we? At eight o'clock, right?"

He kissed her on the forehead. "Yets, Mama."

"I know, sweetheart. I know..." She nodded. "You would never give up on me, either." *While everyone else will say goodbye to me,* she thought, *Brian will only say goodnight. Our bond is eternal.* "You promise?" she asked him.

He stuck out his pinky finger. Mama locked on and they shook.

"Go nigh nigh, Mama," he said. "Go nigh nigh."

She patted the bed beside her. "You can sleep with me tonight, sweetheart. Is that okay with you?"

The word "okay" wasn't completely out of her mouth when he was already lying beside her, wearing his giant smile. Reaching into his pajama bottoms pocket, he took out his lucky white rock and placed it into her other hand. "For Mama," he whispered.

"Oh Brian, I can't take that," she said. It was as if he knew she was struggling to hold on with every breath and needed all the luck she could get.

He closed her hand around it. "For Mama, you," he said again.

"Thank you," she said, and held it to her thumping chest. "You ready...for tomorrow?" the old woman asked, still panting through the pain.

"Mmm..." he said.

"Use your words...sweetheart," she moaned. "We...don't mumble."

"Yets," he said.

She ignored the spikes in her side to pull the covers under his chin, and then kiss his forehead. Though he lived in the body of a grown man, his chestnut eyes were still as innocent and kind as a five year old boy's.

"Low Mama," he yawned, and then giggled when she leaned closer to his ear.

"And I love you, too. You are...the beat of my heart," she managed against the typhoon of pain. "Don't you ever...forget it."

"Yets, I knew." He paused for a second and half-shrugged. "Mama skee."

"Scared about starting the new job...tomorrow?" she asked, pulling away a little to study his face.

He nodded. "Yets."

"We talked about this, Brian. It's nothing...to be afraid of," she said, pausing to catch her breath. "We can do anything...we put our minds to. We've proven it...for years together." She nodded. "Just believe in yourself...and know that both me and the good Lord...are right there with you."

He nodded.

With a kiss on his cheek, the tiny, Italian matriarch eased herself onto her back and exhaled heavily. "Yes?" she asked, relentless in making him exercise his vocabulary.

"Yets, Mama."

"That's my boy," she grunted, still struggling to get comfortable.

For a moment, there was silence. And then Brian yawned, "Mama, nigh nigh." His was still the sweetest voice she'd ever known.

Smiling, the old woman nodded her curly, silver head. "Tomorrow night...at eight o'clock...we'll talk about how good you did at work, okay?"

"K," he said and snuggled right up next to her. He smiled and, within seconds, he was sleeping.

"Okay then," Mama said. She grabbed the crucifix that hung around her neck and kissed it. "Goodnight, Brian."

## About the Author

Steven Manchester is the author of *Twelve Months* and *Pressed Pennies, The Unexpected Storm: The Gulf War Legacy* and *Jacob Evans,* as well as several books under the pseudonym, Steven Herberts. His work has appeared on NBC's *Today Show*, CBS's *The Early Show*, CNN's *American Morning* and BET's *Nightly News*. Recently, three of Steven's short stories were selected "101 Best" for the *Chicken Soup for the Soul* series. When not spending time with his beautiful wife, Paula, or his four children, this Massachusetts author is promoting his works or writing. Visit: www.StevenManchester.com